Odyssey

Odyssey

KATRINA VINCENZI-THYNE

Black Lace novels are sexual fantasies.
In real life, make sure you practise safe sex.

First published in 1996 by
Black Lace
332 Ladbroke Grove
London W10 5AH

Typeset by CentraCet Limited, Cambridge
Printed and bound by Mackays of Chatham PLC

ISBN 0 352 33111 9

Chapter One

The night was warm, the sky a dark velvet, and the stars were shining as *Calypso* sailed smoothly through the dark, oily waters of Piraeus, leaving the lights of Athens behind. In the air-conditioned luxury of the lounge, Merise Isabella Van Asche accepted a glass of champagne from a passing waiter, crossed her long, spectacularly beautiful legs, and smiled inwardly.

As always, Rupert was right: there *was* something special about the first night of a cruise. There was an air of suppressed excitement among the passengers gathered in the lounge for the captain's introductory cocktail party, a discreet yet tangible hum of anticipation. It clung to the air like musky perfume. Too sophisticated, too rich, too world-weary to display true enthusiasm, they still betrayed themselves with restless eyes and voices pitched perhaps just a little too loud.

It was not merely that they were embarking on a

1

cruise, not just that for the next two weeks, in pampered luxury, they would sail the Mediterranean, lounging under the hot sun, dancing under the stars, and stopping at exotic ports of call, free of the constraints of the outside world, dedicated to nothing but their own pleasure.

No, there was something more, she decided. A sense of adventure, perhaps? It was, after all, a 'discovery' cruise with no fixed itinerary, the ports of call depending on the weather, the prevailing winds and the captain's whim. Still, even that didn't account for the atmosphere, heady, potent, almost intoxicating. Strangers mingled and sipped champagne, eyeing one another surreptitiously, even speculatively. Yes, that was it: it was the covert sexual speculation of dedicated pleasure seekers.

It was a small group by cruise standards, no more than sixty passengers; a perfect number, allowing either intimacy or anonymity, casual liaisons or discreet affairs. And two weeks, mused Merise, was really a lovely length of time, the ideal interval for the liaisons she preferred. How convenient that the end of the cruise would provide the natural, inevitable end to the affair.

'Darling,' Rupert had coaxed, 'you must come. You'll simply adore it. It has everything. Spas, salons, first-class cuisine – even expert lecturers for the culture vultures. The most refined hedonism, perfect for a Sybarite like you. I promise you a deliciously decadent time.'

His bright-blue eyes had flashed even brighter, like blue diamonds in his thin, tanned, clever face.

'Decadent?' Merise had echoed, admiring the slim, strong lines of his body, draped uncomfortably over her Rietveld chair. In black jeans and black polo-neck sweater, his glossy black hair tied back in a ponytail and one gold earring glinting, he looked like an androgynous sexual pirate. 'Decadent? How could it be otherwise with you as ship's purser? And how on earth did you land that job?'

'Really, darling, a boy has to have some secrets,' Rupert had replied, fluttering his eyelashes and camping it up outrageously. 'Seriously, Merise, say you'll come. A divine opportunity to observe the human comedy. And if that palls, some gorgeous sites and scenery. The Aeolian Islands, Malta; have you ever seen those massive fertility statues? Huge breasts and beautiful rounded bellies? Yum!'

'But why would one join a cruise when one has one's own yacht, one's own friends, and one is perfectly capable of doing it oneself?' she had asked sweetly, deliberately using the Van Asche 'one' and arching a slanted dark eyebrow.

'Darling Merise, too dull, too dull. Too predictable. I can offer you the decadence of the unknown – strangers – not your practised little coterie of acolytes.' Rupert spoke too quickly and made an extravagant, sweeping gesture with his right hand, sloshing single malt Ne Plus Ultra, and then apologies, over the hardwood floor.

Merise smiled, recalling the conversation. She could never deny Rupert anything. His mere request was enough to ensure her presence; but she was puzzled by his insistence. It was true that she could have made the voyage on her own yacht, as true as the fact that Rupert, if he chose, never needed work again. But he had found something in this raffish existence, something that he was determined to share.

3

And, she was forced to admit, there was something rather exciting in sipping vintage champagne among strangers as the ship made her way out to sea. Perhaps it was the sensual throb of the engines, the almost imperceptible thrumming vibration as the ship gained way. Perhaps it was the aura of glamour: bronzed men and women in evening dress, the whisper of silk and the mingling scent of expensive perfumes. Or perhaps it was the sheer opulence of their unfamiliar surroundings: the gleaming hardwood fittings, the watered-silk wall hangings and butter-soft leather sofas and chairs. It was voluptuously overblown: the plush grey carpeting inches thick and overlaid with Oriental jewel-toned rugs, tapestry cushions adorning every chair and sofa, the rather magnificent Art Deco wall sconces shaded with tinted glass. It was the work of someone who had barely restrained themselves from adding tassels.

The decor, Merise reflected, was not really to her taste. A dedicated voluptuary only in the sexual sense, she preferred a more Spartan setting, clean lines and harsh planes, an uncompromising background for her own striking, enigmatic beauty. But she had to admit that there was something rather vulgarly appealing about such unabashed, sumptuous luxury.

Deliberately she had taken a chair on the periphery of the party and now she glanced idly around the room. With the second or third glass of champagne, laughter was flowing more freely and people were beginning to circulate. Waiters were offering hot and cold hors d'oeuvres: tissue-thin smoked salmon, oysters on a bed of seaweed, prawns and langoustines with garlic mayonnaise, cold asparagus in vinaigrette

4

and feather-light pastry parcels with a delicious, spicy filling.

Clearly, some of the people were here mainly for the food, thought Merise, watching a plump brunette greedily devouring pastries. Her ample hips were already straining against the confines of her red silk dress. In a few years she would look like an overblown peony; just now there was something enticing in her lush ripeness. A succulent hors d'oeuvre, decided Merise, rather like the pastries she was consuming; a delicious morsel for an afternoon, something to whet the appetite, tempt the palate for more robust pleasures.

She smiled as Rupert caught her eye and surreptitiously winked at her. He was standing beside the captain, resplendent in a white uniform trimmed with gold braid. He had, she noticed, kept the ponytail as well as the earring, and still managed to look uncompromisingly male. Perhaps it was the effect of the uniform?

No, that wasn't fair to Rupert. Like herself, she thought complacently, he was the most adept of bisexuals, capable of adapting himself to any gathering, to any sexual scenario. She had seen him aggressively macho and languidly effete, coyly flirtatious and bluntly predatory – the perfect sexual chameleon.

They had been friends now for almost twenty years, she reflected, ever since he had joined the Van Asche household in Vienna as her father's valet. It had been Rupert who had amused the lonely child, comforted the confused adolescent; Rupert who had encouraged her to be herself, to rebel against the repressive Van Asche code of conduct; Rupert who had gently, tenderly, and with skilled eroticism relieved her of the burden of her virginity; Rupert who had led her to an understanding of her true carnal nature. Rupert, her very own sexual *eminence grise*.

She could never look back on those days in Vienna without a secret, inward smile. He had taught her to savour and relish the contrasts, the long, slow thrusts, the short, stabbing jabs, the intricate delicacies of prolonged anticipation, of prolonged stimulation. He had taught her how to take pleasure freely, without shame or guilt, without inhibition. He had taught her that there was no act, no matter how bizarre, that was forbidden between lovers.

Vienna was many years ago, she thought; she was now past thirty, which meant that Rupert must be – good heavens – almost forty! Yet he seemed not to have changed at all.

Nor, she thought complacently, had she. Her body was still slim and firm, her breasts still high and pointed. Her rich black hair was as yet untainted by the premature Van Asche grey and the meticulous beauty regime she had followed since the age of fourteen had given her the skin of a woman ten years younger.

Standing to deposit her empty glass on a passing waiter's tray and accept another, she caught sight of herself in one of the bevelled, gilt-framed mirrors adorning the salon. She was pleased with her reflection. She had dressed dramatically in a slick black sheath that left her arms and shoulders bare, loaded her arms with the heavy, sculpted silver bracelets she adored, and left her hair loose in snaky curls down her back. Her dark, slanting maenad's eyes were ringed in black, and her full, faintly rapacious mouth was crimson.

It was a strong look, sensual and bold, that would

appeal to a certain kind of man, or, indeed, a certain kind of woman.

Glass in hand, a faint smile curving her crimson lips, Merise prepared to join the party.

Julia felt invisible. It wasn't that David was ignoring her. The act of ignoring someone involves some minimal acknowledgement of their presence, a conscious *not* noticing that is tantamount to recognition. No, David wasn't ignoring her. He was utterly oblivious to her, chatting to the captain, describing the lectures he had prepared on the sites they were to visit, his plans for the various tours, his ideas. And somehow his unawareness of her transmitted itself to everyone around them; by some strange alchemy Julia, his partner, colleague, lover and almost-but-not-quite fiancé, became invisible.

She should be used to it, she thought, sipping her champagne. David was naturally flamboyant, a vivid, colourful character utterly unlike the typical, quietly drab professional historian. Force of personality more than scholarship had made him the rising star in the small universe of ancient history and had secured this contract to lecture on *Calypso*.

David was striking, his prematurely grey hair a foil for his youthful face and deep brown eyes, his aggressive enthusiasm and natural charm making him the centre of any group. Beside him, with her indeterminate looks – her hair somewhere between blonde and brown, her hazel eyes neither green nor brown, neither tall nor short, somewhere between slim and plump – Julia often felt she paled to insignificance.

But if living in David's shadow was sometimes annoying, the alternative was far, far worse. If it

7

wasn't for David effortlessly garnering attention, she, Julia, might actually *have* to make conversation. With the imposing figure of the captain, severely impressive in dress uniform. With the intimidatingly sexy dark-haired man on his right. With the lovely, expensively dressed woman with the haughty face who even now was laughing and laying a manicured hand on David's arm.

Conversation, idle conversation, simple social chit-chat, was utterly beyond her. How did people manage, she wondered? She was the conventional academic, an archaeologist at home with sherds and bones, rubble and soil samples, artefacts that spoke to her in their own language. That was the dialogue she enjoyed; people intimidated her.

'Just think of them naked,' her only friend Celia had kindly advised.

It was a piece of advice with unexpected consequences.

At her next faculty meeting she deliberately took a seat next to the chairman, a stern, vigorous, thick-set Scot in his late forties whose piercing grey eyes terrified her as much as his abrupt, brusque manner.

As the minutes of the last meeting were read by the secretary, she tried to imagine him naked. And failed. It was impossible. He was wearing too many clothes, the obligatory tweed jacket and sweater beneath, a shirt and tie.

She let her eyes glaze over and concentrated harder. The jacket would be heavy, dense and faintly scratchy to the touch, but lined with cool silk, Julia decided, mentally stripping him of it. The sweater was cashmere, luxuriantly soft to the touch. She would run her hands down from his shoulder, lightly grazing his

8

nipples, drifting down his powerful torso to reach the hem of the sweater. Perhaps her hands would linger there, brush against the thickening mass at his groin, before slowly lifting the sweater over his head.

Now the paisley silk tie. She would look him straight in the eyes as she loosened his tie, those piercing, arctic grey eyes that would be soft and warm, because no man, however stern, however austere, could remain unmoved by such an intimate gesture.

The shirt, surely Egyptian cotton, would be fine as silk, warmed by his body. Would she begin at the top, expose the strong column of his throat, the muscular planes of his chest, or at the bottom, gently tugging his shirt from trousers, knowing the subtle friction would only increase his growing arousal? A delicious dilemma.

The top then, to prolong the suspense, because he was hard already; he must already be hard. She undid one button, then two, then three, pausing to lick his throat where a pulse was beating madly, then drawing the thin fabric aside to find his nipples. His chest would be coarsely pelted in black and grey, the nipples small and blunt.

She would take one in her mouth, suck it gently, wait for it to harden, swirling around it with her tongue as her hands continued their downward journey, downward, ever downward, until they met the barrier of his belt buckle.

She could feel herself becoming aroused at the thought, a liquid warmth flowing through her veins, pooling between her legs. Startled, she brought herself back to reality and darted a quick glance at the chairman. Fully clothed, he was glaring at someone who had dared question the minutes.

Yet her fantasy had not deceived her. He had removed his jacket and loosened his tie; under the soft cashmere sweater were strong shoulders, the blunt, well-muscled torso of her imagination, and even a tuft of grey and black hair escaping from his loosened collar.

There was something strangely erotic in the knowledge that he was powerless against her make-believe seduction, that she had already licked his skin, tasted the hard nub of his nipple, grazed it with her teeth while her hands rested at his belt, feeling his stomach muscles tighten.

And there she would linger, waiting until he grew harder, until she was sure the constriction of his trousers was almost painful against his massive erection. He would be massive, this blunt, austere man, thick and tensile, at the mercy of his cock and her hands and mouth.

She would flirt with the belt buckle, run her nails along the metal zip of his trousers, feel the heavy weight of his organ straining towards her, feel the power she had over him.

At the thought her heart began to beat faster. Her mouth was dry and she swallowed convulsively. Shifting in her seat she was aware of the new heaviness in her groin, the tautly coiled tension of desire.

When she freed him, slowly, ever so slowly, he would be rampant. And she could lick him, learn him, explore him with her tongue, draw him into her mouth, or merely tease him with her breath. She could do anything.

By the end of the interminable, three-hour-long

10

meeting, Julia had mentally stripped every man in the room, nuzzled the dense bushes of their pubic hair, gently weighed the soft, plump pouches of their testes, caressed the contours of their penises – some long, thin and curved like scimitars, some short and thick – all of them hard, engorged with blood, engorged with wanting her, and she was unbearably aroused.

Her breasts felt full and tender, straining against her bra, the nipples half-puckered, roused by her sensual imaginings, mindlessly anticipating the hard, pulling suckling of a man's mouth. She was hot, too hot, almost flushed, but grateful for the fluffy cardigan that concealed her breasts, grateful too that she was a woman, that her swollen arousal was invisible.

She was wet, her labia slick and engorged, swollen leaves pressing against her panties, turgid, moist and ready. She could feel the thud of her heart echoing deep in the pit of her belly, a heavy, insistent pulse. She had never felt so avid, so greedy, so needy for the deep, sure thrust, the necessary friction. She wanted their tongues lapping at her, sucking deep on her clitoris, their mouths on her breasts, their teeth at her nipples, their cocks thrusting into her.

A separate, reserved part of her mind marvelled at herself, astonished by the vividness of her fantasy, the depth of her physical response. No lover, not even David, had ever brought her to this pitch of excitement and the thought made her feel vaguely, irrationally guilty.

She didn't speak up at the meeting; not because of her customary shyness, but because she was afraid her voice would tremble.

Gradually, tentatively, she learned to control the depth of her fantasies, the extent of her own arousal.

11

It was a harmless diversion, she reassured herself, and one that allowed her natural shyness to translate as poise. And if her fantasies had become more adventurous, more perverse, it was a secret no one but she knew.

Unbeknownst even to herself, she was beginning to see the world differently, beginning to develop some subliminal awareness of the deep, throbbing, utterly physical nature of life and living.

Now, standing awkwardly invisible beside David, she summoned her imagination.

Rupert mingled, gently ushering passengers toward the dining room, his blue eyes sparkling. It was, he thought, rather like the beginning of a play: the cast was assembled, the stage was set, the drama about to unfold. And he was looking forward to this play, watching the script write itself.

Decadence he had promised Merise, and decadence she would have. How could it be otherwise, with such a rich assemblage of players? Rich both in terms of dramatic potential and actual wealth, bored, idle pleasure seekers who wanted culture fed on a silver spoon and the illusion of adventure. What could be better?

The rich, as darling F. Scott had put it, were different. And how he enjoyed watching them as they played their roles. There would be flirtations, liaisons, casual fucks and intense romances, loves and lusts, all with the sweeping, dramatic beauty of the Mediterranean in the background.

Already he had identified some promising types: the faintly haggard looking older woman sporting too many diamonds and clinging to an effetely gorgeous golden youth; a louche looking type with corrupt, cynical eyes and gambler's hands; an Armani-clad couple with eyes for everyone but each other; the statuesque brunette whose hands trembled as she reached for yet another glass of champagne. Oh, yes, it was a promising company, he thought gleefully.

They would feed his desire and delight as they played their roles, amuse him, intrigue him, interest him, perhaps even involve him in their plots and ploys. His was not, he thought, guiding the Armani-clad couple to their places, a starring role; merely that of an attendant lord, to swell a progress, start a scene or two. Mentally he took himself in hand. Fitzgerald was one thing, T. S. Eliot quite another, and wholly unsuited to the atmosphere.

Rupert Harrison had always been something of an emotional voyeur, but his was a kindly nature, tempered by a genuine interest in people. Had fate, or his own, fatal, foolish predilection for folly not intervened, he might have become an excellent psychiatrist or gossip columnist. An ill-spent youth (it was something of an achievement to have been sent down from Oxford in the liberal seventies on grounds of incorrigible dissoluteness) had matured to a decidedly ungenteel hedonism that had led him around the world, from lover to lover, from job to job, always in search of adventure. He had fished for pearls in the South Seas, felled trees in Canada, taught Latin to the son of a Sheikh in the Middle East and sold dubious antiques to credulous tourists in Rome. Privately he considered his own personal low had been keeping chickens in Provence; his finest hour, the creation of Merise Isabella Van Asche.

He watched her now as she moved to her place at

the captain's table. She had become the woman he had envisaged: superbly beautiful, supremely self-confident, a sexual huntress whose prey went joyfully to the kill. There was no resemblance to the prim, perennial virgin the Van Asche dynasty usually produced; yet he had become conscious of a slight inner disquiet whenever he thought of her. There seemed to be a coldness in Merise that even her innate sensuality had not thawed, an austerity that disturbed him.

It was why he had coaxed her to join the cruise: he wanted to see her alone, among strangers, observe her and reassure himself.

There is a certain kind of conversation that prevails among a certain kind of people who meet for the first time and are travelling together. The search for common ground ('Oh, yes, we loved Venice') quickly becomes competitive ('Of course we always stay at the Gritti Palace') and often degenerates into sheer vulgar braggadocio ('I usually fax Harry's Bar to make sure they save my table').

And there is another kind of conversation that prevails among people meeting for the first time. It is wordless, conducted with the eyes, the body, the careless, casual, almost accidental touch. It, too, can often quickly become competitive and sometimes quite vulgar.

Merise, who would no more indulge in touristic one-upmanship than she would set foot in Harry's Bar, toyed with her caviare, listened with half an ear to the captain, and began a quite wordless conversation with the man seated across from her.

He was, physically, a type she liked – tall, lean and dark, with long fingers and a curving, sensual mouth.

14

Merise always looked first at a man's hands – not, as other women might, to find a wedding ring or the tell-tale patch of too white skin – but to decide if they matched her mood, if she would enjoy them moving over her body, moving inside her. There was much to be read in a man's hands, whether the nails were manicured or merely pared, whether the fingers were calloused or soft, long and artistic or short and thick.

His hands were white and faintly furred with silky dark hair, the fingernails blunt and unpolished. He held an unlit cigarette in one hand; in the other, a gold lighter with which he was tracing a small, circular pattern on the white linen tablecloth. Not especially subtle, Merise thought.

His eyes, brown and thickly lashed, were fixed on hers.

Merise let her eyes drop casually to the slim gold wedding band on the ring finger of his left hand and raised her brows slightly.

He shrugged slightly, gave an infinitesimal nod to the woman seated beside him. It was the plump brunette Merise had noticed earlier, the lush hors d'oeuvre in red silk.

Seemingly absorbed by her plate, Merise took her fork and carefully separated one glistening black pearl of caviare and pushed it delicately to one side. She licked her lips, assumed a faintly quizzical expression, as if she was debating with herself, then added another pearl of caviare to the first. She took a sip of wine, nibbled on a toast point, then added a third.

Then she looked up and smiled.

The challenge had been issued. She watched as his eyes widened, as surprise and then calculation changed the expression on his face from complacent sensuality to intrigued interest. It was a novelty to him then, the thought of sharing his wife with another woman. But it appealed.

A waiter hovered solicitously, anxious to serve the second course. Almost casually, Merise manoeuvred the three pearls of caviare on to the tine of her fork, lifted it to her mouth, and let her tongue slip out to capture them. She pressed them to the roof of her mouth, enjoying the rich, oily explosion on her palate.

Then she smiled graciously at the hovering waiter, nodded to him to remove her plate of almost untouched caviare, and withdrew a packet of cigarettes from her evening bag.

As she had expected, the gold lighter flashed even before she had placed the cigarette to her lips.

'Allow me.' His voice was pleasant, a mellow baritone with deep vowels. American, perhaps.

'I may,' replied Merise, as the tip of her cigarette met the flame. She barely inhaled, disliking the smoke. Cigarettes were bait, nothing more.

'Ah.' He cleared his throat. 'Let me introduce myself. My name is – '

'Unimportant,' said Merise softly.

'You're very direct,' he commented.

'I know what I want,' she replied. And she did. Tonight she wanted sex, hot and hard, with no pretence of seduction. No names. Brevity and anonymity, the distillation of lust.

'I see,' he said, and absently touched his wife's arm.

'Difficult?' asked Merise. She ran the tip of her tongue lightly over her upper lip.

'Um. No. No, I don't think so. Er. Midnight? Our

16

cabin?' he ventured softly, sliding a key across the table. He then turned to his wife. 'Darling? More wine?'

Merise stifled a smile.

Rupert, observing this byplay from a lower table, found himself torn between reluctant admiration and disappointment. Merise had struck swiftly, with unerring skill, like some sexual cobra. And like a cobra, cold-bloodedly. There was no passion, no tension, no emotion to season and spice the encounter. Unconsciously he frowned, then turned his attention back to his own table.

Here the undercurrents were subtle but unmistakable. The guest lecturer was deliberately charming the table, flirting with the wife of a Texas oil tycoon, and partaking rather too freely of Chardonnay. His companion and colleague was silent but watchful – jealous, perhaps? The oil tycoon, some years older than his wife, was watching with a benevolent air; did he encourage his wife's flirtations or was he merely amused by them? No politics had ever interested Rupert as much as sexual politics.

He began some subtle flirting of his own.

It was midnight. Merise paused outside the stateroom, idly fingering the room key, wondering whether to use it. The brief jolt of lust she had experienced at dinner over caviare had dissipated almost completely by dessert, drowned by the pedestrian, predictable flow of her chosen mate's conversation. Could he possibly be as banal in bed? Was it even worth finding out?

Mentally she shrugged, then fitted the key to the lock.

The room was dark, the only source of illumination a pool of pale light that spilled across the bed. The woman lay nude, sprawled bonelessly across the white sheets, her arms and legs spread wide. Her skin was pale, so pale that the dense vee of curling dark hair at the apex of her thighs seemed somehow shocking. The man lay beside her, his mouth fixed to her breast, his fingers tangled in the nest of her pubic hair.

He half turned his head as Merise approached, and kept his eyes fixed on her as his tongue curled out to caress the rosy nipple at his mouth, as his hand delved lower to part the shining coral lips of the woman's labia. The woman moaned softly, but barely stirred.

So. Perhaps not as banal as his conversation, thought Merise. He had arranged this tableau to intrigue her, displaying his wife and himself in full arousal.

Her gaze lingered on the woman. Her breasts, full and creamy, were swollen, the nipples firmly erect. Her plump white thighs were open, revealing the soft folds of her labia, the protruding nub of her clitoris. As Merise watched he slipped one finger inside her, then withdrew it. In the pale light, it glistened slickly.

Gently he traced the path between the turgid leaves of the labia to the tip of the clitoris, massaging the flesh delicately in a rotating, circular rhythm, cleverly arousing all the sensitive tissues. He retraced the path to the mouth of her vagina, swirling his finger around the entrance to her body until she gave a soft, inarticulate cry.

He inserted one finger and then another. With the

palm of his hand he cupped the fleshy folds and began gently squeezing and releasing.

Watching, Merise felt the familiar ache begin, the quiet heaviness in her groin, the first flicker of desire. She knew the delicious susurration of sensation within and without, the pooling warmth that became scalding heat. For a moment, she focused on the woman's face. Her eyes were closed and despite her obvious arousal she seemed barely conscious. Too many liqueurs after dinner. Perhaps.

Her eyes drifted to the man. He was lying on his side, his body angled so that she saw the powerful shoulders, the silky dark hair furring his chest that arrowed to the dense bush at his groin. He was fully tumescent, red, thick and hard. His prick seemed to quiver a little under her gaze and his hand stilled at the woman's groin.

Briefly Merise shook her head, and slowly began removing the bracelets from her arms. She lingered over the process, enjoying his anticipation, relishing the cool friction of metal sliding over her skin. She kept her eyes fixed on his hand as he resumed the rhythmic palpation of the female flesh beneath his fingers.

Her dress slithered to the floor. She heard him catch his breath sharply, and stifled a smile. It was not merely that her breasts were high and firm, her belly softly rounded, her hips shapely, her legs long and beautiful; nude, Merise flaunted the body of some barbaric goddess.

Her nipples were pierced with delicate gold hoops studded with diamonds. Another diamond flashed from her navel. Her groin was smooth and hairless, like polished satin, and when she tilted her pelvis the

19

glint of tiny diamonds embedded in her labia caught the light.

He was, as she had known he would be, shocked, faintly repelled and fascinated, lewdly, pruriently curious.

It never failed.

His eyes wide, he lay back, the woman at his side forgotten.

Merise stood at the foot of the bed, flaunting herself and her diamonds, taunting him, gently fingering the hoops at her breasts. Piercing had made her nipples more tender, more readily roused to the slightest stimulation and she could feel them puckering beneath her fingers. A hot, erotic tingling threaded through her, arcing from her breasts to her groin. She felt herself moistening, growing wet.

She let one hand slip to the smooth juncture of her thighs and deliberately caressed herself as he had caressed the woman lying beside him. She slid a finger inside herself, withdrew and held it glistening to the light. Delicately she traced the path to her clitoris, circling the tiny diamonds in her labia with one long, curved nail. More sensitive since the piercing, her flesh swelled to the touch.

The man rose up on one elbow and made as if to reach for her. Swiftly she walked to the side of the bed and gently pushed him back. Then, taking care not to disturb the woman beside them, she lowered herself to his mouth.

His tongue was tentative at first, exploring the diamonds, the bizarre contrast of soft, slick heat and cold, hard stone. On her knees, she rocked above him, forcing a long, smooth stroke from the tip of her clitoris to the mouth of her vagina. His tongue fluttered and probed as his hands lifted to clutch her buttocks, as he tried to impose a rhythm of his own. Softened by the warm, wet wash, Merise was still.

He nibbled at her delicately with his teeth, tasting the diamonds. Heat flowed as he sucked, drawing the tender flesh into his mouth, swirling it with his tongue. The friction was almost painful, adding a sharper edge to her pleasure.

The pleasure was now a tangible thing, hot and thick. Her groin was heavy, her clitoris swollen and erect. His hands were firm on her buttocks, clasping and unclasping, and she felt one finger trace the cleft of her cheeks to her anus, exploring tentatively, as if expecting some jewel there as well.

She felt herself ripening, becoming ready. The sudden wash of orgasm drew closer, rippling and swelling. She closed her eyes and concentrated on the sweet suction of his mouth, the plunging fluttering of his tongue. Warmth became heat as his teeth closed gently on her clitoris, sending a searing streak of flame through her body.

She stiffened and drew away. His hands tightened on her buttocks, trying to force her down, but she resisted, squirming out of his grasp and slithering down his chest until she rested on his groin. Beneath her she could feel the hard, rigid length of his prick, trapped between her thighs. His chest was rising and falling rapidly, his breath coming in short gasps. She lowered herself full-length upon him, fitting herself breast to breast, thigh to thigh.

She breathed deeply, relishing the hot, panting body beneath hers. He smelled of sweat and lust, a musky heat, uniquely male. Her mouth filled with saliva. She drew her tongue along the line of his collar bone, licking him, tasting him. He was salty, faintly coppery. She quelled the impulse to bite deep and taste the blood.

Beside them, the woman stirred and then nestled close, seeking the familiar heat. In a sleepy, dazed caress, her hand slipped from Merise's shoulder to the slope of her breast. One finger caught in the diamond-encrusted hoop piercing her nipple, and an exquisite frisson of sudden, unexpected pain shivered through her.

The man stirred beneath her, jutting his hips, urging his prick through the slick, fleshy folds to the mouth of her vagina. Merise shifted, tightened her muscles, denying him.

Instead, still lying full-length upon him, his wife's lax hand at her breast, she reached for his hand and drew his index finger to her lips. With the tip of her tongue she rimmed the nail, delicately, almost flirtatiously, then caught it between her teeth. The pad of his finger rested on the lush swell of her lower lip. She let her tongue flutter over the tip of his finger as she gently rocked her hips, pressing his prick hard against her inner thigh.

For long moments, she lavished the skilled attention of her mouth on his finger, as though it were his penis, circling it with her tongue, flicking the tender underside, dragging it against her teeth and then pulling it deep into her mouth; a small taste of what she could do to his cock. Another time, with another man, she might have been tempted to display her erotic artistry, and transform his body into a flaming tangle of shuddering nerve ends merely by the touch of her mouth and tongue.

He groaned as he withdrew his finger, swiftly,

urgently, tangling his hand in her hair, pushing her, urging her down to his cock. She let herself be drawn downward, revelling in the slick friction of his hard torso against her body, the thick pressure of his prick against her belly. A hot pain streaked through her as the diamond hoop pulled hard at her nipple.

Gently Merise disengaged the woman's hand from her breast, gazing at her curiously. Her eyes were tightly shut, her breathing shallow and quick. Arching her back, she carefully placed the woman's hand between them on his groin. Almost reflexively, it seemed, her fingers sifted through the dense thatch of pubic hair to close around his cock.

The man stiffened, his eyes open wide.

Merise smiled.

With one fluid movement she raised herself to straddle his prick.

Grasping the head with her fingers she drew him close to her moist heat, stroking him with the soft, fleshy lips of her labia, the sweet abrasion of tiny diamonds, stroking herself with the hot, velvet tip of his penis on her clitoris.

She could feel the muscles in her thighs begin to tense and tremble, the clenching deep in her belly that presaged orgasm. She was hot and swollen, turgid, ready to come. She tightened her inner muscles, prolonging the sensation, and guided him inside her.

Slowly, ever so slowly, she lowered herself, assimilating the fullness a fraction at a time, sheathing him until at last she reached the barrier of the woman's hand, still closed at the base of his cock. She swayed forward, until her clitoris lightly grazed the woman's hand, then back, arching her pelvis until she could feel its thickness pressing against the wall of her rectum.

The red haze enveloped her.

Heat.

Fullness.

Tides, sweeping closer. A molten core about to explode. She hovered on the edge, waiting to fly.

It caught her like a swift gust of wind, lifting her. Her body soared and spasmed.

Helpless beneath her, denied the pumping friction for orgasm, caught by the clasping hand of his wife, the man felt the spasms like a series of tiny shocks. He almost groaned in relief when he felt her lift herself, waiting for the hot, fluid release as she rode him to climax. He lay back, eyes closed.

It was almost a full minute before his brain interpreted the sounds he had barely recognised: the soft clink of metal, the rustle of fabric. He opened his eyes to find Merise fully clothed, carefully placing the stateroom key on the bedside table.

'Why you – I haven't – you bitch!' he spluttered.

'Shh,' cautioned Merise softly. 'You don't want to wake your wife.'

Chapter Two

Julia stood on deck, her hands clasping the rails, staring blindly at the frothy wake as *Calypso* breasted the sea. Her thoughts were in turmoil and her body ached dully with the frustration of arousal denied fulfilment. Again and again, with the repetitious monotony of some ancient record stuck in a groove, she kept seeing images of the night.

David's hands slowly caressing the naked back of a woman in plunging white silk. The sinuous flow of their bodies as they moved to the music. The bulge of his erection, clearly visible, as they moved apart.

Julia closed her eyes.

After dinner there had been dancing in the Starlight Lounge; Starlight because the roof was glass, the only illumination the magnificent constellations above. No great dancer herself, Julia knew that as David's assistant, and therefore nominally part of the 'crew', she had to join in the entertainments; she was happy enough to make an appearance and then melt into the background.

David, of course, was David in his element.

Strange, she had never noticed how blatantly sexual dancing really was. Body movements echoing, mirroring each other, mimicking sex itself. And the music itself, sometimes soft and slow and languorous, sometimes hard and pounding. And David using his body on the dance floor as if he were in bed, exuding a raw, sexual energy.

But it was, of course, only dancing.

David's hand slowly caressing the naked back of a woman in plunging white silk. The sinuous flow of their bodies . . . Julia bit her lip.

He hadn't danced with her.

But it was natural, she argued with herself. Of course David's head would be turned by all the attention, all the women coyly clustering. Rich women. Money had always impressed David. And at any rate, it was all part of the cruise; some liners even hired men to dance with women, didn't they?

David's hand, the flow of their bodies, the bulge of his erection . . .

Unnoticed, Julia had left.

He had returned late to the cabin, flushed with too much brandy and reeking of expensive perfume.

'Dancing,' he explained. 'Fabulous band. I looked for you, but you'd gone. Fabulous band, wasn't it?'

'Yes,' she had replied colourlessly, turning away from him and drawing the sheets up to her neck. She closed her eyes and pretended to sleep as he fumbled with his clothing, bumping into unfamiliar furniture and grumbling as he groped with the light switch.

Either he wasn't fooled or didn't care. He had reached for her clumsily, almost roughly, turning her to him and fixing his mouth to her breast, sucking hard as one hand searched between her thighs. She had struggled a little, resenting his arrogance, his lateness.

He jammed one finger inside her, then another. 'You're ready,' he said thickly.

'No,' she protested. But she was. Her body, responding mindlessly, reflexively, had moistened, opened for him.

It was over almost before it had begun, leaving Julia achingly aroused, frustrated, and David fast asleep.

The cabin suddenly seemed stiflingly small, redolent with the scent of sex. She had slipped out of bed, grabbed her dressing gown, and made her way on deck.

Had he been making love to her, or some other woman, she wondered dismally. David was usually so gentle, so considerate.

David's hand, slowly caressing the naked back of a woman in white silk . . .

Merise padded softly along the deck, savouring the cool night air on her heated skin, savouring the physical satiation that follows climax. She felt deliciously replete, pleasantly tired, and was looking forward to the solitude of her cabin and a large brandy.

As she drew near to the corridor which would lead to her stateroom, she noticed someone clinging to the ship's rail. Rather late to be star gazing alone, she thought without much interest. An amateur

27

astronomer? A drunk? A suicide? Well, it was no concern of hers.

But it might be of Rupert's, she thought, suddenly struck. Oh, God, if it was a suicide, it would probably be highly inconvenient for him. She had a vague vision of officious officials, burials at sea and forms to be filled in in triplicate, and suppressed a sigh.

'Excuse me,' she said coolly, as she drew near the rigid figure. 'Are you – all right?'

The figure turned and Merise saw a pale girl, eyes red with weeping, wearing nothing but a rather shabby dressing gown. Not a suicide, she decided with relief; surely no one would be caught dead wearing that.

'Oh, ah, no, thank you,' Julia stammered. 'It's just a man,' she added bitterly.

'Just a man,' repeated Merise, raising her brows. 'Well then.' She gave an eloquent, dismissive shrug of her shoulders, and walked away.

Rupert was waiting for her in her stateroom, lounging in one of the large, overstuffed silk chairs and sipping brandy. A second snifter stood on the tiny hardwood table, and as she walked towards him he splashed a large measure into the glass and stood to greet her.

'Darling, I didn't expect you to wait for me,' she said, lifting her mouth for his kiss.

Their mouths met gently, softly, like old lovers' past passion, tongues stroking, tangling, remembering. A loving kiss, curiously platonic, infinitely satisfying. It lasted a long time.

'Is it late or early?' she asked when their lips had parted.

'It rather depends on your point of view,' said

28

Rupert ironically, handing her the brandy. 'I wasn't sure whether to expect you at all. It's just past two.'

'Later than I thought, then,' she yawned, sipping her brandy and then setting it on the table.

'Time flies when passion soars,' suggested Rupert, resettling himself in the chair.

'Hardly, my love,' replied Merise with a small laugh. 'No more than a four out of ten, if that. Although a decent enough four,' she concluded fairly. It was a rating scheme they had devised many years ago. A certain amount of ingenuity was required to reach a five; anything over seven ranked as truly memorable.

'I shouldn't have thought you'd bother for a mere four,' remarked Rupert dispassionately as Merise began to undress. 'By now, surely, you can tell that – my God, Merise, what have you done?' he exclaimed.

Laughing she tossed her dress on to the bed and faced him, fingering her nipples. 'Don't you like them?' she asked, drawing attention to the diamond hoops piercing her fleshy buds, and tilting her pelvis so that the precious stones flashed from her navel and her labia.

'Vulgar,' reproved Rupert. 'Quite, quite vulgar. Come closer and let me see.'

With the impersonal air of a connoisseur he examined the jewellery at her breasts. 'Small but flawless,' he commented. 'And a lovely fire.'

Her nipples rose to his touch and a sweet, warm lassitude flowed through her body. It was a comforting warmth, serene and pure, like the gentle glow of candlelight, the perfumed blush of a rose petal. His breath was warm on her belly as he inspected the diamond in her navel, his fingers cool and soothing as he parted her labia.

29

'These are fine,' he judged, stroking the sensitive flesh. 'And the navel – well, perhaps for evening dress. But not, darling Merise, definitely not the nipples. Too fussy. It spoils the lovely line of your breasts.' With clever fingers he turned the hoops, found the catch, and released them.

'Oh, I suppose you're right,' she said sulkily. She'd rather liked them; but she acknowledged Rupert's taste as flawless. 'The things I do for you. My nipples. My jewellery.' She snorted inelegantly, decidedly grumpy. 'Speaking to strangers and rescuing stray suicides and you're not even grateful.'

'What on earth are you babbling about, darling? Come and sit here,' he said, patting his lap. 'And have some more brandy.'

'Oh, nothing,' grumbled Merise, reluctantly soothed by the warmth of his body and the brandy. 'Some silly creature hanging over the rails.'

His body tensed. 'Merise, where – '

'Oh, don't worry, it's nothing like that. But I thought that it might be, and so inconvenient. Just some dreary creature. A lover's quarrel, I imagine.'

'A man? A woman?'

'Oh, a woman,' said Merise impatiently. 'A one, nothing more.'

'What did she look like?' probed Rupert.

But it transpired that Merise really had no clear idea. She wasn't tall, by any means, but not short. Not fat, no, but not slim. Her hair might have been dark, it was hard to tell. Not fair exactly. Red eyes and a shabby dressing gown were the only details she remembered.

Not a passenger then, thought Rupert. Merise's description, vague as it was, struck a chord of memory. The assistant lecturer – what was her name? Julie? Juliet? Something like that. Absent-mindedly he stroked Merise, who had curled around him, boneless as a cat.

'Merise,' he said thoughtfully, 'have you ever considered the idea that a one can be much more interesting, much more intriguing, than a four?'

He looked down at her, the perfect golden body wrapped around him, the dark hair like a raven's wing in the soft light.

Merise was asleep.

David awoke full of energy and his customary high spirits. Julia, who had passed a restless and fitful night, lay lethargically in bed and watched him, through heavy-lidded eyes, as he dressed for the day. Despite herself, she couldn't help admiring the strong lines of his naked body as it disappeared beneath the white cotton shirt, the khaki trousers.

'There's an early morning briefing with the captain,' he was saying as he rolled up the sleeves of his shirt to expose bronzed forearms furred with silky dark hair. 'With the prevailing winds we'll have rounded Cape Sounion – he was thinking of going through the Doro Channel, and . . .'

Julia promptly lost interest and leant back into the pillows, closing her eyes.

'Tired, Julia?' he interrupted himself, and bent to drop a kiss on her cheek. 'Don't worry, there's no need for you. I'll just be doing informal lectures, chatting, you know, giving them the big picture. No need for boring archaeological detail,' he continued blithely, neatly slighting her speciality. 'They don't want history, they want romance.'

31

So, thought Julia bitterly, do I.

'Have a lie-in, and I'll see you later.' The door closed on his words.

For a while she tossed and turned, but true sleep eluded her. At last she turned to her fantasies.

The man with the dashing ponytail and piratical gold earring; the clever face with bright-blue eyes, and the gently malicious wit. At dinner she hadn't spoken more than a few words to him; now she summoned him to her.

He would undress slowly, his eyes never leaving her face as he stripped off the white, gold-braided jacket, revealing his torso, slim and sinewy, and hairless but for a few scant tendrils ringing his blunt nipples. He would smile as he unzipped his trousers, as his erection, strong and thick, pulsing with desire, sprang free. And he would stay motionless, letting his eyes and body speak for him, showing her how much he desired her.

His eyes caressing like fingers, travelling over her mouth, the curve of her jaw, her throat, to the slope of her breasts. Lingering at the nipples, sucking them, laving her breasts. Down the slope of her belly to the curly triangle between her legs, his breath gently rustling, then dipping to the tender skin of her inner thighs. Tracing the contours of her legs, the sensitive curve to the knee, flowing over her calves to the delicate arch of her foot.

At her pleasure he would come to her, warm and hard. Explore, with tongue and lips, teeth and cock, all the soft, hidden places, the tender skin just behind the lobe of her ear, the nape of her neck. Straddling her, he would offer himself, search the line of her brows with his prick, the curve of her cheekbones, the

32

contours of her mouth before placing himself at her lips.

She could taste him, bittersweet, hard steel sheathed in milky silk. Moistened by the touch of her mouth, he would follow the line of her throat, imprinting himself on her flesh, caressing her nipples with the velvet tip of his prick, making her feel the hot, hard power of him. The plangent thickness against her belly. The strident, insistent heat against her thigh. One swift, sure thrust to the heart of her, branding her with his length, his strength.

A swift withdrawal. The moist warm wash of his tongue where his prick had been, fluttering, stroking, tantalising, making her throb in newfound emptiness, craving the fullness. The hot coiling deep in the pit of her belly.

His mouth at her clitoris as his fingers probed deep inside her.

The heat. Gathering, twisting, snaking through her.

The pulse at her core, beating like a second heart.

The swift rush of his entry.

Julia soared.

When she woke, hours later, it was almost eleven; too late for breakfast, too early for lunch. Idly she pondered the day. She felt refreshed, the ghosts of the night before exorcised by sleep. She had been over-reacting, imagining things, she told herself irritably. Now she should, she decided, search out David, resume her appointed station by his side, ready to offer any advice or information. But his remark about 'boring archaeological details' rankled, and she was strangely disinclined to do anything resembling work. Some time for herself, some time to herself, she thought, leafing through the glossy brochure outlining the *Calypso*'s many amenities: spas and whirlpools, a hydrotherapy clinic, an aesthetics centre – nothing so crass as a beauty parlour here, she noted. You could lose five pounds in a morning, wrapped in damp cloths like an Egyptian mummy, refresh and revitalise yourself with a seaweed scrub, punish your body with an array of tortuous-looking exercise machines and then soothe it with aromatherapy and massage.

Oh to be one of those rich and pampered women for whom facials and manicures were as commonplace as brushing their teeth! The pool, at least, was within her reach, and it looked incredibly inviting in the picture – a glossy azure oval on the foredeck with a magnificent view of the sea.

She pawed through her case, deciding to leave the boring business of unpacking to another time, and extracted a slim black one-piece swimsuit. It was new, bought especially for the cruise, and cut high on the thighs, flattering her hips. A thin, kimono style cover-up and dark glasses, and she felt unexpectedly chic, almost glamorous.

The morning was warm, promising heat, the sea air soft and salty. *Calypso* sparkled gleaming white in the sun as Julia made her way to the foredeck. The pool, she was pleased to see, was deserted, with only a few people lounging on the deck chairs scattered along the edge, offering burnished, oiled bodies to the sun. A man, so deeply tanned his skin was the colour of mahogany; a couple absorbed in the morning papers; a white-coated steward offering cold drinks. A striking, dark-haired woman, in two scraps of gold lamé that only emphasised her near nudity, reading a lurid-looking paperback.

It was the woman who had spoken to her last night. She ought to say something, Julia realised dismally, erase any future awkwardness that her silly behaviour might cause.

'Um, good morning,' she ventured tentatively, standing at the foot of the lounger. Taking off her sunglasses, she essayed a smile.

Merise looked up. 'Good morning,' she responded, her voice cool.

'I just wanted to thank you for last night,' Julia persisted, perching awkwardly on an adjacent chair.

'Last night?' echoed Merise, raising her brows. This wasn't the plump brunette with the lovely, pale skin.

'Yes, it was kind of you,' said Julia doggedly.

'Kind?' said Merise. Memory returned. The shabby housecoat. The drab creature crying over the rails. Perhaps not quite so drab as she remembered. 'Not at all,' she replied, with perfect truthfulness.

For some reason, her patent disinterest put Julia at her ease. 'I was just being silly,' she said. 'I must have had too much to drink. David could never be unfaithful to me,' she added softly, almost to herself.

'He's dead, then?' queried Merise, her interest mildly piqued.

'Dead? Of course not,' exclaimed Julia.

'Impotent then?' offered Merise maliciously. Really, it was almost amusing, the way she flushed with colour. More amusing, at any rate, than the paperback Merise had been struggling through. Heralded as a raunchy, racy, sexy read it was proving sadly banal – as banal as this silly creature agonising over her lover's fidelity. Was there anything more trite?

'No, I mean, never,' stumbled Julia.

'Then of course he'll be unfaithful,' yawned Merise.

'Why do you say that?' asked Julia earnestly.

'The nature of the beast,' said Merise lightly. 'A prick, of course, has no brain. And it takes so little, so very little to make it hard, and a man helpless.'

This was so close to the colour of her fantasies that Julia found herself unconsciously nodding in agreement.

Merise shifted on to her side and let her gaze slide across Julia's body. 'Do you doubt me?' she smiled, provocatively running the tip of her tongue over her lips. The implicit challenge was irresistible and the imp that was her libido stirred. Her voice became low and sultry. 'To allure, to tempt, to seduce with your eyes, your voice, to promise that it will be longer, hotter and deeper and infinitely more exciting . . . oh, it's the simplest of the erotic arts.'

Julia's throat was dry. A thrumming pulse of sexual heat seemed to flow from Merise, charging the air. Her words, heavy and humid, hung between them.

'I could make him want me,' she continued softly. 'Make him want me enough to forget anything else.' She made a graceful, idle gesture with one hand, emphasising the swell of her breasts, the golden triangle between her thighs, glittering in the sun. She let her hand rest on her thigh, long, beautiful fingers splayed suggestively.

Potently, wordlessly, that mere gesture evoked the powers and pleasures of the flesh, the heady swirl of arousal, the susurrating rustle of desire.

'As I could make you,' whispered Merise. 'Make you wonder what it would be like, the soft, gentle flow of a woman's mouth on your body, knowing, as a man never can, all the delicate, sensitive, secret places, knowing how to lap and tongue, and circle and tease and please.'

Julia was motionless, mesmerised by the hypnotic rhythm of Merise's voice, the erotic portrait she was painting.

'Making you hot and wet with my tongue, making your breasts swell, making your nipples ache for my mouth. Making you cry out for me, sob for me, burn for me. I can make you come that way, you know, just my mouth on your breast, sucking endlessly until nothing exists but twin points of fire.'

Julia tensed. It was as clear, as compelling, as extravagant as any of her fantasies. She could almost feel that red, rapacious mouth at her breast.

'I could make you feel things you've never felt,' promised Merise seductively. 'And I can make him no more than a blind cock, urgent, mindless, wild to rut, frantic, fervid.'

And then she laughed, breaking the spell. 'So, do you doubt me?' Merise asked in her normal, cool tones.

'I – ' began Julia, then stopped, speechless.

'And now, of course,' said Merise, sounding pleased, 'you'll always wonder.' A tiny smile played about her mouth. There was something infinitely satisfying in playing carnal cat and mouse, especially when you were the cat.

'Yes, yes, that's true,' said the mouse, surprising her.

Merise had merely been amusing herself, toying a little with the mouse, flexing her claws for the fun of it; now it seemed that she had struck an unexpected chord. The girl's eyes seemed focused yet faraway, rapt and absorbed. Was she so sensually susceptible?

37

Julia's thoughts flowed swiftly, crystal clear, like a waterfall. In some bizarre, perverse way it seemed exactly right that this woman with the feral eyes should seduce David. Make him blind and mindless. If she could, it would prove something. Like some ancient rite of purification, some ritual cleansing, it would free her, remove the mantle of invisibility that David always cast upon her. She did not know how she knew this, but she did know it.

'Yes,' she heard her voice say, 'I should like you to seduce David.'

'How very curious,' observed Merise, rather taken aback. 'Why?'

'As you said, now I shall wonder if you could. If you would,' replied Julia. Impossible to explain the invisible cloak; impossible to explain the ingrained fantasy world that inexplicably made this the right thing, the only thing to do.

'Ah, yes, there is a difference,' agreed Merise. Now she was becoming intrigued. 'But why should I?' Her eyes narrowed. 'You're not, I hope, seeking a co-respondent for some tawdry divorce action?'

'Oh, no, we're not married,' said Julia, shaking her head. 'We're sort of almost engaged.' And that too was strange, she thought for the first time.

'Then I repeat, why should I?' Merise inquired, one eyebrow arched.

'Because otherwise you might wonder,' Julia said.

'Merise, my darling. And Julia, what a pleasant surprise.' It was Rupert, flopping, exaggeratedly limp, on a chair next to Merise. 'My dears, I require vast quantities of champagne at once. I've narrowly escaped the adoring throng clustering around our esteemed historian. So wise of you to absent yourselves. A

38

highly coloured version of Mycenae mixed with the sack of Troy. And someone was wearing Chanel No. 5, a scent I simply cannot abide.' He rattled on amusingly, his eyes darting from Julia to Merise.

A most unlikely pair, he conceded, wondering at finding them together. Was Julia the lovelorn waif Merise had happened upon? Ever willing to aid the course of true – or, indeed, untrue – love, he made a mildly bitchy remark about David's scholarship, and waited for Julia's reaction.

Julia fumbled a little, disconcerted by the sudden appearance in the flesh of the man who only that morning had played in her fantasy. 'Um, well, David wants to give them the big picture, you see. Not scholarship, necessarily, but romance.'

'Ah, romance,' sighed Rupert theatrically, rather amused that she had not leapt to his defence.

'So David, then, your sort of almost fiancé, is the historical lecturer and a romantic?' Merise asked Julia.

'Yes, well, yes and no. I mean yes, he's here to lecture, but no, I don't think he's a romantic.'

'That certainly makes it easier,' remarked Merise ambiguously, with a smile so familiar, so unambiguous that Rupert was quite surprised. 'Julia – it is Julia, yes? – wants me to seduce her sort of almost fiancé,' she explained blandly, turning to Rupert.

'Darling, what fun,' said Rupert, eyeing Julia with interest. 'And how original. It's usually the other way around.'

Julia felt the heat rise to her cheeks. Silently she toyed with her sunglasses.

'Not really a challenge, I would have thought,' continued Rupert. 'From what I've seen he's quite susceptible to the fair sex. But why? Is it a challenge?'

'No,' said Julia quite calmly. 'It's a dare.'

'No,' corrected Merise. 'It's a game.'

'Excellent,' enthused Rupert. 'Can I play too?'

Applause rippled from the darkened lecture theatre as David concluded his talk. He gave a warm smile and a slight, mock bow to the audience, enjoying the adulation. It was well deserved, he knew. For almost an hour he had amused them, entertained them, shown slides and given them a taste of the big picture.

'Ladies and gentlemen, thank you. I'll certainly be available later to answer any of your questions. Now I understand that cocktails are being offered at the swimming pool on the foredeck.' Another warm smile and he pressed the switch on the lectern that lit the room.

He gathered his notes together as the passengers left the room, their progress spurred by the thought of cocktails. But one woman detached herself from the throng and made her way towards him.

She was striking, he thought, slim and elegant with masses of dark, silky hair. She moved with the graceful arrogance of one of the big cats. In a saffron-yellow silk halter dress and chunks of amber around her wrists and throat, it looked as though she was wrapped in sunlight.

'He summoned his best professional smile. 'Something I can help you with?' he asked.

'Oh, yes. Yes, I think so,' replied Merise, her voice husky and inviting.

The heat in her eyes astonished him. She was looking at him as though she were licking him, eyes flicking over his body to his groin, hungrily, greedily. Explicitly.

She held her hand out to him as she went up to the stairs to the podium. Unthinkingly he reached for it, intending a brief, informal handshake. But she tangled her fingers with his.

There was the silence that follows a vague and unanswerable remark – an awkward silence. And Merise exploited it, watching him, making him aware of her physical presence, still holding his hand. It was not an intimate clasp, but it was unexpected. Just enough to disconcert him slightly.

She let the silence grow as a small smile played around her lips.

David broke it, awkwardly. 'Some question perhaps? It was a very general introduction.' His voice trailed away at the look in her eyes.

Her dark eyes were hot and feral, challenging, disturbing. And she was standing close to him, too close, not touching but breaching the invisible barrier of space that strangers maintain. He could smell her perfume, something sweet and musky. It seemed to cling to his nostrils.

'An introduction of sorts,' said Merise vaguely.

Slowly, deliberately, she placed their entwined hands at his groin, her eyes never leaving his face.

David froze in shock and sudden lust. This was unreal, surreal, the distillation of fantasy. Her fingers moved knowingly, tracing the line of his shaft, exploring him, and he felt himself begin to harden reflexively.

The woman was mad. But her fingers – her fingers were magic, firm yet subtle, skilfully seeking and finding the sensitive ridge of his prick, closing on him. He had to stop her, wanted to stop her, yet wanted just a moment more of this exquisitely shocking stroking, this bizarrely exciting encounter.

Abruptly he shook his head, as if to clear it, tore his eyes away from hers and nervously scanned the room.

'No one can see,' purred Merise seductively. 'And no one need know.' Her fingers fluttered persuasively on the head of his shaft as she leant across to flick the light switch on the lectern. The room was plunged into darkness, the only illumination a white glare from the empty slide projector playing on the screen behind them.

'I – ' David began hoarsely.

'Haven't you ever had it like this? Wanted it like this? A stranger in the dark?' Her voice was molten. 'Ah, yes, you like this,' she said, feeling him stiffen under her hand. 'Imagine my mouth, hot and warm, wrapped around you, sucking you. You want that, don't you?'

Her fingers were insistent, demanding. He could feel the blood pulsing to his prick; the lust, swift, fierce and urgent.

'I'll stop if you don't want this,' she said. A taunt? A promise? Her fingers were deft, clasping and unclasping, making him even harder.

'No,' he heard his voice say.

It happened so quickly. In a moment her mouth was where her hand had been, the barrier of his clothing swept aside. It was like being licked by flames. Her hands and lips moved ceaselessly; the rhythms she used changed constantly. He was caught in the warm, red vice of her mouth, trapped by the snare of her snaking tongue.

She knew how to tease, drawing her tongue softly around the line of his retracted foreskin, how to

42

please, sucking him hard against the roof of her mouth, and she knew how to taunt, scraping the sensitive skin with her teeth.

It was madness. But when he reached out blindly, tangling his hands in her hair, it was to draw her closer, to surge into the hot, sucking cavern of her mouth. Never had he felt like this, rock-hard and heavy as lead, urgent as a boy. All he knew was the coiling heat in his groin, the pulse of her fingers swirling on the sensitive skin of his balls, the lewd insinuation of a finger between his buttocks.

Kneeling at his feet, Merise shifted David's position slightly ensuring that both he and she would be in perfect profile before the empty white screen.

For Julia, too, it was the heart of fantasy. Never before had she felt the voluptuous lure of the voyeur, the sly, secret titillation of watching others, of violating taboos. The cool carnality left her breathless. Invisible by choice, alone in the screening room, she watched and it was as though they served her pleasure by proxy. Transfixed, she could not tear her eyes away.

The phallus, boldly outlined on the white screen, thick and engorged, pulsing with life.

The flickering tongue, swirling along its length.

Lust observed was lust shared.

She felt the warm tingling awakening between her thighs, the heat of arousal.

Watching, for the first time she absorbed the pleasure of the male, the tumid, mindless, primal urge to mate, to spill; watching, she absorbed the carnal expertise of the female, the erotic poetry of her mouth and hands.

Unseen, she was an accomplice to their arousal, a

phantom partner, a lover alone yet not alone. She felt an ambiguous pleasure.

With cool, impersonal pleasure Merise felt him begin to shake, the muscles of his legs begin to tremble. His climax was close; she could spur him on or check him, frustrate or fulfil him according to her whim. That was the source of her own swift rush of pleasure, the exhilaration of pure sexual power. Knowing that Julia was watching sharpened the edge of her pleasure.

And mindful of Julia's eyes fixed on them, she remembered a whore's trick, learned in Paris.

When she felt his body tightening, gathering, pulsing with the need to come, she sucked him hard against the roof of her mouth, and then dragged her mouth away as he began to spurt, carefully tilting her head so that the semen flowed, arcing through the air from his prick to her waiting lips.

Chapter Three

'So, tell me, what did that prove to you?' asked Merise.

It was twilight. The sun had met the sea, disappearing below the horizon with a brilliant burst of flame, and the sky glowed softly in reminiscence. Merise and Julia were sitting beside the pool, Merise curled languidly on the lounger like a drowsy cat, sipping gin and tonic. Julia's drink stood untouched on the table between them.

'Something,' replied Julia slowly and hesitantly. 'Something significant.'

'Yes?' prompted Merise, selecting a handful of peanuts and delicately licking the salt from each one. She felt sexually complacent, if not sated, and rather curious about Julia's reaction.

'When I saw him with you, something changed. He was at the same time more and less than I believed him to be. Does that make sense to you?' asked Julia, reaching for her glass.

'No,' replied Merise baldly. 'What you saw was a man as he is – a blind phallus, nothing more. I asked what it proved to you.'

'Well, perhaps no more than that.' Julia's tone was thoughtful. 'But it made me see both of us in a different light.'

The hot, white glare of the empty slide projector illuminating David's swollen shaft. The jutting arc of semen as it flowed to Merise's waiting lips. The illicit, complicit thrill as she watched, unobserved.

'David, you see, overpowers me,' she continued. 'And to see him so easily overpowered himself . . .' Her voice trailed off.

'Overpowers you?' repeated Merise, vaguely amused. David had been so pliant, so easily aroused, so susceptible. Of course, she had served the male ego, the male fantasy – swift, sharp, anonymous sex, a woman on her knees before him, overcome with lust – really, it was all so easy. A predictable one, she decided, mentally scoring the encounter. But remembering her own surge of pleasure, from knowing that Julia's eyes were avidly devouring her every movement, she raised it to a four.

'He has so much charm, so much energy,' explained Julia, tasting her drink for the first time. 'At first I was – what, flattered that he was interested in me? It was exciting. And then it became – I don't know – somehow easier. David casts a long shadow. I was happy in the shade, I think.'

'How dull of you,' said Merise lightly with a faintly malicious smile. She was surprised at the sudden fire in Julia's eyes.

'Not any more,' replied Julia flatly.

'No? So what do you propose to do now? Break off

your almost but not quite engagement? Bring him to his knees, as I did? Well, metaphorically at least.' Merise's voice was silky.

Again the image of David and Merise flashed before her. David aroused and shaking with need, Merise so potently powerful. She felt the tingling echo of their lust feather down her spine.

'Yes and no,' said Julia, feeling her way to an answer. Sex was not the answer, or was it? It was certainly part of the equation, or part of the question. A means, or an end, she wasn't sure.

'Darlings, here you are,' said Rupert gaily, emerging from the shadows. 'I've been scouring the decks for you. Simply too bad of you to start comparing notes without me. After all, who masterminded our little vignette of this afternoon?'

Of course it was Rupert who had carefully shepherded away the passengers to cocktails on the foredeck; Rupert who had thoughtfully locked the door behind them; Rupert who had arranged for Julia to sit alone in the screening room. He was gazing at them now with the eager expectancy of a child on Christmas morning, greedy for gift-wrapped gossip.

'And who played the starring role?' Merise said sweetly. 'Rather brilliantly too, I might add.'

'Darling Merise, was there ever any doubt?' He knew the sensually compelling force of her hands and mouth, the skilled eroticism of her touch. After all, he had taught her himself. 'Julia?'

Blue eyes alive with mischief scanned her face. To his surprise, the dull aura that had seemed to encase her had faded; her eyes seemed brighter, more green than hazel. He found himself mentally remaking her as she fumbled a reply. A striking haircut with some

47

added colour; dramatic shadow in vivid colours to bring her eyes to life; bold artifice could create a quite stunning creature, if cleverly applied.

'It was quite remarkable,' said Julia slowly, groping for the right word. 'I felt – free.'

'I'm sure that's not all you felt,' commented Merise, her red lips curving in a knowing smile.

'No,' acknowledged Julia honestly. The dull throb of observed desire still echoed in her own body. 'But it was the most important.'

'Important?' queried Rupert.

'Because it was invented. We made it happen. I can invent something else. Reinvent myself, perhaps.'

'And what do you want to be?' asked Rupert curiously.

'I want the power Merise has,' Julia replied without hesitation. 'The sensual power. And I want what David has. The acclaim, the reputation. I want to overpower him, myself. In every way.'

'Hmm.' The mischief faded from Rupert's eyes, replaced by swift calculation. This was promising material. His fondness for the role of Svengali had never left him and Julia, so outwardly drab, so unexpectedly adventurous, might prove a rewarding creation. And her academic qualifications were a considerable asset. Honed, moulded, reshaped, recast, she might become a second string to his bow, as Merise was his first.

And she might serve as the catalyst in the highly explosive, exceedingly complex web of intrigue he had been contemplating weaving for some time. Loose threads, he mused. Toss one skein to Merise, another to Julia – perhaps together they could spin a net to snare the prize.

He had not allowed himself to think too closely about the affair. True, he had connived and contrived this role as ship's purser as a perfect cover; true, he had persuaded Merise to join him in the vague expectation that should he decide to act, he might need her. But he had never expected that fate would provide such a perfect pawn as Julia. Seemingly repressed, yet sexually adventurous – no prude would have crossed swords with Merise in such a strange scenario; an experienced archaeologist thoroughly discontent with her lot and her lover; on the face of it, quite, quite perfect. But was she bold enough? Worse still, could she be plagued with the uncompromising morality of the conventional academic? That would never do at all.

'Ambitious,' drawled Merise, finishing her drink and signalling a passing waiter for another.

Yes, mused Rupert, his thoughts flowing freely, ambitious and audacious, deliciously so.

'And quite improbable,' concluded Merise.

'Not necessarily,' corrected Rupert, roused from his reverie.

Alone in her cabin, Julia prepared to change for dinner. She was preoccupied, wondering at her own, uncharacteristic outburst and the feelings that had provoked it, wondering too at Rupert's enigmatic remarks. Since meeting Merise and then Rupert she had been behaving completely out of character. She was astonished at how much she was enjoying it.

Or was it out of character? Immersing herself in the tiny shower, enjoying the play of cool water on her naked body, she considered for the first time the heady effects of the fantasy world that she had created

49

for herself. It had begun as no more than a harmless distraction, a ploy to combat her shyness, her reserve. But the barriers between fantasy and reality were becoming more fragile. It had raised her sexual curiosity, her taste for adventure. No other explanation was possible for the way she had responded to Merise's challenge.

For challenge it had been. She could still hear that beautiful, husky voice. *I could make you feel things you've never felt. And I can make him no more than a blind cock, urgent, mindless, wild to rut, frantic, fervid.*

Despite the cool water, she felt her body begin to heat at the memory. Dreamily she soaped herself, savouring the delicious tingling as her nipples hardened under her fingers.

Over the sound of the shower she heard the door to the cabin open and then close: David was back.

Did she blame him, she wondered absently, turning off the shower and reaching for a towel. It was hardly fair to expect him to resist the powerful lure of Merise when she herself had already succumbed. Yet she was conscious of a deep resentment, a resentment that had nothing to do with sex. How curious that the issue of his fidelity, once so crucial, now seemed meaningless.

Should she confront him with it? She could do it wordlessly, effortlessly – go to him now, mimic Merise by placing her hands on his groin, make him hard with her fingers, then take him between her lips and draw him deep into the cavern of her mouth, as Merise had done, releasing him slowly – yes, then surely David would know.

The idea had a certain, bizarre appeal, a sort of sexual symmetry.

'Julia, are you almost finished in there? I want a

quick shower before dinner.' David's voice was impatient.

Julia glanced at herself in the misty mirror. Her eyes were bright, her face faintly flushed. She let the towel she had wrapped around her fall. 'Come in, David,' she called.

'There's hardly room for both of us,' he grumbled, opening the door. 'And I need a shave.' Oblivious of her nudity, he edged toward the sink.

It was simple, then, to ease between him and the sink, press her naked body against his, reach down and cup his groin.

'Julia, honey, really, there's no time . . .' David's voice trailed away.

Julia ignored him, concentrating on recapturing the rhythm she had observed, fluttering her fingers along the outline of his shaft, stroking him until he began to harden. She felt a glowing surge of triumph as he thickened at her touch. It was enough.

'I hadn't realised it was so late,' she said casually, turning away.

In his office below decks, Rupert smoked reflectively. He seldom indulged in cigarettes, preferring the occasional cigar, but the occasion seemed to call for a packet of Gitanes and a stiff whisky and soda. The captain, influenced by the prevailing winds, had set their course for the Turkish coast, bypassing Chios and Lesbos; inspired perhaps by David's florid stories, he was talking of a shore expedition to Troy.

It was too much of a coincidence; fate was clearly dealing Rupert a winning hand.

From the point of view of a ship's purser, the proposed visit was ludicrous. Passengers expecting

51

rocky grandeur and spectacular vistas, the lofty towers of Ilium, were going to be confronted with a jumble of gullies and ditches, rubble and overgrown bushes and some rather fine walls, all of which would fit comfortably in the concourse of London's Euston Station.

On the other hand, from the point of view of an antiquarian not averse to dabbling in the black market who was masquerading as a ship's purser, the proposed visit was a remarkable stroke of luck. There was unfinished business there for the man who had once sold dubious antiques to credulous tourists in Rome. He had kept his contacts and friends from the old days and rumours still reached him: rumours from Egypt of intact tombs being secretly and skilfully plundered by unscrupulous custodians; rumours from South Italy of a cache of priceless Apulian vases – and rumours from Turkey of a secret treasure trove of Trojan gold.

With cheerful impartiality, he was on the best of terms with both cops and robbers, thieves and those set to trap them; neither side had managed to penetrate the veil of secrecy surrounding the new Trojan treasure.

Set a thief to catch a thief – an overworked ploy, these days, that often resulted in narcotics officers setting each other up for deals, and undercover art squads from different countries investigating each other. But someone completely innocent, with impeccable credentials, someone unknown, might succeed where the professionals would fail.

Someone like Julia, perhaps.

Rupert lit a fresh cigarette, surprised to find nearly

half the packet gone and his ashtray full. Shortly he would have to make his appearance at dinner.

Meditatively he blew a smoke ring.

Except for those invited to the captain's table, seating at dinner was informal. Already little groups were beginning to coalesce; the dedicated non-smokers, the wine drinkers.

Merise paused at the doorway and glanced casually around the room. She was aware of several speculative looks cast her way, and an icy glare from one man who looked vaguely familiar. Raising her eyebrows, she recognised him from the night before. She smiled, a warm, knowing, utterly seductive smile, and entered the room with the vague intention of joining their table. It would be amusing to discover just how much his luscious little wife remembered; amusing, too, to toy with his hostility.

'Darling Merise, you'll join us, of course,' said Rupert, suddenly appearing by her side and gesturing to the table where David and Julia were sitting. Julia was apparently engrossed in the wine list; David was chatting animatedly to a haggard-looking brunette wearing too much make-up and too many emeralds.

'Really, Rupert,' Merise began to protest, then felt the subtle pressure of his fingers on her wrist at the pulse.

'It's important,' he whispered softly.

Eyes narrowing in surprise, she turned to look at him. She couldn't mistake the mischief in those bright-blue eyes, the aura of barely suppressed excitement.

'You're up to something,' said Merise. She recognised that look, that suspicious gleam in his eyes. He had looked much the same the night he had appeared in her apartment in New York with a purloined Renoir to finance mining for gold in the Yukon.

'Mmm,' he replied unresponsively, urging her towards the table.

For a moment she hesitated, and then, mentally shrugging her shoulders, gave in.

'But why? And what do you want me to do?' she asked curiously. In her mind, David and Julia had already been relegated to the realms of history where, by virtue of academe, they already belonged. An afternoon's whim. A mere flexing of her sexual muscles.

'Be yourself, my darling, which you do so well. Captivate our dreary lecturer, draw him out – '

'I did that this afternoon,' Merise retorted, unable to resist the pun.

'And *so* artistically, my pet,' approved Rupert. 'Just follow my lead, and if it should happen to lead to your cabin, well, I'm sure Julia – and I – will be suitably grateful.'

'You and Julia?' Merise blurted, almost tripping in shock.

'Merise, my darling, it's not what you're thinking – or, at least, not quite. I'll tell you everything later. And I'll need your help, I think,' said Rupert rapidly, hastily pulling out a chair and bestowing a charming smile at the table at large. 'David, Julia, you don't mind if we join you? I don't think you know Merise Van Asche, one of our most delightful passengers, and Mrs Armitage, you're looking resplendent tonight, those emeralds are truly to die for, but I've interrupted you, David, what were you saying?'

There was a brief, frozen moment as David recognised Merise. Mrs Armitage smiled coyly and fingered

54

an emerald earring before flitting off to her own table. Julia set aside the wine list and smiled.

The table was set for eight. Another couple joined them, and then another. Introductions were made, names exchanged. As if from some great distance, David heard his own voice responding, saying all the right things, laughing politely at some sally of Rupert's, while the blood drummed thickly in his ears.

'And here we are, sailing the seas that Odysseus once sailed and the mighty Agamemnon.'

'We really came for a rest, just to get away from everything.'

'The spa is divine, I don't think I'll even leave the ship.'

'Oysters, how lovely, just what I was craving.'

It was Merise's voice, low and husky, that broke the spell. With a start, David came to himself. Before him, artistically arranged on a bed of cracked ice, were half a dozen oysters; beside him was Julia, discussing the works of Homer and Schliemann's early excavations with the purser, Rupert; across from him, delicately licking an oyster shell, was the woman who, a few short hours ago, had been licking his penis with equal finesse and concentration.

He caught her eye and she smiled at him. A swift, conspiratorial smile that seemed to promise discretion. David began to breathe more easily.

'Of course, if it wasn't for Homer's *Iliad*, we wouldn't think of it at all – just another small city in the Mediterranean, one of thousands.' Julia, speaking calmly, authoritatively.

Reflexively David interrupted her. 'Julia, really. Troy is one city that stands for all cities – rise and fall, the great siege, the mighty destruction, all for the sake of Helen, whose beauty launched a thousand ships.' That was better; he was on form now. He prepared to captivate the table with the tale of Schliemann's discovery, how the self-taught, self-made German millionaire had pursued a childhood dream to discover the lost city. It was a good story, and he told it well, only peripherally aware of Julia and Rupert conversing in low tones.

Had he been listening, he would have been quite surprised.

For Rupert and Julia were having a technical and complicated argument over the identification of Homer's Troy.

'The identification of Troy VIIa, a paltry site – '

'The date fits, mid-thirteenth century, when the great royal palaces of Mycenaean Greece – '

'Ah, but the pottery dates are unreliable.'

'When you consider how much Schliemann actually destroyed . . .'

'But no other rival site has been identified in the area, and it must be the north-west corner of Turkey.'

Merise, listening with half an ear to both conversations, was becoming bored. A champagne sorbet was offered to cleanse the palate before the *boeuf en croute*; a rich, full-bodied Burgundy replaced the Chardonnay. It was unnecessary to captivate David; he was engrossed in his tale, and in love with the sound of his own voice.

Later, perhaps, if Rupert wanted to slip away with Julia, as he had implied. But why on earth should he?

Then one word caught her attention.

'Gold?' she asked, turning to Rupert. 'What gold?'

* * *

56

Dessert was a sinful dark chocolate mousse decorated with swirls of white chocolate and almonds followed by a selection of cheese and fresh fruit, coffee and brandy. With the removal of the main course, conversation once again became general, then flagged.

Obedient to the subtle pressure of Rupert's thigh, Merise recalled her promise to divert David. It wasn't difficult; an intimate smile, a caressing look, a flattering reference to his wide and varied knowledge, a few subtle remarks couched in the language of *double entendre* and innuendo.

David hardly noticed when Julia excused herself and when, a few moments later, Rupert followed her.

The purser's cabin was below decks. Compared to the luxurious fittings of the passenger's staterooms, it was sparsely furnished. No inviting settees lounged cosily against the walls; no pictures adorned the walls; there was no television, no built-in stereo. The furnishings consisted simply of a wardrobe, a desk and a single chair. And a double bed.

Julia, accepting a snifter of brandy from Rupert, felt her eyes drawn irresistibly to the bed. 'Let's discuss a theoretical proposition,' Rupert had said, inviting her to join him in his cabin.

She had accepted eagerly, without hesitation. She was enjoying their discussion about the ancient site of Troy, surprised to find his knowledge so detailed. Even David quailed at the chronology of Late Helladic pottery; Rupert seemed to revel in it.

And she was well aware that physically, emotionally, she was as drawn to Rupert as she was to Merise: together they embodied something she had only envisaged in her fantasy world. Somehow they were more vivid, more colourful, more *alive*.

Now, alone with him in his cabin, a cabin that seemed utterly dominated by the big double bed, she felt both excited and nervous, wishing simultaneously that she had never agreed to come while anxiously waiting for him to make some move. Any move.

Unaware of her nerves, Rupert was calmly reaching for another snifter, whistling softly. A tiny, detached part of her mind noted the tune was incredibly complicated and that he was completely on key.

'Please, Julia, make yourself comfortable,' he said, turning to her. 'I'm afraid there's only the one chair, or . . .' He smiled and nodded at the bed. This, Rupert decided, was going to be decisive. If she was going to be a perfect pawn, she would have to be prepared to use her body as well as her wits.

And use it well.

Face to face, she was suddenly even more conscious of him physically; the slim, strong lines of his body, the bright-blue eyes.

'Um, the chair is fine,' she said, taking a gulp of brandy. 'Thank you.'

He half turned away, hiding his amusement, and settled himself comfortably on the bed.

'You said something quite interesting to me, you know,' Rupert began.

'Oh, the redating of Late Helladic Three B sherds as it relates to Schliemann's stratigraphy,' interjected Julia, relieved and disappointed.

'No,' said Rupert gently. 'Fascinating as it may be.' He took a moment to let his eyes travel over her, assessing her primly crossed legs, lingering on her breasts, making sure she could feel the touch of his gaze. 'Earlier, when you said you wanted to reinvent yourself.'

Julia flushed slightly, recalling her words. 'I suppose we all say silly things – '

'And there was something else you wanted.' Rupert's eyes were fixed on hers. His voice was steady, measured.

I want the power Merise has. The sensual power.

Her words hung between them, as surely as if she had repeated them.

'It is possible,' said Rupert slowly, swirling his brandy glass and delicately inhaling the fumes, 'that I can help you. That we can help each other. But I would have to be sure.'

'Help me? Sure of what?' Julia stammered.

'I said I had a theoretical proposition for you,' said Rupert. 'Let's abandon theory, for the moment, and concentrate on the proposition.'

'What – what proposition?' She regretted the words as soon as she had said them. The proposition was abundantly clear, even if the motives were obscure. For some reason, Rupert was willing her to test her sexual powers, offering himself to her fantasy.

'Just pretend,' he said softly, unconsciously echoing her thoughts, and in her mind the phrase almost obliterated his next words. Later she was to recall some disjointed phrases – seductive interrogation, a passing reference to Mata Hari – at the time, all she heard was 'pretend'.

In her fantasy, he had come to her, aroused her, caressed her, tantalised her with his mouth, his tongue, his prick. Reality was the obverse: he was waiting for her to come to him. Challenging her to arouse him.

Instinct told her he was sexually more sophisticated, more knowing; instinct did not deceive her.

'No, not yet,' he said softly, shaking his head, as she stood and began to remove her clothing.

'No, not yet,' he said again, as she knelt beside the bed, her fingers struggling with the buttons of his jacket.

She felt frustrated yet excited. Prolonging the inevitable was a delicious torture.

'Slowly. Make me want your mouth. Like this.'

A fleeting kiss at her temple, his breath warm against her skin. The tip of his tongue, outlining her lips, his mouth a breath away from hers. She parted her lips, only to feel the delicate brush of his fingertip exploring the sensitive swell of her lower lip. And then he drew back. Waited.

They were lying face to face, fully clothed. Hesitantly Julia drew herself up on one elbow and looked down at him. She had expected to feel his mouth hard on hers, possessive, demanding, urgent; not this delicate minuet.

Rupert's face was expressionless, but his eyes were watchful. Tentatively she reached out, traced the lines of his thin, clever mouth with her finger. His lips were cool, but his eyes were warming. She let her hand glide over his face, along the strong lines of his jaw, faintly stubbled with dark hair. Down the sensitive column of his throat, until her fingers met the fabric of his jacket.

'Slowly,' she repeated, beginning to understand.

Rupert smiled and closed his eyes. Her mouth and hands were light as she explored him, delicately erotic. With subtle movements of his body he guided her to the pulse at his temple, his inner wrist, all the places men, as well as women, love to be touched. He checked her impatience, restrained her eagerness as skilfully, wordlessly, he taught her the artistry of anticipation.

Clothing was no hindrance when the starched cotton of his uniform could be used to vex his blunt, male nipples, chafe the thickening length of his prick; the silk of her dress, too, seemed to heighten sensation, not veil it.

It was a long time before he allowed their mouths to meet.

A chaste kiss, a mere mingling of breaths.

Swollen with anticipation, sensitised now to the merest movement of his body, his mouth, Julia sighed with pleasure as his tongue caressed hers, softly and delicately, then arched in a swift spasm of erotic shock as he plunged deep into her mouth, withdrawing only to thrust again and again in blatant mimicry of the act itself.

His mouth was hard, devouring, his hands all soft persuasion as they flirted with her nipples, a heated contrast of sensation. Senses swimming, she dimly recognised that he wanted the same from her.

Alternately fierce and tender, passionate and passive, he led her through the carnal spectrum, from the soft warmth of a gentle kiss to the swift flash of red heat as his teeth closed on her nipple. And gradually, almost imperceptibly, he allowed her to take control, to remove his jacket, her dress, his trousers, until at last they were both nude.

Julia felt as if she were on fire, her body melting and flowing into his. The pulse between her legs was beating like a second heart; she wanted him inside her, wanted the deep, rhythmic thrusts to stroke her to climax. But she had, almost unconsciously, absorbed his erotic instruction, and so she too was alternately fierce and tender, digging her fingers hard into the muscled globes of his buttocks as she delicately licked the tip of his penis, gliding the moist lips of her sex along his shaft as she scraped her teeth across his nipples.

Time blurred as their bodies tangled. He brought her to his mouth, sucked hard on her clitoris as his fingers fluttered at the mouth of her vagina, then reversed their bodies as he felt the first, faint contractions of her inner muscles. He caressed the cleft between her buttocks, fingered the taut mouth of her anus, then offered himself to her hands. Every sensitive, secret crevice was tasted, licked, explored.

Flesh met flesh, curled and meshed. When he finally surged inside her, Julia climaxed at once, a fierce convulsion that lifted her body like a wave.

Floating in the sea of mindless pleasure, she was barely aware of Rupert's withdrawal.

It could have been minutes or hours later when, drifting back to consciousness, she opened her eyes. Rupert was once again fully dressed in his uniform, sitting on the chair beside the desk, sipping brandy and smoking a cigarette. He had a strange, secretive look on his face, as if his thoughts were far away.

While Julia had slept, Rupert had slipped away to the ship's communication centre and made four calls.

The first to an old friend, now highly placed in the Turkish archaeological service.

The second to a schoolmate from Oxford, who owned a most respectable antique shop in New Bond

Street, a front for one of the more sophisticated smuggling rings in Europe.

The third to a contact at the British Embassy in Athens.

The fourth to the Helen and Menelaos Snack Bar in Tevfikiye, a dilapidated, crumbling structure just at the outskirts of the site of Troy.

From the first he received exuberant greetings, a few pointed, tersely guarded observations, the promise of immediate assistance with any necessary documentation, and the scent of danger.

From the second he learned a name.

To the third, he gave a few, discreet hints, just sufficient to kindle attention without attracting undue interest.

The fourth, to his surprise, failed to respond.

This was because the proprietor of the Helen and Menelaos Snack Bar, both friend and lover, and Rupert's most reliable informant, was lying dead, his throat cut from ear to ear, his blood slowly staining the dirt floor as the telephone rang and rang.

Chapter Four

Julia stretched slowly, cautiously, relishing the dull ache between her thighs, the echo of orgasm. Never before had she truly experienced the rosy, enveloping blush, the blissful languor of complete satiation, the physical resonance of utter fulfilment. It was as if some hitherto unknown string deep within her had been plucked, a mysterious note sounded.

She was exquisitely conscious of her body, ripe and sensitised, lush and full. Like a peach, she thought hazily, a rainbow, a desert flower in the sun after a rain shower. He had led her through a spectrum of sensation, an erotic extravaganza, tuned her body like a virtuoso and made her vibrantly, throbbingly aware of herself. Through half-closed eyes she watched Rupert and let her mind drift, relishing the mindless, purely physical enveloping contentment of a body well used.

Rupert sensed she was awake. For a moment he hesitated, unwilling to disturb her, his strategy still hazy. Now was the time to begin to lead her gently into his plot, while she was still warm with sex, pliant from passion. Thoughtfully he lit another cigarette and sipped his brandy.

The truth, he decided, but not all of it – just enough to allow her to play the role he was devising. A few lies – just enough to ensure his safety and hers. And a few necessary evasions.

Briefly, uncharacteristically, he hesitated. What he had in mind was certainly risky, quite possibly even dangerous. But, he reminded himself, it was Julia herself who had unknowingly made the first move. The circumstances were simply too, too compelling. Who was he, after all, to resist the role of fairy godmother?

Smothering a wry smile he rose, stubbed out his cigarette and walked over to the bed.

'Julia?' he said, reaching down to caress her cheek. 'You're awake?'

'Mmm, yes,' she replied. Her eyes were slumberous, her body still faintly flushed, still sensitive to his touch.

'It was good.' Half statement, half query. His hand slipped lower to cradle the swell of her breast.

'Oh, yes,' she breathed, feeling her nipples tighten reflexively.

'I thought it would be,' Rupert murmured with a little smile. 'You wanted something different, a little more exciting, a little more adventurous?' With the palm of his hand cupping her breast he pinched her nipple between his thumb and forefinger, rolling it firmly between them with a hard, insistent pressure that he knew would send shivering red darts straight to her groin.

'Poor Julia,' he said softly, lowering the sheet and tangling his other hand in the fleece of her mound. 'Life should be more interesting, shouldn't it? Not following meekly in David's shadow, but casting your own, isn't that right?' He tugged gently at the hair curling around his fingers, opening the slick lips of her vagina.

'I can help you do that, you know,' continued Rupert. His touch was firmer now, plucking her nipple to the point of pain, pulling harder on her hair.

Helplessly Julia gazed into his bright-blue eyes. Heat was snaking through her body. She was dizzy, dilating with desire. His fingers were as compelling, as persuasive as his words. At that moment she would have agreed to anything he asked only to prolong the haze of pleasure sweeping through her.

'I have contacts in Turkey, you know,' he said, easing one finger down to the bud of her clitoris, feeling her arch to his hand. 'And there are rumours, Julia, exciting rumours of lost hoards, of secret treasures.

'With your knowledge, with your expertise we could work together,' he coaxed. Her eyes had fluttered closed and her breathing was rapid. He had lost her, Rupert realised, brought her too quickly, too close to climax for his words to have any impact at all. She was still caught in the aftermath, the sensual realm where even minor stimulation evokes a stronger response. His hands stilled.

'Julia,' he chided gently, 'You're not paying attention.'

'Attention?' she gasped, eyes flying open. God, he couldn't stop now, not when every nerve in her body was singing, straining, surging to release.

66

Apparently he could. 'To my proposition,' he reproved with a laugh.

'Not now – more, please – finish,' she murmured disjointedly.

He slid down the bed, parted her thighs with his hands, and blew gently on the slick flesh of her mound. 'Are you listening, Julia?'

'Oh, yes,' she breathed.

'Good, good.' His tongue flickered swiftly over her clitoris and then was gone. 'Now, I was saying?'

How could she concentrate, with his breath warm on her sex, her body taut as a bow? Some sort of game, she thought dimly, some sort of test. 'Turkey – Turkey and treasure,' she recalled. 'Smuggling?' she asked, stiffening involuntarily and drawing away from his mouth.

Oh dear, sighed Rupert mentally, scruples. Damn. 'My dear girl,' he said with a plausible attempt at outrage, 'Do I look like a smuggler to you?' He didn't wait for an answer. 'I'm merely an antiquarian, an enthusiastic amateur. Oh, I'll admit, some of my contacts have fewer scruples, but they have their uses. And sometimes it's convenient to have one foot either side of the fence,' he added vaguely.

'What, then?' she asked curiously, her mind beginning to focus even as his tongue slipped between the plump folds of her labia.

'A coup,' replied Rupert. 'The archaeological coup of the century.' This, at least, he reflected, had the virtue of absolute truth.

'But the Turkish authorities, the foreign schools,' began Julia, puzzled. It was, she realised dimly, possible to separate mental and physical. Her body, under the sensuous sway of Rupert's tongue, was in

67

thrall as her mind struggled sluggishly to reassert itself.

'My dearest Julia, you of all people should know how overstretched the Turkish archaeological service is, how rich in ancient sites, how impossible to control with such a huge coastline. And gone are the days when they'd welcome the foreign schools to make their discoveries for them. Who can blame them, after the last two hundred years? But we can strike at the heart of the matter.'

As if to emphasise his words, his mouth closed on her clitoris, sucking hard, pulling the sensitive tip between his teeth. Liquid heat surged through her.

'Oh, yes,' she said, mind and body melding on the verge of climax.

'But you must', said Rupert sliding one finger inside her, and then another, and then a third, 'be prepared to put yourself completely in my hands.'

'Yes, yes, yes!'

'But I still don't understand,' Julia said later, sipping the brandy he had given her and smoking an unaccustomed cigarette.

Rupert was busily making notes and muttering to himself. 'Off the boat ... illness, of course, perhaps something infectious ... ship's doctor ... a makeover, nothing too obvious ... *on* the boat, since we're in the back of beyond ... damn Nazem, have to call again ...'

'Rupert,' Julia interrupted, her voice insistent, slicing through the plumes of smoke from her cigarette. 'I need to know more. If I'm going to help you.'

'Details, my dear Julia, details. You'll leave the cruise when we dock for the shore expedition for

Troy, the day after tomorrow, or perhaps before. It doesn't give us much time. You'll have all the necessary documents and credentials, and almost as crucial, a decent haircut. I'll arrange a meeting with Nazem and he can introduce you to the right circles. He can lead you to Tarik, I'm sure.'

'Exactly what is this all about?'

'Exactly? The lost city of Troy, my dear, and the real Trojan gold.' Rupert raised guileless blue eyes to hers. 'Didn't I make that clear?'

Under Julia's persistent questioning, the story unfolded, Rupert-like, in fits and starts. The unconfirmed discovery of a site near the mound of Hissarlik, rich in gold. ('I just adore gold, don't you? Silver is all very well for daytime wear, but it just doesn't work in the evening. And this is old gold, the gold of warriors, the gold of princes.') A cloistered freemasonry of illicit traders protecting the secret, headed by a Turkish industrialist known as Tarik. ('Industry is so grubby, so tacky, I've always thought, but it seems to pay.') An old friend, ex-MI5, who had somehow infiltrated in to Tarik's circle. ('You'll love Nazem, Julia, everybody does, such fun for you, and he'll help you every step of the way.')

Her cover? Posing as the expert adviser to a reclusive American billionaire and private collector determined not to be outdone in the growing market for smuggled artefacts. ('But of course my darling, we're on the side of the angels, protecting the cultural inheritance for Turkey, for generations to come, for – dare I say it? the world.') She, Julia, armed with academic expertise, could plausibly insinuate her way into Tarik's circle, evaluate the finds, and then blow the scam wide open to triumphant acclaim. ('What a coup! What an adventure!)

'What about,' said Julia slowly, rather shaken, 'Another brandy?'

Merise was bored. Distracting David wasn't difficult; he had followed her eagerly to the Starlight Lounge to dance, and now the hard bulge of his erection was pressing between them. He held her closer, apparently smugly confident that she would be impressed, excited.

She was not. She accepted the involuntary engorging of his prick as no more than her due. What man could fail to respond to the sinuous movement of her torso against his, remain unmoved by the closeness of her body? Especially a man who had already experienced the erotic expertise of her mouth, the flashing climax she had so expertly bestowed. She would have been surprised, perhaps even faintly intrigued, if he had remained limp.

No, the only faintly intriguing aspect to the evening was Rupert's interest in Julia, his fleeting reference to gold (which he had hastily diverted), and his insistence that she distract David. But not, she thought firmly, all the way to her cabin, as Rupert had suggested. Playing cat and mouse with Julia, with David as bait, had been amusing; the thought of sex for the sake of it was dull, dull, dull.

He would be, she mused, a clumsy lover – unimaginative, uninspired, the type who prided himself on knowing where the clitoris was without having the faintest idea of what to do with it.

Still, for Rupert's sake she would keep him amused for an hour or two, and then, having safely dispatched him to his own cabin, she would find Rupert and demand to know exactly what he was playing at.

Decadence he had promised her, and decadence she would have. Decadence was decidedly not dancing with some boring historian she had already sampled; decadence was not decoying some lecherous lecturer while Rupert played his own mysterious games.

Decadence was ... She let her mind wander. Well-matched debauchery, experience and inexperience, two men, even three, awakening a woman to the homoerotic delights of the flesh, initiating an innocent to the dark delights of pain and pleasure.

'This afternoon,' David breathed, close to her temple.

'Yes?' murmured Merise, dragging herself back to the present.

'You were – are – astonishing,' he said softly.

'True,' she replied evenly, her red, rapacious mouth softening to a smile.

'I couldn't believe it. And then you left so suddenly. And when I saw you at dinner ...' David's voice trailed away.

'Yes?' she prompted, tilting her head back to look into his eyes.

'Well, I thought ...' He pressed a little closer to her.

He seemed to be having a great deal of difficulty finishing a thought. 'Yes?' she prompted.

'Well, I was afraid it might be awkward. I mean, you and I at the same table, together, and Julia my ...'

'Wife?' interjected Merise wickedly.

'No, no, we're more partners,' corrected David. 'But I wouldn't want her to be upset. She's a bit old-fashioned.'

If only you knew, thought Merise, smothering a

71

smile. Julia's bourgeoise attitude to sex and fidelity had undergone a startling sea change. 'And you are not?' probed Merise.

'It's different for a man,' replied David with a smile.

Was there ever a more old-fashioned rationale, mused Merise. True, as she had said to Julia, a prick has no brain, but women were just as susceptible to the lures of the flesh. Their sensuality was more diffuse, less concentrated on a single organ, and thus, often, more easily aroused. She felt a brief, unfamiliar pang of sympathy for the creature that had been Julia, agonising over David's fidelity. She also felt rather pleased with herself for helping to obliterate that creature.

'I'm sorry, what did you say?' asked Merise, aware that she had lost the thread of David's words.

'I said we'll have to be discreet,' David said softly.

I must not laugh, Merise warned herself, as a bubble of pure amusement welled within her. No, no, laughter would be absolutely fatal. As inconceivable, as ridiculous, as utterly bizarre as it appeared, this man actually appeared to think he could use her as she had used him. How quaint. How naive. How very, very, wrong.

And perhaps, just perhaps, she would show him just how wrong.

Julia walked back to the cabin she shared with David. She felt strangely wayward, unsteady, as if her bones had melted. Her senses were both blurred and preternaturally acute. She was overwhelmingly conscious of the thick carpeting beneath her feet, the faint strains of music floating from the orchestra in the Starlight Lounge, the sweet scent of roses in the air, yet she made her way like a sleepwalker, relying solely on instinct to guide her to the cabin.

A mélange of disjointed images floated through her mind. Rupert's fingers, long and brown, cupping her breast; his eyes, bright as blue diamonds; the barely suppressed excitement in his voice when he spoke of the Trojan gold.

Her fingers trembled as she bent to unlock the door to the cabin. Suddenly she felt a wave of apprehension. She couldn't face David, not now, not with her mind in disarray, her body still warm from Rupert's last embrace. Quietly, stealthily, she opened the door and found the cabin dark and empty.

She closed the door and leant back with a sigh of relief. For a long time she simply stood there, eyes closed and breathing deeply, until she began to feel calmer.

Sleep. She needed sleep, the healing oblivion of unconsciousness. In the tiny bathroom she quickly washed her face and brushed her teeth, avoiding her own eyes in the mirror. She should shower, she realised, erase the heady scent of sex from her body, but she was simply too tired. A warm wash of cloth between her thighs, a spritz of cologne would have to suffice.

Yet once in bed, snuggled deep beneath the covers, sleep proved elusive. Her body might be exhausted, but her mind was clearing. The lost city of Troy and the real Trojan gold, a conspiracy, Tarik . . .

Impossible, she thought irritably, turning over on to her side. Troy had never been lost in any real sense; Homer gave its general location near the Dardanelles, along with landmarks, the islands of Imbros and Samothrace, Tenedos and Mount Ida. Impossible that a site so exhaustively excavated, so intensely studied, could yield a treasure trove. There was no need to try and recall all the details, the early explorers, the first excavations, the flaws in Schliemann's chronology: modern academic consensus decreed that of the settlements uncovered, Troy VIIa, a rather modest establishment destroyed by fire around the mid-thirteenth century BC, was the Troy of the Trojan War.

But did it matter?

With a sudden shock of surprise, she realised that she had been thinking exactly like the dull academic she had vowed to reinvent: plodding, pedestrian, obsessed with evidence, constrained by detail.

Did it really matter, she wondered with a rising tide of excitement. Did it matter whether Rupert was an amateur antiquarian, as he claimed, or someone with shady black-market connections, as she had begun to suspect? Did it matter whether the lost city and Trojan gold was a figment of his imagination, an elaborate hoax?

Wasn't it enough, more than enough, that Rupert was offering an adventure, a chance to break free, to escape into an unknown future?

Now wide awake, she rolled over on to her side to turn on the bedside light, and just as quickly thought better of it. She didn't want David to come in and find her awake. David. Her mind balked at his name. But it was necessary, she acknowledged, absolutely necessary, to think about him now. If she decided to go along with Rupert's plan and leave the cruise, she was also leaving David.

Irrevocably.

Was that what she wanted? Or could she have it both ways? Rupert had suggested she feign illness to leave the cruise. She could return from her foray into the unknown, completely recovered and with David none the wiser.

But if – just supposing if – if there was a treasure; if there was a lost city; if it was the archaeological coup of the century. How wonderful it would be to stand in the spotlight, with David, slack-jawed and incredulous, on the fringes. A series of images, each more flamboyant than the last, crossed her mind. She, Julia, on the cover of *The Times*, bedecked with gold, bracelets, earrings, necklaces, much like Sophia Schliemann had posed a hundred years earlier; David burning with rage and envy. Chat shows, interviews, book contracts; David slinking into academic obscurity. Julia a celebrity, and David crushed, pulverised by her success. Perhaps he'd turn to liquor for solace, or drugs. He'd lose his job, come crawling to her for help, for money, for forgiveness.

She was astonished at how intensely, deliciously, wonderfully pleasing the picture was. Mentally she shook herself, rather shocked. She was far, far more bitter than she had realised.

That, at least, solved the problem of David.

With a sigh of relief, she snuggled back under the covers. When, a few moments later, the cabin door opened and David sidled surreptitiously into the room, she was fast asleep.

'Decadence,' snorted Merise, her fine nostrils flaring. 'Refined hedonism! Decoying some pompous historian while you steal away his drab little wifelet is hardly my idea of decadence, Rupert. What are you up to this time?'

She had, Rupert realised, worked herself up into a

fine temper. He watched admiringly as she stalked around his cabin, the space too small to comfortably accommodate her rage. And she looked magnificent, her body quivering with tension, her dark eyes spitting.

'Darling Merise,' he began.

'Don't darling me, Rupert,' she hissed, stalking over to his desk and pouring herself a huge brandy. 'Tell me.'

Standing behind her, he fitted her to his body, cupping her buttocks to his groin, her long, lovely back to his chest, and gently kissed the nape of her neck. 'I will, my darling, I will. Relax for a moment.'

He held her until she suddenly softened against him, as he had known she would.

'So?' she asked, after a time, shifting away from him to sprawl on the bed.

'Gold,' he replied simply, with a smile. 'Old gold, exquisitely crafted, thousands of years old. A priceless treasure.'

'Treasure?' she scoffed. 'How much of that brandy have you had?'

'Merise, my love, I'm quite, quite serious. Tell me, how much do you know about Bronze Age Greece?'

'Little,' yawned Merise. 'And I care less.'

Rupert sighed and tried again. 'Homer describes three cities rich in gold – Troy, Mycenae and Orch-'

'Rupert.'

'-omenos. Schliemann excavated – '

'Rupert.'

'But I'm trying to explain,' he protested. 'Imagine, just for a moment, the shaft graves at Mycenae.'

'Oh, God.'

'Five graves, Merise. Nineteen men and women.

76

Two children. All covered in gold.' Some note in his voice caught her then; aware of it, he began to speak more rapidly. 'Funeral masks of hammered gold, breastplates, diadems, gold and silver drinking cups, glowing in the torchlight. Bronze daggers with golden hilts inlaid with silver. Hundreds of gold discs shaped like flowers, spirals, animals and fishes. The tomb of mighty warriors, the most magnificent, dazzling display of wealth and artistry of the ancient world.

'Old gold is different, you know. Softer, purer. It's like liquid sunshine, and it glows in a way new gold never will.'

'Oh,' said Merise, reluctantly impressed. It was the tone of his voice more than his words; he sounded like a visionary describing paradise.

'Well,' said Rupert, coming out of his trance, 'They found gold at Orchomenos and gold at Troy, but not as much at Troy as you might imagine for the booty that Paris is supposed to have stolen.'

'Paris?' asked Merise.

'Darling, that extensive convent education utterly ruined you,' reproved Rupert. 'Paris, Prince of Troy, who seduced Helen, wife of Menelaos – '

'No, no, really Rupert, that's too much,' interrupted Merise. 'Just get to the point.'

'Actually, that is the point,' said Rupert. 'There have been rumours recently that the real Trojan gold was never found. The academics, of course, know nothing – not their circles. The black market works in different ways. Luckily, though, their evidence supports the rumour, as the gold from Troy is a thousand years too early to be Helen's dowry.'

'Oh, I see,' said Merise scathingly, with a sudden flash of inspiration. 'So that's where Julia comes in.

You and your tame archaeologist jump ship, set off into the sunset with pick and shovel and dig up the treasure. Delusions of Indiana Jones, my dear.'

'Listen to me, Merise. Who knows most about any ancient site, who can conceal the secrets before they are ever discovered?'

She yawned, blatantly, and drank more brandy.

'The workmen, Merise, and their families. It's been established now for generations, a sort of freemasonry of traders. A network almost impossible to penetrate. But with the right decoy, a decoy with an impeccable cover and credentials, led gently to the right contacts, who knows what could happen?'

'And Julia is your decoy? A rather drab little decoy, darling, I must say.'

'Ah, but we can change that,' said Rupert confidently.

'We?' Merise inquired coldly.

'Of course "we",' Rupert said. 'A makeover in one of the salons, a bit of the polish that you know so well how to impart. And the reward for you – a little taste of decadence.'

'Decadence?'

'The corruption, my dear, of an innocent. I'm sure she's never been with a woman before. Wouldn't you like to awaken her to the pleasures of the flesh? Create a new sexual being?' Rupert was gambling here, and he knew it. But he sincerely wanted to placate Merise, and the experience would do Julia no harm. It might even prove another milestone on her journey to self-discovery.

'I don't know, Rupert, I really don't,' complained Merise, unconvinced. 'The whole affair sounds most improbable.'

'Not at all, my love, not at all. Did I ever tell you about the time I kept chickens in Provence?'

Julia, feigning sleep, lay in bed and listened to the sound of the shower. She and David, she mused hazily, seemed to have reached some unspoken accord. He hadn't woken her when he had returned to the cabin last night, and she knew that if she only continued to lie back, eyes closed, he wouldn't waken her when he left this morning.

The shower ceased, replaced by the whine of his electric shaver. She turned over on to her side, her back towards the door, as he entered the cabin to dress. He was trying to be quiet, but so self-consciously that he made twice as much noise as usual. At last she felt him move to the side of the bed where he paused uncertainly. Their customary brief kiss? No, evidently he thought better of it, for he moved away and the next thing she heard was the cabin door closing.

With a giggle of relief, she sat up and snapped on the light. She felt unexpectedly light-hearted, buoyed with anticipation, with expectation. The day beckoned. She relished the moment. It had been so long, so very long since she had awoken with such pleasurable expectancy. She felt like a child with some long-awaited treat in store, and laughed again at the image.

Room service, she decided greedily, reaching for the phone. Something truly fattening, to celebrate, like eggs benedict and bacon. Coffee, of course, and orange juice, and fruit, strawberries perhaps. By the time she had placed her order she was starving.

She showered, a long, hot, luxurious shower, then briskly towelled herself dry, revelling in the tingling friction against her naked skin. A red crescent moon on the whiteness of her breast, faint bruises on the insides of her thighs where Rupert had gripped her too tightly, reminded her of the night before.

She smiled at herself in the mirror, a voluptuary's smile of remembered pleasure.

It was a look David would not have recognised.

Breakfast arrived and she ate hungrily. It wasn't until she had finished and poured a second cup of coffee that she noticed the pale-blue envelope resting beside her bowl of strawberries.

With eager fingers she opened it.

'Meet me at The Spa at 11:00. R.'

His handwriting was neat, precise, his initial scrawled boldly. She felt a shiver of excitement as she stared at it.

The Spa was one of *Calypso*'s highlights. Encompassing one entire floor below deck, it offered everything: aesthetics, body sculpting, hydrotherapy, Swedish or Japanese massage, aromatherapy, mud baths, the trendiest techniques, the newest fads.

Decorated in flattering tones of peach and apricot, it was a temple to narcissism where plain women could acquire the patina of beauty, and beautiful women became even more beautiful. Under the watchful eye of Miko, a Japanese former supermodel, manicurists, pedicurists, stylists and make-up artists devoted themselves to enhancing, and sometimes transforming, nature.

Julia hesitated a little uncertainly at the double doors, her earlier buoyancy fading a little. She felt nervous and awkward. It was one thing to envy the polished creatures who frequented such places as if by divine right, quite another to find herself confronting the reality. She had never had so much as a facial in her entire life, she realised with a sudden feeling of panic.

She was relieved by the appearance of Rupert, walking down the corridor towards her.

'Julia, my dear, you got my note? How delightfully prompt you are.' Chattering away, he led her through the double doors. 'I've spoken to Miko and she knows exactly what we want. I know she'll find us a look – the look. I trust her implicitly, but implicitly! Ah, there you are, Miko my pet – my dear friend Julia, whom I place in your lovely hands. And now, darlings, I must dash, have tons of fun, my dears.'

It all seemed to be happening so quickly, thought Julia dazedly, as she followed the terrifyingly beautiful Japanese girl to a private cubicle and accepted the white towelling robe handed to her. The room looked like some strange hybrid of an operating theatre and a courtesan's boudoir with silk-covered walls and huge mirrors, a white and gilt vanity covered with an array of jars, bottles, tongs and tools all arrayed with surgical precision, and a chaise longue that mysteriously managed to suggest a hospital bed.

Miko was studying her intently, a furrow of concentration creasing her flawless forehead. 'Rupert has explained everything,' she said in her soft voice. 'Please, you will disrobe so that I may judge.'

A little awkwardly, Julia began to undress. Uncomfortable under Miko's intent scrutiny, she would have scooted into the towelling robe immediately, but Miko stopped her with a gesture.

'Not too fat, not too thin,' she murmured. 'A few pounds less here, perhaps, to create the waist.' Her hands, delicate as butterflies, rested for a moment

81

under Julia's ribs, then flowed to her thighs. 'A complete waxing, one must never use the razor.' Her hand fluttered uncertainly at the cluster of pubic hair. 'More definition here, more style.'

Miko seemed utterly absorbed.

Why, I'm nothing more than a body to her, thought Julia. An example of flesh, pure and simple. Her awkwardness began to ease.

'Sergio for your hair, a rinse, some highlights.' She stroked her fingers through Julia's hair, and then again lightly touched her mound. 'And here of course, too. One must be thorough. You will relax, and simply enjoy, yes?'

The next three hours passed in a blur of mindless physical sensation. Heat, constriction and tingling as she was wrapped from torso to thigh in a sculpting sheet. An almost painful sensitivity from the waxing, as if her skin was being burnished. The scrape of pumice on the soles of her feet. The soothing comfort of creams and oils massaged all over her body. It was like some out-of-body experience, the real Julia was detached, floating, observing, while her flesh was pliant to unknown hands. She began to feel a wonderful sense of anonymity, of otherness, one of the most seductive of feelings.

She watched as Sergio played with her hair, combing it this way and that. If he spoke to her, she wasn't aware of it. The interminable, tedious process of tinting, cutting and styling passed in a haze.

She was a butterfly emerging from her cocoon, a new, green shoot budding forth from an old plant. There was a dim, erotic unreality in submitting mindlessly to his hands. She felt no embarrassment as he parted her legs and delicately painted the vee of her

82

pubic hair with the tinting brush, only a self-satisfied, pleasurable glow.

With the same, detached interest she watched as Miko recreated her face, enlarging her eyes with shadow, dying her lashes a darker shade, finding her cheekbones and narrowing her nose with shades of foundation.

It was not until Rupert reappeared that reality surfaced.

'Well, Julia,' he whistled softly. 'Very, very well.'

She smiled at him and looked back at the mirror.

'Stand up and let me see,' he said.

Unselfconsciously she stood and slipped off her towelling robe. The sculpting had narrowed her waist, emphasising the swell of her hips, so that her figure now seemed more voluptuous than undistinguished. Her flesh glowed. Her lightened hair warmed her skin, the fashionable blunt cut drew attention to the shape of her face. And her eyes, no longer some indeterminate shade, were triumphantly green.

'So, the little duckling becomes a swan?' commented Merise with more than a trace of acid in her voice.

They were in Merise's cabin, Rupert and Julia enjoying a late lunch provided by room service while Merise merely sipped champagne. Never one to underestimate the value of a good hair cut and flattering make-up, Merise was still astonished at the change in Julia. In some strange way it seemed to come from within, owing nothing to artifice.

'Something like that,' Julia agreed equably.

'Clothes,' said Rupert indistinctly, munching asparagus. 'Not much, jeans and khaki, but truly sexy lingerie, black and high cut, silk, yes, definitely.'

'What the well-dressed archaeologist is wearing this season?' mocked Merise.

It fell flat.

'Absolutely,' enthused Rupert. 'The ship's boutiques are bound to have something, you two can browse this afternoon. It'll be such fun for you, Merise. Oh, damn,' he exclaimed as his beeper shrilled out. 'Must go, my darlings, I'm sure you'll keep each other amused. I shall return *à bientot* because I think, I truly think, we'll shift our plans to dawn. We should be close enough to shore, one of the zodiacs will suffice, five o'clock perhaps . . .' The door closed on his words.

The two women were silent after he left.

'So, you know about Rupert's plans?' asked Julia at last, before the silence became too oppressive.

'Lost treasures?' scoffed Merise. 'My dear, Rupert has been searching for lost treasures all his life. One madcap, harebrained, ill-conceived scheme after another.' And that was not completely untrue, reflected Merise, thinking of him keeping chickens in Provence. While she had no real desire to interfere with Rupert's plans, the transformation of the drab little mouse galled her in some inexplicable way. This was no longer some innocent to be debauched, as Rupert had insinuated; there was a new, elusive, sensual awareness about Julia that had nothing to do with simple vanity.

'An amusing way to live,' returned Julia lightly, seemingly unperturbed.

An unexpected response, thought Merise with a tinge of grudging respect. 'If you can afford it,' she countered. 'Can you?'

The question had nothing to do with money, and both women knew it. Julia paused before replying.

'I'm not sure,' she replied honestly. 'But it will be worth it to find out.'

She was surprised at the smile that lit Merise's eyes. It was frank, approving, open, and, for the first time, honestly friendly.

In the ship's communication centre, Rupert stood, white-faced, the receiver dangling from his hand.

Impossible.

Inconceivable.

Nazem, friend and lover, the poor Turkish peasant who ran the Helen and Menelaos Snack Bar, Nazem, ex-MI5 and Rupert's most reliable informant and contact, was dead.

The details disjointedly offered by his grieving brother, Mabik, were unclear. Random violence? In the tiny, sleepy, dusty village of Tevfikiye, no more than a collection of rude dwellings and stray goats? A warning? An old score settled?

Rupert was shaken. Murder and violence played no role in his schemes, and while a frisson of danger always enhanced his delight when snaring a prize or outwitting an adversary, he had never spilled blood to achieve his ends. It was too, too messy, he thought distractedly.

He would grieve, in his own way and his own time, but first he had to decide what to do.

Abandon the lure of lost treasure?

Trust Mabik to lead Julia through the complex network Nazem had known?

What price the Trojan gold?

Chapter Five

'We have a – a problem,' announced Rupert abruptly as he entered Merise's cabin. Julia and Merise, still dawdling over lunch, looked up in surprise as he strode over to the table, unceremoniously plucked the champagne bottle from its ice bucket, splashed some into a glass and downed it in one swallow.

Merise was concerned when she saw the look on his face. He was pale, his eyes like flat blue stones. 'What's the matter?'

'Nazem is dead,' he said flatly. 'Murdered.'

'Oh, no,' gasped Julia faintly. 'How do you know? I mean – what happened?'

'And who is Nazem?' asked Merise.

Rupert looked at her distractedly. He hadn't troubled Merise with the details; her interest in the Trojan gold had been perfunctory at best. 'A friend,' he replied slowly. 'A good friend. And my contact in Turkey.'

'Contact?' queried Merise.

'An ex-government agent turned freelance,' explained Rupert impatiently. 'He ran the snack bar at the edge of the site as his cover while he pursued his investigations.'

'How did you find out?' asked Julia.

'I called just now and spoke to Mabik, his brother. The stakes seem to be much higher than I realised,' he added softly, almost to himself.

'What happened?' persisted Julia.

'It's almost unheard of,' continued Rupert randomly. 'There are always risks, but for the most part, we don't like our treasures stained with blood. How did it happen? His throat was slit.'

'How horrible,' shuddered Merise.

'And you think Tarik is behind it?' ventured Julia, some of the colour returning to her cheeks.

'Who is Tarik?' asked Merise.

'Who else?' shrugged Rupert irritably, ignoring her.

'Well,' said Julia, consideringly, 'you said he was ex-MI5. It could be an old enemy, someone who had discovered his whereabouts. Perhaps it was personal. A jealous husband, a debt or something. What did his brother say?'

'Mabik was careful,' replied Rupert thoughtfully. 'He did say that Nazem was expecting me, and as the new head of the family he would arrange the welcome Nazem would have given us. We were speaking French; he used the verb *arranger*.'

'Which means?' prompted Julia.

'Which suggests,' corrected Rupert, 'that Mabik may be carrying on Nazem's work. Or was merely being polite, extending Turkish hospitality.' Or it might be a trap, he thought to himself. *Arranger* could mean almost anything – to set in order, to arrange, to contrive. Or settle a quarrel. Mabik might belong to the other side, family ties notwithstanding and if that were the case, he would have a score to settle with Rupert himself. God, what a mess. Duplicity, deception, and double dealing were Rupert's forte, not Julia's. He would have trusted Nazem with her life; Mabik was an unknown quantity.

And now the knives were out and first blood had been drawn. Rupert had no morals and few scruples, but he couldn't in all conscience send Julia in like some ritual lamb for slaughter. Too late now to arrange anything else; they would have to abandon their plans.

'But we still go ahead, don't we? Even without Nazem?' asked Julia. She could see the answer in his eyes, even before he spoke. A sickening wave of disappointment rushed through her.

'Rupert, we must,' she said quickly, words tumbling out in a torrent. 'My cover is perfect, you said so yourself. Even without Nazem's help, I can manage, make such a stir that it's bound to flush Tarik out. Mabik will help.'

'And has it occurred to you that Mabik may not be on our side?' suggested Rupert sardonically.

'Of course,' she surprised him by saying. 'And if that's the case, he'll lead me to Tarik all the sooner.'

She had a point there, Rupert conceded. 'It may be dangerous, Julia, much more dangerous than I anticipated.'

He was surprised by the hot glow in her eyes. 'Oh, yes, I know that,' she replied.

Good God, she actually likes the thought of it,

Rupert realised. He had seen that reaction before, the slick excitement, the sudden, nervous energy. The thought of danger was an aphrodisiac to some, but he couldn't have imagined Julia as one of them. Not quite a lamb to the slaughter, then.

'Julia,' he began.

'Or I'll go on my own.'

Rupert was silent. She meant what she said; her voice was flat, matter of fact. He turned the question over in his mind, fruitlessly. Julia knew too much already, enough to seriously endanger everything.

Merise's cool voice interrupted his thoughts. 'I have no idea who this Nazem is, or Tarik, or Julia's cover,' she said. 'And no desire to know. But it's not like you to be so spineless, Rupert. Think of those chickens in Provence.'

A decisive hit, Rupert acknowledged wryly. 'Please, God, not chickens,' he muttered.

'So we'll do it?' asked Julia eagerly, understanding only the note of weary capitulation in his voice.

'Yes, we'll do it,' he agreed. The decision made, he seemed to regain some of his old sparkle. 'So, then, details, details. I'll speak to Mabik again, arrange to meet. Merise, you can help Julia pack the right things – no, select them yourself, charge them to my account.'

'Right things?' asked Merise.

'Professional but with a provocative edge,' explained Rupert. 'And Julia, you'll have to remain here, out of sight. I'm afraid, my dear, that you're about to become very, very ill. So ill that the ship's doctor insists that you be flown to the nearest hospital. There's a helicopter on board for emergencies. I wonder, appendicitis? A coronary? No, you're too young, just sudden, shocking, undiagnosed pains, severe, but not life threatening. A sudden onset, so sudden that there was no time at all to inform David. Do you know, I rather think you've already left?'

'I must go to her,' protested David weakly. 'I mean, she'll need me.' Damn Julia, he thought furiously, just when the cruise was beginning to get underway, just when he was finding his stride among all these rich, influential people, just as he was making an impact, she had to spoil it all. Just to get his attention, he was sure of it. And the hell of it was – it worked. He had to be shocked and concerned, desperate to rush to her side – his image of himself would accept nothing less – but inwardly he raged.

'My dear, dear chap,' began Rupert soothingly.

He sympathised eloquently with David's distress; managed to convey his deep understanding of a man torn between his public and private duties; even (was he going too far here, wondered Rupert gleefully) mentioned a 'stiff upper lip'.

And by the time he was finished, David had begun to feel that there was something, well, noble, indeed almost heroic, in abandoning his almost-but-not-quite-fiancée to the hands of an unknown doctor in a foreign country while he valiantly remained with the cruise.

'Professional, but provocative,' pronounced Merise, tossing some packages on to her bed. 'Open them and see what you think.'

From the delicate folds of tissue paper a symphony of silk emerged, vivid scarlet, inky black, creamy white, celestial blue, saffron yellow, bras and panties

90

so suggestively cut, so superbly seductive, so low on the breasts, so high on the thighs that they would make mere nudity seem modest. And soft, so soft that they seemed to slither through Julia's fingers.

'You like them? Try them on,' suggested Merise.

Julia turned to look at her. There was a note in Merise's voice, a look in her dark eyes that made her hesitate. But only for a moment. She had played cat and mouse with Merise before; perhaps the new Julia could turn the tables? Would a woman, especially a woman with a newly voluptuous figure, a striking new style, a woman about to embark on a dangerous adventure in a foreign land, hesitate to remove her clothes? For anyone?

Probably not, she decided.

No, definitely not.

She felt a sudden surge of delicately wanton energy.

She slipped out of the sundress she was wearing and hastily discarded her white bra and pants. No striptease: her clothes simply weren't up to it. Finally naked she faced Merise, confident in the polished glow of her skin, the now seductive swell of her hips, the sleek, honey-coloured vee of hair between her thighs.

'Mm,' mused the new Julia. 'What colour suits me best, do you think? The black, perhaps?'

She plucked the black bra from the bed and held it against her breasts. A mere wisp of fabric, barely covering her nipples, designed to arouse. She turned from Merise to admire herself in the mirror. The black silk made her pale skin seem paler, and her nipples, thrusting against the lacy edges, looked like raspberries.

'Or maybe the red?' Moving back to the bed, she let

the black bra fall and reached for the red panties. Saucy sister to a G-string, they moulded to her sex, a rich, enticing triangle that made a flattering counterpoint to the swell of her hips and warmed her skin.

'Which do you prefer?' she asked Merise, exulting at the flicker of surprise she detected.

'I think, don't you, that the white would be more appropriate,' said Merise.

'Why appropriate?'

'Pure and virginal,' suggested Merise lazily.

Another challenge. Should she rise to it, ignore it, pretend to misunderstand? Merise was watching her with the indulgent tolerance a parent might display to a precocious child: amusing, but not to be taken seriously.

'But I don't feel pure and virginal at the moment,' retorted Julia. Slowly she peeled off the red panties, relishing the whisper of silk along her legs, and reached for the black. Her full breasts swelled from the delicate cups and the black vee between her thighs was a startling, suggestive contrast to the whiteness of her skin. She turned to Merise, teasingly, almost flirtatiously. 'Well?'

'Provocative, Julia, is also a state of mind,' commented Merise with a slight smile. 'Try the other things.'

Khaki trousers, finely cut to emphasise her waist, with a line of gold buttons instead of a zipper. A tailored white shirt with oversize pockets at the breast and gold buttons that subtly, almost subliminally, suggested the nipples beneath. Two pockets on the arms. A pair of jeans so tight they clung like a second skin and a matching denim shirt, again with pockets at the breasts.

In her delight at such superbly cut, strikingly spare clothes that seemed at once to make her taller, more sophisticated, Julia preened unselfconsciously. Sensual innuendo was forgotten; she was, quite simply, thrilled with the way she looked. 'Merise, they're perfect,' she said. 'What a beautiful fit. I love this white shirt. What a clever idea to have all these pockets.'

'Yes, it's very nice,' agreed Merise, honestly amused. Cat and mouse again. Julia was like a kitten, trying to flex her newfound sexual claws at one moment, distracted by a ball of string or its own tail the next. It was rather disarming. 'But remember what I said.'

'What?' asked Julia, her back to the mirror, awkwardly craning her neck over her shoulder to admire herself from the rear.

'Provocative is a state of mind,' reminded Merise. 'A moment ago you tried to flirt with me a little, yes?'

Julia's head snapped back. She flushed a little, and said nothing.

'Without clothes, or with the armour of sexy little lingerie? Hmm? And now you're all dressed up and not sexy at all.'

'Oh,' said Julia in a small voice.

'To provoke, to tempt, to intrigue, you must always be as erotically aware of your body as you were wearing nothing but a little scrap of red silk.' Languidly Merise rose from her chair and came to stand behind Julia at the mirror. 'So, you like this white shirt, but you don't understand it. See how cleverly the pocket swells the line of your breasts, the gold buttons over your nipples. If I press down – like this – I find the very tips of your nipples, don't I? And these buttons, here, on your trousers, leading down your belly, until the very last one, just below the bone, no? If I press down – here, like this – I'm close, very close to the heart of you.'

Julia was transfixed by the image in the mirror. Merise's hands, slim fingers and scarlet nails, closing around the gold buttons, brushing against her nipples. She could feel her breasts swelling in response, the sweet puckering as her nipples hardened, the tingling warmth that arced to her groin.

Merise's hands, drifting to her waist, gliding down the line of gold buttons that bisected her belly until they reached the last button, the button that pressed against her mound, the button that, yes, was so close to the furrow of her inner lips, so close to her clitoris that if the pressure was only a fraction harder she would be unable to restrain a quick spasm.

Already she was growing moist and tumid, the fluttering of arousal deep in her belly.

'You are aware of it now, I can see,' murmured Merise. 'To seduce, to tantalise, you must make me aware of it too.'

Their eyes met in the mirror. Merise smiled and moved away, returning to her chair. Julia, aroused and frustrated, like a horse curbed and spurred at the same time, stood trembling before the mirror.

'Wear your clothes like a lover,' said Merise softly. 'Think of them as an embrace, not to conceal your body, but to caress it. And as you respond, others will too.'

Julia gazed at herself in the mirror. Beneath the white cotton shirt, black silk cupped her breasts, black silk pressed against the damp, plump folds of her sex. To think of them as a lover's hands, soft and secretive, enfolding. In the mirror she saw her hands raised to her breasts, finding the gold buttons, tracing the path down her body that Merise had drawn.

Layers of silk and cotton made a faint, pleasurable friction, a thrumming, rippling warmth. Her body simmered.

To her surprise, watching Julia, so absorbed in her reflection, Merise found herself becoming faintly aroused. Perhaps it was because she herself had stirred Julia to this response, she mused.

'But I thought, Julia, you were trying to seduce me, not yourself,' said Merise mockingly.

Startled, Julia turned away from the mirror. Had she tried to seduce Merise, she wondered confusedly. She had wanted to flaunt her new body, her new beauty, wanted Merise to acknowledge her as – as an equal, she realised.

She had already made her decision when she chose the black.

'Both of us,' replied Julia. Guided by sudden intuition, she turned back to the mirror and slowly began to strip off the white shirt and khaki pants, the scraps of black silk underwear. 'You can teach me, and I will learn from you, but first I want what David had. To even the score.' She closed her eyes.

She heard a low laugh, a rustle of discarded clothing. Hardly daring to breathe, she waited.

A soft, lapping warmth between her thighs. The questing arrow of a pointed tongue insinuating between her inner lips. Teeth closing on the nub of her clitoris.

She felt herself engorging, becoming hotter, wetter. Her clitoris was being sucked deeper and deeper into an avid cavern. The world contracted to the rhythmic sucking, the friction of tongue and teeth. She felt the pulse of her inner walls, rising and contracting like a tide. A moist, burning heat engulfed the delicate tissues of her flesh.

Poised on the edge of orgasm, knowing that the next suckling, pulling pressure, or the next, would fire the flames of her climax, she hovered, hot and trembling.

Her senses began to swim, and then suddenly dissolved in the spiralling rush of oblivion.

The enveloping haze that engulfed her. Lifted her. Raised her.

Consumed her.

And so it began.

A long, lascivious, lubricious odyssey that lasted well into the night.

She learned the strange yet familiar geography of another woman's body, another woman's touch, the unerring skill of a lover who knew exactly what sensations were evoked by her touch. For the first time she tasted the sweetness of a woman's flesh, the heady glow as a nipple hardened under her lips, a clitoris pulsed beneath her tongue. She learned to vary her strokes, her rhythm, to prolong stimulation to the point of pain.

Unconsciously she absorbed the lesson that Rupert had taught Merise so long ago: when flesh meets flesh there are no rules, no boundaries.

It was a glowing, vibrant Julia who met Rupert the next morning at dawn, glossy with the rampant, sexual vitality that only forays into the forbidden bestow. Dressed in the white shirt and khaki trousers, carrying only a large tan leather pouch, she seemed to hum with energy.

Rupert had wondered what had transpired last night in Merise's cabin. He had returned later, wanting to speak to Julia, and found the cabin door locked, the 'Do Not Disturb' sign unequivocally barring his way.

Anything was possible, knowing Merise. She might have tried to intimidate her with some carnal trickery, frustrate her, even ignore her. But no, it seemed that Julia had emerged not just unscathed, but positively triumphant. Her eyes, glowing green, and her mouth, ripe and rosy under a thin coat of gloss, sent one message, while her body, severely clad in the almost military chic of white and khaki, sent another, contradicting the first – or emphasising it, he wasn't sure. She seemed almost virile.

'Hurry, Rupert, it's getting late,' she urged, tugging his arm.

'Yes, yes, of course,' he said hastily.

The zodiac, an inflatable rubber raft with its own outboard motor, slipped easily away from the sleek, looming lines of the *Calypso*. At the helm, Rupert guided it across the waves, carefully checking the currents, the wind. The current which sweeps down the Dardanelles was powerful, requiring all his concentration.

Julia, clutching a line that was threaded along the inside of the bulbous plastic bulges that constituted the sides of the zodiac, as she perched precariously on the billowing edge that dipped perilously close to the sea, was exultant. She narrowed her eyes, searching for the coastline, a mere haze of brown and yellow in the distance. A sudden wave of sea water sloshed into the craft, wetting her from waist to ankle, and she laughed aloud.

Her khaki trousers and black silk panties were sodden. Wet, salty, lover's hands, she thought joyously. The pulse of the outboard motor thrummed along the plastic skin of the zodiac, a low, humming vibration, subliminally sexual, that echoed her own, inner excitement. Truly alive to her own physicality for the first time, she relished the feeling. If she were a man, she decided, she would already be hard.

Calypso receded into the distance. Ahead lay the Turkish coast, a range of low hills just becoming visible. Ahead lay the future, Mabik, the mysterious Tarik, and the Trojan gold.

'Where are we going?' she called across to Rupert.

'Canakkale,' Rupert called back distractedly, concentrating on the current. 'There, can you see the minarets? The fortress at the south of the quay? No? They'll be clearer soon. It's quite a busy little port, the largest on the strait. The car ferry from Gallipoli docks there. Mabik will meet you.'

'You're not coming with me? Then how will I know Mabik? How will he find me?'

'No,' Rupert tossed over his shoulder. 'We decided that you'll be more conspicuous on your own.' And it was just possible that if the port was being watched, Rupert might be recognised. Unlikely, but possible. He decided not to burden Julia with the implications of that. 'Mabik knows what you look like. He'll make it look like a pick-up. A lot of village men hang around the docks, smoking, drinking tea, looking for tourists to rip off. He'll mention the Helen and Menelaos Snack Bar to identify himself.'

'Wonderful,' laughed Julia, 'a code word. Now I

feel like a real spy. All I need now is a sinister little handgun and a cyanide capsule!'

Not for the first time, it occurred to Rupert that Julia wasn't taking the affair quite seriously. 'You have one,' he said flatly, removing a small package from his pocket and tossing it to her. 'A nice, ladylike little pistol, some Turkish lire, some American dollars, and a few letters to establish your authenticity.' At least they didn't have to bother with fake ID, he reassured himself. Julia's own identity and academic credentials were perfect.

'Oh,' said Julia, taken aback, but slipping it into her bag.

'We're almost there,' said Rupert, gesturing to the coast. 'You can see the minarets in the distance.'

In the early morning haze, the graceful spirals were barely visible. The sun was just beginning to cut through the vapour.

'Use the ship's telex,' Rupert began to remind her again.

'I will, I will,' interrupted Julia with a laugh. 'And, yes, I'll be careful.'

There was little time for more. As Rupert cut the engine, the zodiac drew up to the quay, bumping lazily against a small fishing boat. Awkwardly Julia made her way to the helm, impatient to begin.

The docks were beginning to come to life. A gaggle of small, dark-skinned boys were playing desultorily with a soccer ball. Beside a row of dilapidated taxis, young men in Western dress were smoking cigarettes. Elderly men hunkered down near impromptu stands spread on the road, offering newspapers and cartons of cigarettes for sale. And among them was Mabik.

She was too excited to pay much attention to Rupert's final, hasty admonitions. She stopped him by the simple expedient of pressing her mouth to his in a brief but astonishingly sensual kiss, and clambered ashore without a backward glance.

Rupert watched her retreating with some amazement.

'Cigarettes, lady, American cigarettes?'

'Newspapers, lady, American newspapers?'

'Taxi, lady, I give best deals.'

Julia walked slowly, shaking her head but smiling. Every port, it seemed, no matter how large or small, had its itinerant entrepreneurs. And they always seemed to assume you were American.

'You need guide, pretty lady with hair like gold?'

Gold. The code word or coincidence? Julia turned and nearly caught her breath. Mabik, if it was he, was tall and dark, wearing tight jeans that emphasised a lithe, powerful body, a black T-shirt and a white linen jacket. He had strong features, a hawk-like nose and liquid brown eyes, and firm, full lips. He was young, no more than twenty, she decided, and positively radiated all the vitality and youthful energy of a healthy male animal. The attraction was immediate. And he was aware of it.

'A guide?' Julia repeated, playing for time. 'Why would I need a guide?'

'To show you the sights, pretty lady.' His eyes were roaming over her body in frank appreciation. 'You come to see Troy, yes? All the tourists come here for Troy.'

'Perhaps,' said Julia neutrally. The day was growing warmer; she could feel the heat of the sun on her back. And the heat of his eyes on her breasts.

'I show you all the best places,' he promised. 'Places tourists never see.'

'Yes?' If it was Mabik, why didn't he get to the point?

'I show you everything,' he said, a teasing glint in his eye. 'And then, when you are hot and tired and dusty, hot with the sun, I will refresh you.'

'How?' challenged Julia.

'With a long, cool drink. I know a little place – the Helen and Menelaos Snack Bar.'

'Mabik,' she acknowledged.

'And you are Julia,' he said softly. 'Friend of Rupert, who was the friend of my brother Nazem.' His expression was unreadable.

'Yes. I'm sorry,' said Julia hesitantly.

'The will of God,' he answered inscrutably.

'Or Tarik?' ventured Julia, watching him closely.

'Shh. Not here,' he cautioned. The teasing light returned to his eyes. 'You are a sexy tourist, and I am giving you the pick-up. All my friends will be jealous. Now you will come with me.'

His car, parked behind the taxi rank, was an ancient Ford with a surprisingly powerful engine, which Mabik drove far, far too fast. Within minutes they had left behind the cobbled streets of Canakkale and turned onto a modern tarmac road, the Izmir highway. Julia looked about, fascinated. To her right a grove of pinewoods sloped down to the shore and to the left was a range of low-lying hills. The scenery flashed past. She caught a glimpse of tiny fishing boats bobbing on the turquoise sea as they left the coast and drove down into a fertile plain.

Fields of wheat and cotton and sunflowers flourished, nourished by irrigation dykes lined with

101

poplars and willow trees. There were cattle grazing, and, much to Julia's delight, camels with gaily woven saddle cloths tethered by the side of the road.

Mabik stopped beside the river, parking the car under the shade of a willow tree. 'Before I take you to the village, we will talk,' he said, and as he spoke pulled a thin, vicious-looking knife from the inner pocket of his jacket.

Julia froze in sudden terror. How stupid she had been, she thought numbly, blindly, criminally, fatally stupid. Rupert had warned her. The gun, his little ladylike pistol, was useless stowed in the tote bag she had flung carelessly, stupidly on the back seat.

'Breakfast,' explained Mabik, producing a loaf of bread and a packet of olives. 'We will sit under the tree and eat.'

'What a good idea,' she said brightly. But, as they left the car, she took the precaution of removing her bag. Even if she didn't know how to use the pistol, she felt better having it near her.

'So, why do you come to Truva?' asked Mabik, passing her the loaf of bread and, she was relieved to note, the knife.

'Truva?' asked Julia.

'We say Truva, you say Troy,' he explained.

'Oh. Surely Rupert explained everything?' Julia prevaricated.

'Not everything,' said Mabik shrewdly. 'But he spoke of Tarik. And I see now why he sends such a beautiful woman.' His dark eyes were openly admiring.

'Tell me about Tarik,' she invited, feeling again the tug of attraction.

'I know little,' Mabik shrugged. 'The elders in the

village know more. He is rich, powerful. He owns many things, many people. And he is feared. He has a weakness for women and old things. He collects them.'

There was something oddly chilling in his description, flat and terse as it was.

'Old things?' joked Julia weakly, guessing he meant antiquities. 'Or women?'

'Old things he saves,' said Mabik soberly. 'Women he breaks.'

'I don't break easily,' Julia said.

'A strong woman, yes? I like strong women.' The light was back in his eyes, teasing, flirtatious, quickly extinguished by her next question.

'Where is he now?'

'Istanbul, I think,' Mabik replied. 'The elders know.'

'And you'll take me to them?' asked Julia.

'Later,' said Mabik evasively. 'After we talk.'

But talk, thought Julia, might be dangerous. The less Mabik knew, the better, until she was sure of him. Perhaps, if she could distract him a little.

'It's getting hotter,' she said idly, undoing one button of the white shirt and then another. His eyes followed her fingers, lingered on the swell of her breasts.

'Yes,' he agreed absently. With visible effort he lifted his gaze to her face. 'Why Tarik?' he asked abruptly. 'What do you want with him? He's a dangerous man.'

Was that a warning or a threat? She realised she still held the knife he had given her to cut the bread. Inspiration struck. Before she could think better of it, she lunged towards him, taking him off guard and knocking him flat on his back. Straddling him, she raised the knife and pointed it at his throat. 'And perhaps I am a dangerous woman.'

To her surprise, he began to laugh. 'Yes, Julia, perhaps you are.'

Beneath her, she could feel him hardening, the thick rod of his prick stirring against her thigh, and she too began to laugh. There was something unreal, surreal about the scene, the dappled shade of the willow tree, the gently flowing muddy brown water of the river, the lush fields, the hot sun, the lithe male body under hers, and the knife in her hand.

She had taken him by surprise. She had no real doubt that knife or not he could easily overpower her, but he made no move, only shifting slightly to ease his erection between her thighs. There was no fear in his eyes, only hot, naked lust.

'So now we talk, Mabik,' she said, rubbing herself against his engorging prick, feeling him grow harder, teasing them both with the rough friction of their clothing, the knife still at his throat. But the real weapon, she realised as his hips began to thrust unconsciously, uncontrollably against her, was her body.

'They wanted me to make sure of you,' he said thickly. 'Before I brought you to them.'

Insinuating her free hand between their bodies, she found his shaft, stiff and throbbing beneath the denim of his jeans. She curled her fingers around him, and as her palm recognised his length she found herself growing almost unbearably wet. 'And does this convince you?' she heard herself ask. 'Or this?' as she tightened her grasp.

'You could persuade me,' he grunted, his hands moving to the gold buttons of her trousers.

Chapter Six

'No, oh no,' said Julia. 'Under the circumstances, I think you persuade me. Tell me about yourself, and what you do, and your connection with Tarik. And then, perhaps . . .'

'But you know all this,' protested Mabik, arching against her. 'For generations my family have worked at the site of Troy. My great-grandfather laboured for Schliemann himself. It is our inheritance, our right. The site provides for its own. Oh, God, no harder, Julia; careful, or I'll come like this.'

Relenting, she loosened her clasp, drew her hand away.

'But I didn't mean you should stop,' he ground out through gritted teeth. There was a faint sheen of sweat on his forehead. 'And you don't need the knife.'

With some surprise, she realised she was still holding the knife in her right hand. She let it drop, a decision made more by her sex than her sense of reason, and placed her hands on his shoulders. They were rocking together now, their bodies effortlessly in rhythm.

'A family business?' probed Julia. It was not unheard of that workmen, especially in poor countries, regarded the finds as their own and often skimmed some of the choicest.

'A long and honourable tradition,' he protested. 'Not like Tarik who rapes our inheritance, as I wish – I wish you would rape me.'

'Rape?' She was amused, intoxicated with the thought. 'Can a woman rape a man?'

'Julia, you have, you are. I am at your mercy.'

He was joking, yet it was not a joke. The knife was within his grasp; yet he had yielded, was yielding to her.

'And if I'm inclined to mercy?' she teased, her hands at his zipper. She widened the opening of his fly. He wore no underwear and his penis, freed from the restriction of his jeans, rose straight into the air. She circled her hand around it triumphantly. He was big, bigger than she had imagined, hot and straining against her fingers.

'Anything,' he promised rashly, thrusting into her hand. 'Anything.'

She rose swiftly and stripped off the khaki trousers and black silk panties, then held herself above his body, straddling him with her knees. He lay motionless, passive, waiting. There was something excruciatingly arousing in his passivity. It lit her blood like a flame.

She lifted his shaft to the slick entrance of her body. Slowly, with exquisite care, she lowered herself, feeling her inner muscles stretch to his fullness. When he was deep, deep inside, she began to rock her pelvis gently. Inflamed, he began to thrust. Their bodies locked together in a frenzy of discordant rhythms that led quickly to a searing, soaring climax.

'So, as an archaeologist, how do I rate as a rapist?' asked Julia some time later as they dressed and gathered up the remains of the bread and olives.

'An archaeologist?' asked Mabik, turning in surprise. 'But we thought – we wondered – '

'What?'

'Well,' he shrugged and looked a little embarrassed. 'The lines from the ship weren't good. Rupert said you were a collector. We were afraid that, like Tarik, you might seek to take our gold.'

The village, thought Julia, was hardly a village at all, more a collection of wood-framed houses with crumbling plaster and exposed wattle with the obligatory mosque and minaret. A gaggle of geese pecked at the muddy street and cows were being driven into a yard by a little boy with a long cane.

'Ciplak,' explained Mabik. 'This is where the great Schliemann stayed when he came here first. My family has always lived here. The elders will soon be gathering for the midday meal. I will translate and they will tell us what can be done.'

They had stopped before the largest of the wooden houses. Julia followed Mabik to the door where he removed his shoes, gesturing for her to do the same. An old woman dressed in black greeted Mabik with delight, darting suspicious looks at Julia from the corner of her eye.

Their conversation was incomprehensible; Julia turned her attention to the room. It was large and simply furnished with a divan along one wall. But the walls were freshly whitewashed, and brightly coloured carpets covered the floor. Turning to Julia, Mabik offered her a pair of slippers, then guided her to the divan where he sat cross-legged.

The woman left then returned with a tray of tiny glasses containing tea. Mabik cheerfully downed three, while Julia struggled with hers. It was a strange flavour, rather smoky, not unpleasant but unfamiliar.

A middle-aged man appeared at the door, and then another. The same ritual prevailed: slippers were offered, glasses of tea drunk. The room began to fill. It was a strange and motley group, with some of the men wearing the traditional, baggy Turkish trousers, others in well-cut Western suits. Determined not to feel ill at ease, Julia sipped her tea and waited.

Once, and not so long ago, she would have been very ill at ease, she thought idly, retreating to her fantasy world, stripping each man with her imagination, revelling in her make-believe seduction. It was no longer necessary. Self-conscious fantasy had become absorbed in a subconscious, physical awareness that was infinitely more satisfying.

'They will speak after we eat,' Mabik whispered to her as the throng began to move to the end of the room.

Lunch was served in a courtyard that opened off the living room, at a long table covered by a white cloth. Jugs of wine and beer were set at intervals along the table. So they're not abstainers, Julia noted, tasting her wine and finding it surprisingly good. The *meze* or hors d'oeuvres, were delicious: pastries filled with cheese and herbs, stuffed vine leaves, soft white cheese, olives, and a variety of spicy dips. This was followed by chunks of lamb grilled with tomatoes and served with potatoes and aubergines. The atmosphere was apparently convivial, with much laughter and repartee, and Julia found herself relaxing.

She was a little surprised when, after baklava and Turkish coffee, the questions came, fast and furious, some awkwardly pointed, some apparently irrelevant.

Who had given her the name of Tarik?

How old was she? Was she married?

Why should they trust her?

Where did she get her degree, where did she study?

How did she know Rupert?

How did he learn of the Trojan gold?

Who was she, a foreign woman, to meddle in the affairs of men?

She replied as best she could, Mabik translating. She was a respectable archaeologist, only posing as an adviser to a reclusive, eccentric American millionaire who collected antiquities; she had no interest in their own affairs; she did not know the source of Rupert's information, only that he wanted her to ingratiate herself with Tarik and authenticate the rumours by examining the artefacts.

At that, an elderly man with a wizened face silenced the others and drew from the folds of his baggy trousers an object which he handed across the table.

It was an exquisite little bowl of rock crystal adorned with a bird's head and neck, an object of fragile, translucent beauty. It caught the sunlight, refracted it. Julia handled it carefully, reverently.

'Mycenaean,' she said softly. 'From the shaft graves. Sixteen or seventeen hundred. And,' she added, raising her head to look him straight in the eyes, 'last seen

109

in the National Archaeological Museum in Athens.'
With elaborate courtesy she handed it back to him.
Then, reaching down for her tote bag, she extracted
the parcel Rupert had given her earlier, handed it over
and watched as he unwrapped it to reveal the pistol,
the sheaves of American dollars and Turkish lire, and
the letters which were given to Mabik to translate.

There was a startled hum of voices which quickly
increased to an angry, incomprehensible babble.

Mabik left his chair and came to her side.

'They will confer,' he said. 'You will wait in the
other room.'

Julia made her way back to the living room and the
divan where, cross-legged, she sat and prepared to
wait.

Deep in the heart of sprawling, teeming Istanbul,
behind the elegant facade of a restored Ottoman
palace, Tarik, too, was seated on a divan, waiting. As
he waited, he let his eyes rove pleasurably around the
room. At the centre of the complex, labyrinthine
network of rooms that comprised the palace, reached
only by a series of antechambers and interconnecting
doors monitored by a sophisticated, computerised
security system, this room was his retreat, his
sanctum.

It glowed with gold.

Museum-quality glass cases lined the room, displaying his treasures. Jewellery of all sorts: bracelets,
earrings, necklaces, rings and diadems that glim-
mered in the dim light; cups and vases, daggers and
breastplates, boxes and plaques and seals – all of
ancient gold.

His thin lips relaxed in a small smile. A fractional

110

curve of the mouth, it still seemed to rest uncomfortably on his face. With strong, almost menacing features, a large, hooked nose, hooded eyes and high cheekbones, it was not the face of a man who smiled often.

A buzzer sounded, alerting him.

She had arrived.

Quickly he stripped, revealing a powerful, bullish, brutish body with a thick pelt of dark hair covering his chest and a dense tangle at his groin. Moving to one of the glass cases, he extracted a mask of beaten gold, the image of a warrior long dead, and fitted it to his face. A death mask, it had been solid gold before Tarik had drilled small holes for the nostrils, thin slits beneath the heavy eyelids. From the same case he took another mask, a heavy necklace of gold links, and two daggers.

At the touch of a button, solid screens of chased metal descended from the lofty ceiling, obscuring the glass cases. The room dimmed to a thin, subaqueous light.

The woman entered. She was tall and slender, with long blonde hair that flowed almost to her waist. She knew what he expected; Tarik had taught her this game. She didn't like it. She was nervous, afraid, and hopelessly excited.

Wordlessly she discarded the white linen shift she was wearing, draped the heavy gold necklace around her throat, fitted the gold mask to her face, and reached for the gold dagger Tarik held in his hand.

The mask was heavy, almost stifling, distorting her vision. Before her he was a blur of black and gold.

Like creatures from some bizarre mythology, they faced each other.

* * *

It was late afternoon and Julia was asleep on the divan, dreaming strange, erotic dreams. Then, the next thing she knew was that insistent hands were shaking her.

'Julia. Julia. Wake up.'

'No,' she moaned, half-awake, half-asleep, struggling to recapture the dream.

It was no use. Mabik's face swam into focus.

'Wake up, Julia. You were asleep,' he said. He looked at her flushed face, her glowing green eyes, and sensed her arousal. If only, he thought fleetingly, they were not in his grandmother's house, but back by the river. He looked away. This woman was outside his experience – not a whore, not a nice Turkish girl who would never dream of so much as kissing in a public place.

He cleared his throat. 'It has been arranged,' he announced.

Julia sat up and ran her fingers through her hair, shaking her head to dispel the dream. 'How?' she asked.

'Celik – one of the elders,' he said to her uncomprehending look. 'He knows a man, who knows a man. Your letters of authorisation have been faxed to Tarik's private secretary in Istanbul, requesting an appointment.'

'Faxed?' retorted Julia in surprise.

'Oh, we are not so primitive as we look here in Ciplak,' responded Mabik with a smile. 'Celik, too, has access to a plane; you will be flown privately to Istanbul when we hear from Tarik's office. Celik,' he added inconsequentially, 'was very fond of Nazem.'

'Oh,' said Julia, frowning.

'No,' said Mabik. 'They do not trust you completely.

112

But they believe you are against Tarik, and they hate him more. And some of them know Rupert from the old days.'

'What more did you learn from them?' asked Julia.

'Little, Julia, very little.' He made a vague, helpless gesture with his hands. 'I think you still don't understand. Here much is left unspoken that is understood. And if it is not understood, it is still unspoken. Celik is one of us, of the village. I do not know how he knows to contact Tarik, how he has a plane, why he has agreed to help you. We do not question because he is one of us. We are always loyal to our own.'

A little like the Mafia, thought Julia, wisely refraining from voicing the thought.

Later she would recall the intervening hours in a series of images, some sharply focused, some blurred and distorted.

The endless cups of tea, drunk from the tiny glasses, as she and Mabik waited.

Mabik's hand, brown and long fingered, triumphantly clutching the flimsy fax that signalled acceptance.

Her hand, trembling a little, splattering blue ink splotches from an old-fashioned fountain pen, as she hastily transcribed a telex for Rupert.

The small room under the eaves where she lay restlessly on crisp white cotton sheets, waiting for morning.

She drifted off, stirring only when Mabik's hands, coaxed her awake.

The bowl of chicken soup incongruously provided for her breakfast by the old woman in the black dress.

The muddy ruts of the road, the freshly tilled earth

of an outlying field that served as an impromptu airstrip.

The sleek lines of the waiting Cessna.

The patchwork quilt of land, brown and green and yellow, as the plane left the earth.

The swift change to rippling blue as it banked over water.

The rippling, vibrating thrum of the plane's engines.

The foggy, smoky haze that heralded Istanbul, and the swift descent to Ataturk Airport.

The waiting limousine.

The vibrant sprawl of the city itself, parks and promenades contrasting cruelly with squalid slums and high-rise apartment blocks. The smell of dust and diesel fumes.

And, finally, the elegant facade of an Ottoman palace.

A predator, she thought, at her first sight of Tarik, striding into the elegant anteroom where she had been left to wait. His large, muscled body moved with the confident ease of a jungle cat and his eyes were black and cold, like chips of obsidian. His hand was cool, the massive palm engulfing her fingers. He held it just a little too long, squeezed it just a little too hard, as if to remind her of his own superior strength.

The room suddenly seemed smaller, dwarfed by his presence. He had a powerful aura of concentrated energy that was almost menacing. She felt the hairs on the back of her neck prickle.

'Miss Symonds.' His voice was deep and low, almost caressing, as if to belie the harshness of his grip, but his eyes were cold and impersonal. 'Please be seated. My assistant persuaded me to see you, thinking that we might share a common interest.'

As an opening, it was subtle enough, giving nothing away. 'Please, call me Julia,' she replied with a smile.

'And I am Tarik.'

'Tarik, then,' she nodded, with another smile.

He was a man who knew the value of silence, and used it like a weapon. He meant it to be unnerving, Julia realised, and it was. It was like chess, or fencing. But she knew how to fill the void, she thought with a sudden surge of triumph, and summoning her imagination she found her tongue. She shifted in her chair, straightened her back so that he fullness of her breasts thrust against her denim shirt, and crossed her legs.

'You have a reputation, Tarik, as a collector,' she said, eyeing him speculatively. Beneath the elegant white Armani suit was a naked male, vulnerable to her mouth, her hands, her body. She had to concentrate on that, remember that she was wearing white silk under denim, challenge him with her own strength.

'Indeed,' he replied, steepling his fingers and casually stretching out his long legs.

'In certain circles,' she modified, uncrossing her legs, mimicking his posture. Expert tailoring couldn't disguise the thick, powerful thighs, the muscular calves. They would lie heavily on her, rough and abrasive with dense, dark hair.

'You know I represent a collector with similar interests,' she continued. Even limp he would be big, too big, perhaps, to take fully in her mouth. She would close her mouth over the head of his shaft, flutter her tongue around the bulbous head, wait for him to swell, to thicken.

And so, while her mouth formed carefully superficial phrases, her eyes told a different story, creating a sensual connection. No man and woman can meet as strangers for the first time without wondering, however fleetingly, what the other would be like in bed. With her eyes, with hesitations and pauses and a faintly distracted air, Julia conveyed a preoccupation that was purely sexual.

It was not entirely feigned. She was going to have Tarik, and had known it from the moment he had held her hand too hard.

'Provenance is not our concern,' she said delicately. 'Authenticity is. You've seen my credentials. And my employer is prepared to pay very generously, provided that the works are original and untraceable.'

'Why come to me?' asked Tarik deliberately, watching her eyes. Most people gave themselves away with their eyes, a flicker of uncertainty, a sidelong glance to avoid the truth. He could see nothing in this woman's eyes but the hot glow of lust, as unexpected as it was arousing.

'You're known,' she replied negligently. 'There have been rumours. And if there were some new cache, unknown and untraceable, of the sort we are interested in, it was suggested that you were the man to speak to. But perhaps I'm wasting my time?'

It was a challenge as much to his prick as to his expertise, Tarik realised with delight.

And so the conversation continued, now on several levels. On one level, delicate negotiation, establishing parameters, an inventory of mutual interests and knowledge, a rapid give and take of information.

116

Current market prices. Export laws. The difficulty of distinguishing modern replicas.

A subtle seesaw, as each tried to second guess the other.

On another level they assessed each other physically.

He would not be a considerate lover, decided Julia, concerned for her pleasure, careful with his body. He would take what he wanted, selfishly, brutally, rutting and thrusting, hard and purposeful. The thought excited her.

She was small, mused Tarik, so much smaller than he that she would be tight, hot and tight around him. That thought intrigued him more than their conversation. She might be exactly what she claimed to be, an expert adviser to a wealthy collector, in which case he might possibly be interested. She might be a plant, a spy, an undercover agent for the Turkish government. In which case he would kill her. But not before he had taken her, at least once. He imagined her nude, clothed only in gold, and felt his body tightening in response.

The possibility of a new treasure trove was lightly touched upon, just as deftly evaded.

'Rumours,' shrugged Tarik dismissively. 'Always there are such rumours. A peasant finds a gold bead in a field and suddenly there is a treasure. And yet, sometimes there is.'

The question of Julia's loyalty to her employer was raised delicately, and just as delicately avoided, with the subtle implication she might not be averse to a little double dealing.

'I receive a finder's fee and a percentage,' she improvised. 'So, naturally, I belong to the highest bidder.'

'A wise policy,' he approved.

Julia was becoming frustrated. So far, she had learned little from their verbal fencing. He had carefully avoided anything incriminating, revealing only the intelligent interest of a true antiquarian. He had not even expressly admitted to owning a collection, which was, of course, illegal. She had laid the bait; he had neither refused nor accepted it.

Think, Julia, she told herself. What was the key that would unlock a man like this? She could sense his physical interest, the way his cold, black eyes roamed greedily over her body. Greed. Yes. The fundamental craving to possess, ravenous and insatiable. The avarice of the collector was a lust, and lust she was learning to understand. She wasn't naive enough to think that she could entrap him sexually; his eyes were too cold, his self-control too assured. And that in itself was exciting.

'While I don't collect myself,' she began, 'I appreciate the desire. The thrill of acquisition. It's a very basic urge, I imagine.'

'Yes,' Tarik agreed blandly. 'So I assume.'

'And I believe, very strongly, in fulfilling basic urges. Don't you?' asked Julia. She let her eyes drop unmistakably to the bulge at his groin.

'Ah, but I never act on impulse,' cautioned Tarik, amused.

'But I do,' replied Julia. 'We have a saying, business before pleasure. Our business is concluded, is it not? I'll await your decision. And so, in the meantime . . .' she smiled and licked her lips suggestively.

'Is this some ruse, some ploy?' Tarik asked lightly. 'Are you going to try and seduce me, win my confidence with sexual favours, pry away at me over

118

pillow talk?' There was an edge of disdain in his voice.

'No,' replied Julia. 'I'm simply going to try and seduce you.'

Nothing carries the ring of conviction as purely as the truth. Tarik's eyes flickered in surprise.

She had been right: he was not a considerate lover. In his massive bedroom faintly perfumed with incense, under the great globe of a chased bronze lamp, on cool silk sheets, he took her quickly, roughly, barely pausing to undress. There was no question of seduction.

He held her wrists, spread her thighs with his knee and sheathed himself in a single thrust that made her gasp.

He was big, massive, as she had known he would be, and each stroke seemed to reach her womb. She quivered and moaned, her flesh clutching in spasm at his thrusts. It was a primal, avid rutting, and she gloried in it, climaxing almost immediately, as he thrust harder and faster.

An answering fury welled up inside her, hot and insistent. She arched upward to meet him, blow for blow.

She bit his lip.

She felt his teeth at her neck and raked her nails down his back to his buttocks.

It was an exquisite savagery. Flesh met flesh, pain and pleasure mingled. Her thighs were bruising with the repeated impact, and his grip on her wrists was harsh. She came and came again. There was no beginning and no end, only a continuous shudder that rose to a peak with each thrust.

His hands dropped to her breasts, rhythmically squeezing and pinching the sensitive nipples as he thrust. She moaned as the heat flooded through her, dissolving her.

His hands slid down to her sides and then to her buttocks, cupping her, raising her for still greater penetration. She screamed aloud, an animal cry of pure triumph.

And still he thrust, harder and harder. Beads of sweat dropped from his forehead to her breast.

At his final thrust, she climaxed again, a violent convulsion that rippled through her body like a shock wave, electrifying her flesh.

She returned to herself slowly, lying alone in the huge bed. Tarik had gone. She stretched tentatively, finding her body deliciously sore and limp. Idly she wondered what to do next. With some vague idea of having a shower, she reached for her tote bag, only to discover that it, too, had vanished. She frowned. She knew she had left it beside the bed; it didn't take much imagination to conclude that Tarik had removed it to search her belongings. Well, he would find nothing suspicious; that might reassure him.

Tarik. She let her mind drift pleasurably back to his performance, his incredible stamina. It was like being ravaged by a force of nature. She smiled to herself, comparing Rupert's studied technique with Tarik's primitive, visceral coupling. Next time, she decided, it would be on her terms.

She was, she realised, becoming a little lost in this game of seduction and deception. She had to remind herself that it was Tarik who was the alleged kingpin of the conspiracy she was meant to uncover, that Tarik was the enemy. Enemy and lover. He had stirred a response from her that she had not known she was capable of – a visceral, vital, purely animal feeling. Already she wanted it again.

Wanted him again.

As if summoned by the thought, Tarik appeared at the door, followed by a manservant bearing a tray and, she was pleased to see, her errant tote bag.

'Julia. I thought you might like some refreshment,' said Tarik, coming to stand at the side of the bed. He looked down at her, pleased with the sight. She looked soft and sweet, her hair tumbled, her eyes still faintly glazed with pleasure. Astonishing to find that she was so wild, so uninhibited. Seldom had he taken a woman whose response met and fired his own so powerfully.

'And my bag, and my passport, and my documents,' she teased lightly.

'And those as well,' he returned, not at all discomposed. 'That will be all, Muhammed. I'll open the wine.' The manservant withdrew noiselessly.

'So it seems that you are who you claim,' said Tarik.

'Hmm?' returned Julia vaguely, admiring the strong lines of his body, now wrapped in a silk robe. He was opening the wine with a deft economy of movement, his large hands dwarfing the corkscrew.

Silently he passed her a glass of wine and waited for her to speak. He was still not convinced by her story, despite the apparent authenticity of her papers, but he had decided to act as if he were. Reassured by his pretence, in the warm intimacy following sex, she would return to the treasure, try to pin him down, prise the details from him. From the nature of her

121

questions, he could learn a great deal. With some surprise, he found himself harbouring the faint hope that she was not a spy, not a government agent.

'This is delicious,' commented Julia, sipping her wine. 'No, no food just yet, thank you. We have, I think, some unfinished business.'

Tarik smiled wryly to himself. So predictable.

She set her wine glass down, rose from the bed, and came to stand beside him. 'I was supposed to seduce you,' she reminded him softly, toying with the belt of his robe. 'Instead, you ravished me. Now it's my turn.'

So, not the treasure, at least not yet, thought Tarik, as her hands stroked his body through the silk of his robe.

He had been rough, impatient; she was gentle, leisurely, tracing the nub of his blunt, male nipples until she felt them tighten, exploring his hard, muscled torso, his thighs, his calves, avoiding, with strict discipline, the area of his groin.

She parted his robe and let it fall to the floor. He made to reach for her, but she stopped him with a gesture.

'No,' she said. 'My turn. Stay still.'

She licked and nibbled and tasted, her hands shifting restlessly over his body. For Tarik, always the aggressor, it was an erotic novelty to remain passive. He was hard long, long before he felt her tongue curl around his penis, lightly circling the engorged tip as her hands cupped his balls, and one slim finger searched the cleft of his buttocks for the mouth of his anus.

She was as inexorable, as insistent as he, the warm, wet wash of her tongue, the delicate scrape of her teeth as powerful as the thrust of his shaft. She sucked him deep into her mouth, as far as she could take him, encircling the root of his shaft with her palm and fingers, clasping and releasing him in a pulsing, throbbing rhythm.

He could feel the ache begin, deep in the base of his spine, the swollen heat gathering to explode. With unaccustomed gentleness, he sifted his fingers through her hair, tilting her face to his.

'Julia,' he groaned.

'Come to bed,' she invited, rising gracefully to her feet.

He responded eagerly, half dragging her to the rumpled silk sheets, but she evaded him, pushing him back with both hands on his shoulders so that he lay beneath her.

'My way, remember?' she teased.

Straddling him, she parted the lips of her vagina with the fingers of one hand, and with the other drew his penis towards her. She was already wet, slick with excitement. Gradually she lowered herself to the swollen tip and rocked against it, making him furrow her flesh, brush against her clitoris.

She felt the first, faint contractions of orgasm, the tiny rippling of inner muscles, and lowered herself, sheathing him inch by voluptuous inch, until he filled her completely. And then she was still, denying them both the hard, wild ride they craved, the only friction the small pulse of her inner muscles clasping and unclasping him, until she could stand it no longer.

She began to move, slowly at first, then faster, then faster still, riding him mercilessly. With each stroke her swollen clitoris brushed against the wiry tangle of

123

his pubic hair, an abrasive, electrifying friction that drove her harder and harder until her frenzy was consumed in a violent climax.

Afterwards they lay together, slick with sweat, too stunned to move.

At last, Tarik spoke. 'My God,' he said devoutly. 'My God.'

'Yes,' she agreed hazily.

'That was – ' he paused to find the word ' – unique.'

'For me too.'

He turned and gathered her to him and, in a gesture that surprised both of them, kissed her gently on the lips. With infinite care he circled her mouth with his tongue, probed delicately between her lips, then, more firmly, tangled his tongue with hers.

It was a kiss of curious sweetness, warming, caressing.

Intimate.

Careful not to awaken her, Tarik eased himself from the bed. As he picked up his neglected wine glass he saw that his hand was shaking. He gulped down the wine and poured another glass, his thoughts a tangle of confusion.

She was everything he imagined, hot and tight and with a wildness that matched his own.

He didn't trust her.

He already wanted her again.

Remarkable. Women seldom interested him for long. But there was a lawlessness in her that he recognised in himself.

And she had said that she belonged to the highest bidder.

What price would he have to pay?

He could test her, take her to his room of gold.

Could he turn her?

If she was telling the truth, she might prove a true gold mine, he thought, smiling wryly at the phrase. Together they could dupe her billionaire, palm off copies of inferior pieces for exorbitant prices, and thus he, Tarik, could buy her with her employer's riches. It was a neat little scheme, he decided.

But only if she was telling the truth. And only if she could be bought.

Chapter Seven

The late afternoon sun streamed through the white latticed walls of the inner courtyard. Flowers bloomed in clay pots, an exotic profusion of purple and crimson, vibrant pink and glowing yellow, perfuming the air with spicy scents. A small marble fountain in the shape of a dolphin splashed into a blue-tiled pool. Green vines crept up the trellises and created a living arbour overhead. It was secluded and peaceful; the traffic from the outside world muted to a dull hum, like bees gathering around the hive.

Clad in only her white silk underwear, Julia, supine, relaxed, and utterly at peace, lay on a cushioned sunbed. Beside her, on a delicate wrought-iron table, wine was chilling in an ice bucket, and olives and fruit, cold meat and cheeses, were temptingly arrayed. She had no interest in the food. Sated with sex, replete with physical satisfaction, she was simply content to drowse in the dappled sunlight, self-satisfied as a cat.

Sleepily she pondered her next move, considered

the effort of a provocative remark, the sort of leading questions that Rupert would expect her to ask, and yawned. This was her time, and, at least for the moment, Tarik was her lover. She could still feel the hot length of him imprinted on her body.

It was enough to simply relish the moment, cherish the sunlight, the warmth of fulfilment.

Across from her, Tarik sat on a wrought-iron chair, dressed again in his white Armani, idly toying with a glass of wine, distracted and disconcerted by both her semi-nude body and her silence. Spy or business-woman, or simply woman, she should be asking questions, probing for answers, or seeking praise and reassurance. But she said nothing, apparently content to bask silently in the sunshine.

'I should go,' said Julia at last, opening her eyes and stretching luxuriously.

'No,' said Tarik forcefully. A little taken aback by his own response, he shook his head. 'No,' he repeated in a softer voice. 'You shall remain here, as my guest.' Immediately he cursed himself for his stupidity; he should have let her go, had her followed, her move-ments tracked, her contacts traced.

'That sounds more like an order than an invitation,' Julia commented, narrowing her eyes against the sun to look at him.

He made an abrupt, dismissive gesture. 'Forgive me if I spoke too harshly. I am accustomed to giving orders. I would be most pleased if you would stay here with me. But perhaps you are expected else-where?' he asked.

'No,' said Julia, 'I've made no plans. My time is my own now that I've made our offer.'

'But surely you have friends, family. Your employer will be waiting to hear from you,' Tarik probed.

Julia shrugged and thought briefly of Rupert. 'He can wait,' she said negligently.

'You are remarkably casual in pursuing his interests,' commented Tarik, puzzled.

Julia laughed. 'You mean I should be badgering you with questions, pestering you for details?'

'It's rather strange that you're not,' he agreed, sipping his wine.

'What good would that do?' she asked reasonably. 'We're at an impasse. Either you decide to trust me, or you don't. If you do, you know I'll require proof. Perhaps my sources misled me. Perhaps you're not the man I want.' There was a sexual challenge underlying her words that he responded to instinctively.

He rose abruptly, setting down his wine glass with a snap and striding over to her. Grasping her roughly by the wrist he jerked her to her feet.

'Come with me,' he said harshly.

He walked quickly, and Julia stumbled a little, trying to keep up with him. She had meant to tease him, not provoke him, and she was aware of an icy trickle of fear snaking down her spine.

He led her through a labyrinthine series of corridors, the marble cool on her bare feet, until they reached a series of massive, interlocking doors. A security console was fixed to the wall. With his back to her, concealing the screen, Tarik pressed a combination of buttons, and the door opened to an antechamber. Another massive door, another security console, another combination.

Julia gasped as the doors opened. The room literally glowed with gold. Amazed, she shook off Tarik's hand and walked into the room. Glass cases on all four walls were full of golden artefacts. She blinked, her eyes dazzled.

She moved slowly around the room, unaware of Tarik watching her like a hawk.

It was a magnificent display, and impossible to take in completely. She vaguely recognised a gold death mask that she had last seen in the National Archaeological Museum in Athens, a necklace of gold filigree she knew to be in the museum in Cairo. Armour and jewellery, cups and vases, plaques and seals, all of solid gold.

'My God,' she breathed, stunned, turning to Tarik.

In her eyes he saw only wonder.

He relaxed a bit, permitted himself one of his infrequent smiles.

'I don't believe it. It's . . . it's . . .' she shook her head in disbelief.

'Would you like to look more closely?' he asked, moving to one of the cases that contained an array of jewellery.

'Oh, yes,' she said eagerly.

'Examine them for authenticity?' he said ironically, opening the case and passing her a necklace.

She handled it reverently as golden pendant acorns shivered from her fingers. 'Beautiful,' she breathed. She examined the workmanship carefully. 'And well-restored,' she added.

'And your expert opinion?' he asked.

'Mmm. Macedonian, I think. Perhaps third century,' she hazarded, recalling an illustration she had seen in some article or other. The archaeologist might be appalled; the woman was entranced.

'Very good,' Tarik approved. 'The outer limits of

my interest, in fact. I prefer rather older examples. Try it on.'

'Oh, no, I couldn't,' gasped Julia.

'Why not?' asked Tarik, amused. 'It was meant to be worn. Here, I'll help you.' Taking the necklace from her, he carefully fastened it around her throat, just as carefully unfastened the clasp of her brassière, pushed her white silk panties down to her ankles, and then stood back to admire the effect.

Against her bare skin, the necklace was warm and heavy. The pendant gold acorns brushed against her nipples, which tautened reflexively. She cupped her hands under her breasts and looked down, marvelling at the intricately crafted gold links gleaming against her skin. An erotic thrill shivered through her.

'So, you like it,' commented Tarik.

She raised her eyes to his and saw something flicker in their black depths. For an instant his impassive face betrayed him, and she saw lust, greed and triumph. The key, she thought confusedly, knowing, instinctively, that she had him.

'Oh, yes,' she said. She had no way of knowing that her features echoed his look of moments before – lust, greed, and triumph.

Tarik recognised her response. It answered his own. He sighed with pleasure.

'Stand there,' he ordered.

And obediently she stood, passive, as he turned back to the case. He fastened another necklace around her throat, and then another, until her breasts were crushed under the weight, only her nipples jutting forth, rasped to arousal by the heavy gold links. He slid bracelets on to her arms, loading her from wrist to elbow with solid gold. There were rings for all of her eight fingers, so thick and heavy that she could barely move her hands. He clasped a belt around her waist, and then another.

His hands were at her feet, urging her to step out of the scraps of white silk lying on the floor, and when she did so, he fastened bracelets around her ankles.

At last he led her to the divan, arranging her carefully on her back, spreading her thighs just slightly.

'You know how they were found?' asked Tarik, his voice strangely muffled. 'Those queens and princesses, noble ladies from long, long ago, draped in gold.' He went to another case, filling his hands with small golden discs shaped like rosettes. 'They think these were attached to some cloth, a winding sheet,' he explained as he carefully placed them on her body in smooth, unbroken lines from shoulder to ankle.

'Yes, yes, I know,' Julia managed. Her body was warming, responding to the weight of the gold. As he placed a series of gold rosettes on her mound she could feel herself moistening. But her arousal was tinged with uncertainty, a trace of fear that sharpened her senses.

'Of course, I was forgetting,' murmured Tarik. 'And then, at last.' He turned to her with a gold death mask in his hand.

'No,' cried Julia, struggling to sit up, suddenly afraid. But the weight of the gold made movement difficult, and he was at her side in an instant.

'Don't be frightened,' he said. 'It's unique to see through the eyes of the past, sex and death gilded by life.' He subdued her effortlessly and fixed the mask to her face.

She could breathe, she realised with relief; there

were tiny holes drilled through the nostrils. And she could see, just dimly, through the tiny slits at the eyes. She cased to struggle and lay passive. When he returned to her line of vision, she saw that he had stripped off his clothes and that he too was wearing a gold death mask.

It was a shocking contrast, an impassive gold face above the hairy, brutish, male body. It was Tarik, but not Tarik. The paradox created another realm, another dimension.

He parted her thighs, releasing a tiny cascade of the gold rosettes that had adorned her mound. They fell between the lips of her sex, and she heard him laugh, a low growl deep in his throat.

She caught her breath as he began to explore the sensitive flesh, not with his fingers, not with his mouth, but with the embossed surface of a gold rosette, coaxing her clitoris free, tracing it from the tiny stem to the trembling head. The gold was hard and cool, faintly abrasive. It was a strange sensation, she thought hazily, as she felt the delicate tissues begin to swell and suffuse with a burning heat.

Again and again he repeated the movement, dragging the rosette along the sensitive nub, back and forth, back and forth until she was slick and engorged.

Beneath the weight of the gold death mask, her breathing was laboured, and she felt herself growing lightheaded, almost dizzy. The world contracted to the hot pulse between her legs, the cool, impersonal friction of cold gold against her.

She could feel his fingers, parting her inner and outer lips, probing, placing the thin golden discs between them, opening her even further. It was bizarrely arousing. The first, flickering ripples of impending orgasm began to pool in her groin.

From behind his mask Tarik could see the gleam of gold, newly lustrous from the musk of her body. The soft, pink, woman's flesh highlighted the warm glow of it. He forced his tongue through the mouth of the mask to taste it.

Moist warmth met cool metal.

Julia moaned, feeling the wet wash of his tongue thrum against her labia, the golden discs pressing against her core. The heat coiled deep within her and unfurled. Her inner muscles began to clench and spasm.

She felt the sharp edge of a golden disc press against the mouth of her vagina and came in a swift, heated rush.

'So,' said Tarik lazily, some time later, 'you approve of my collection and its uses?' He had set aside the death mask and was sprawled naked on the divan, watching Julia as she carefully removed the gold bracelets from her arms and ankles, studying each piece in turn.

'Magnificent,' she agreed. 'And you are right, these were meant to be worn,' she added, admiring the sinuous curve of a coiled gold snake, each scale perfectly etched, the eyes a pair of small, glittering rubies. 'As for its uses . . .' she let her hand fall to a gold rosette and fingered the embossed surface that had caressed her clitoris.

'Keep it, if you like,' offered Tarik with one of his rare smiles.

'Oh, I would like to, very much,' said Julia eagerly, then hesitated. 'But it would be a shame to break up a collection that's intact.' Even as she spoke her fingers closed protectively over the rosette.

'Never mind,' he said negligently. 'I have many, and there are many more awaiting me.'

Her heart began to beat a little faster. 'So it's true then,' she ventured. 'There is some new treasure trove?'

'Did I say so?' he parried.

'Not in so many words,' she admitted, defeated.

He was almost tempted to laugh at her crestfallen expression. 'Later, Julia,' he said easily. 'Now I think it must be time for dinner. We shall return here, when we have eaten, and then we can explore my collection more thoroughly.'

Rupert presided over his table on board the *Calypso* with the easy charm that was second nature to him. No one, not even Merise, would have detected his preoccupation as he flattered and amused, captivating his audience with improbable tales and lurid stories – most of them, he reflected to himself, all too true.

A skilled raconteur, he had them all in the palm of his hand: they hung on his words, devouring his stories as eagerly as they devoured the sumptuous dishes placed before them.

Over king prawns roasted with lemon and dill, served on a bed of saffron rice, he discoursed wittily on the travails of life as a ship's purser, and privately considered the telex he had received early this morning from Julia in Istanbul where she was with Tarik. He still had friends in Istanbul. He could contact them tonight, ask them to keep an eye on her. In the absence of Nazem, it might be a wise precaution to establish a shadow, a tail.

A boysenberry sorbet to cleanse the palate. An almost scurrilous anecdote involving a prominent political figure. The annoying, nagging doubt that there was something he should have done, something he should have taken into account before embarking on this improbable scheme. Yes, most definitely he would have a watch set over her, he decided.

Sea bass, grilled with ginger and spring onions, more succulent than any lobster. A naughty, ribald tale dating from his school days at Oxford. His thoughts roamed from Julia to Merise, resplendent in gold lamé at the neighbouring table. He had neglected her, he chastised himself, too caught up in his own interests to consider hers. And yet the opportunity might arise from this scheme for a little decadence, of the sort that she preferred. She seemed satisfied enough, left to her own devices, preparing to cut a sexual swathe through the more dubious elements of the passenger list, he mused. She had even, much to his surprise, agreed to his request and continued to toy with David. Yes, certainly she deserved a reward for her patience, he thought. The man was an egotistical bore.

Meringues filled with chestnut purée and topped with whipped cream. Nostalgic reminiscences of other cruises, other continents. Rupert's mind wandered back to Julia. He hoped that her newly found confidence hadn't deserted her, that she was enjoying her taste of adventure. He also fervently hoped that she could persuade Tarik to disclose the location of the Trojan gold. His cut from the coup, a few choice *objets* discreetly skimmed from the cache, would provide a tidy sum, ensuring a comfortable retirement. And banishing forever the spectre of chickens in Provence.

* * *

Freshly bathed and scented, and clad in a silk dressing gown thoughtfully provided by Tarik, Julia sat facing him across the polished surface of an elegant dining table. Like all the rooms she had seen in the palace, it was simply furnished, almost curiously austere. His passion, she guessed, was reserved for gold, for his collection.

Well, not entirely, she corrected herself, feeling his eyes upon her as she sipped cool cucumber soup. She felt an answering tug of attraction and lowered her eyes to her dish. It would be easy, dangerously easy, to forget the role she was supposed to play and simply succumb to this attraction.

She had meant to make a mental inventory of his collection so that when he was exposed she could describe each piece, ensure that it was all returned to the Turkish government; already her memory was fading, narrowing to the embossed gold rosettes he had slipped between her thighs. A single gold rosette now lay in her pocket. She knew already, right or wrong, that she would keep it for herself.

How strange to think of plotting his downfall even as her body warmed under his eyes. Strange and disconcerting. Tarik, she reminded herself, was the enemy; a man who had plundered his country's heritage for his own selfish pleasure.

So it was something of a shock to find herself admiring him, the blunt, bold strength of his will. He knew what he wanted and he took it. In a strange way, he reminded her of Merise. Both were arrogant, unscrupulous at achieving their ends. But she felt a bond growing between them, and that was truly dangerous.

She had learned to give her body freely; deeper

emotions had been obliterated in sensual rediscovery. She felt a warm affection for Rupert, a grateful awe for Merise. Mabik had been an indulgence, a celebration of the new Julia. But Tarik was something else again.

It would be a cruel irony to fall in love with her own victim.

No, she told herself, it was lust, nothing more, could be nothing more. She must be as unscrupulous as he if she were to succeed.

When they next returned to his room of gold, she would keep her wits about her, she decided.

'Your thoughts don't please you, Julia,' observed Tarik, watching the play of emotions cross her face. 'Or is it perhaps the soup?'

With a start she realised she was still holding her spoon untasted, halfway to her lips. 'No, no, the soup is delicious,' she said hastily.

'But you looked troubled,' he persisted.

Dear God, was her face that easy to read? She must be careful, she warned herself, summoning a smile. 'Just a stray thought,' she said lightly.

He looked dissatisfied, as though he would have pursued it, but fortunately they were interrupted by a servant bearing a platter of roast lamb, redolent with mint and garlic, surrounded by rice and aubergines stuffed with tomatoes and onions.

'Tell me about yourself,' Julia said, intending to divert him. In her experience it was a conversational ploy few men could resist.

'As you see, a simple man with simple tastes,' he said as the servant poured local red wine into their glasses and then departed.

'Hardly simple,' she countered, tasting the wine. It was rich, full-bodied, and surprisingly good.

'I disagree,' said Tarik. 'I know what I want. And how to get it. That makes life very simple.'

Uncanny to hear him echo her thoughts of moments before. She nodded in agreement.

'And you, Julia, what do you want?' he asked.

'Power,' she replied unthinkingly. Rupert had asked her that question not so long ago, she remembered. Then she had said she wanted sensual power, acclaim, reputation. Perhaps it all simply distilled to power.

'An unusual ambition for a woman,' he commented, intrigued.

'But there are many kinds of power,' she said thoughtfully, drawing the rosette from her pocket and turning it in her fingers.

'True,' he agreed, his eyes fixed on the rosette.

'The power of sex,' she mused turning the disc to the light and admiring its sheen. 'The power of gold. The power of money. The power of power. The power to be yourself.'

'All those things,' he agreed. 'But surely the greatest is the power to enjoy them.'

'Mmm,' she murmured.

'Your employer, for example,' probed Tarik. 'Does he collect from lust, or merely to invest? Will he ever drink wine from a gold rhyton drinking cup, placing his lips where ancient warriors once drank, and feel the thrill of history against his lips? Will he ever drape a woman in gold simply to see the warmth of it against her skin, or will his treasures lie lifeless in some vault?'

'Mmm, in a vault, I suppose,' replied Julia.

Almost worse than a museum,' he scorned. 'Untouched, unused, unloved. A waste.'

She ran a finger over the bumpy surface of the rosette. She could almost, she thought, almost sympathise with what he said. It was the force of his conviction, and the memory of the afternoon when she had felt the weight of ancient gold against her breasts and thighs.

'Perhaps,' she said non-committally. He was wrong, of course he was wrong: a country's heritage belonged in a museum, displayed for all to enjoy. But the jewellery, so carefully crafted, so intricately fashioned, had been meant to be worn, as he said.

'You feel so strongly, I'm surprised that you deal at all,' Julia offered, finishing her lamb and her wine. Tarik immediately poured her another glass.

'Ah, but ancient gold is not American dollars,' Tarik pointed out blandly, watching her carefully.

She had the sense that some bait, some lure had been extended. 'But if there is some new treasure trove, wouldn't you prefer to keep it for yourself?' she asked slowly, feeling her way.

'Infinitely,' said Tarik.

'But you want the money,' suggested Julia cautiously.

His face was its usual, expressionless mask. He made no reply.

She thought of the bond she recognised between them and felt the glimmerings of an idea forming in her mind. 'You want it all, don't you?' she asked.

That was something she understood, had grown to crave. If the coinage of her desire was different to Tarik's, the essential desire was the same.

'What do you mean?' Tarik demurred.

'The money and the treasure,' she answered softly. 'That's why you've been so cautious with me, so careful. You couldn't bear to part with any of your own collection, could you? It's not for sale,' she mused aloud. 'And the thought of more: it's irresistible, really. There *is*, there *must* be a new trove, or you wouldn't have even bothered to see me. You want it all,' she repeated.

Something flickered in the black depths of his eyes. She mustn't push him too hard, Julia cautioned herself.

'An intriguing idea,' commented Tarik, inwardly exultant. She had divined his intent without the slightest provocation, which meant she was perceptive; she had shown no surprise or outrage at the notion, which might mean she was as unscrupulous as he. And therefore as untrustworthy. Or she might simply be testing him.

She was already on the shady side of the law, he reflected, a supposedly respectable academic involved in the decidedly unrespectable trade in ancient arte-facts, a woman who had claimed she belonged to the highest bidder. And he saw the hunger in her, the greed that echoed his own. His was for gold, hers was more vague, more diffuse, more sensual.

'And, theoretically at least, not so difficult,' Julia replied.

'No? Tell me, theoretically, how it could be accomplished,' Tarik invited.

'Copies,' said Julia slowly, toying with her food. 'Reproductions. You obviously have access to some fine craftsmen who have done that sort of work for you before.'

'What makes you say so?' asked Tarik sharply.

'I recognised several pieces,' she explained simply. 'The death masks, for one. Currently on display in the National Archaeological Museum in Athens. Either theirs is a copy, or yours is. And I rather doubt that it's yours.'

'Ah,' Tarik nodded.

'Under the circumstances, laboratory testing is impossible,' Julia continued, thinking fast. 'My employer has to rely completely on my word. So if you duped me, or persuaded me, into authenticating the copies, you could retain the originals as well as their purchase price. A simple double-cross.'

'And how, theoretically, do I persuade you?' asked Tarik.

What possible motivation could she have, wondered Julia frantically. Inspiration struck.

'By giving me the site,' Julia said.

'What?' exclaimed Tarik.

'The trove is intact, isn't it?' she asked with some trace of anxiety. 'Because if it's not, I'm not interested.'

'It's intact,' Tarik assured her, inadvertently confirming, for the first time, its existence. Julia felt a sudden wave of triumphant relief. 'But what do you mean, "give" you the site?'

'I want to know the location, examine it myself. Then, after you've cleared the trove, or most of it, I want to be able to "discover" it as an archaeological site. My employer will believe I skimmed off the best for him from my new site, while at the same time it will make my reputation in academic circles,' she said. 'I'll have my finder's fee, and grant money for years. It couldn't be more perfect.'

'I see,' said Tarik, consideringly. It sounded plausible enough, and her obvious self-interest reassured him.

They both fell silent as the servant returned to take their plates and offer sweet pastries, coffee and brandy. Conversation resumed on a more general plane and the treasure was not referred to again.

Until they returned to the room of gold.

'I could force you to tell me,' mocked Julia playfully, half-serious, half-teasing. In her hand she held a golden dagger, the hilt decorated with a hunting scene engraved in silver. Tarik was naked beneath her, the head of his penis poised at her entrance. She held the tip of the dagger to his throat, then traced a line to his nipple, not hard enough to draw blood, leaving only a faint, pink line against his skin. His flesh tightened against it and his hips arched convulsively against hers.

Deliberately she contracted her inner muscles, allowing him only the faint pulse of her flesh against his.

'Tell you what?' groaned Tarik.

'The site of the treasure,' she laughed, sliding her body down his.

'Or I could beg you,' she whispered against the dense bush of his pubic hair, blowing softly on his swollen testicles, delicately licking the tender skin, swirling her tongue to the root of his penis.

Gold was his aphrodisiac; sensual power was hers; and so their desire was conjoined in the room of gold.

Lost in carnal make-believe, unbearably aroused by Tarik's assumed passivity, she became more inventive, more demanding.

'Or even torture you,' she suggested, sliding a

heavily beringed finger between the cleft of his buttocks and finding his anus.

And Tarik held himself back brutally, gave himself to her utterly, allowing her to torment him, knowing from the hectic flush of her cheeks, the tumid slickness of her inner lips, that she was as aroused as he, knowing that she was only playing an erotic game like some wayward child, knowing that he would never disclose the site of his treasure trove.

For Dmitri, the Turkish-Greek who had agreed to help Rupert and observe Tarik's movements, the days passed slowly. Parked some distance from the elegant Ottoman palace, he watched as servants left and returned, and smoked too many cigarettes. He was used to the utter boredom of surveillance and was careful not to let his guard drop once he had established the routine comings and goings of the household. He read the newspapers with one eye, listened to American rock and roll on the radio, smoked his cigarettes and waited. Dmitri was a patient man.

Rupert was becoming impatient. As *Calypso* made her way across the Aegean to mainland Greece, further and further away from Julia and Tarik and Troy, he began to curse each nautical mile separating them. Julia should have contacted him by now, he fretted. Reports from Dmitri failed to reassure him. This complete lack of action on any front was as disturbing as it was suspicious. Julia's proposal was a simple one: Tarik could either refuse or agree. If he had refused, Julia would have left days ago. If he had agreed, they should both have left days ago.

Had Tarik guessed that Julia was involved in some

scheme to expose him? Even now she might be lying dead, her throat cut from ear to ear like poor Nazem. He tried to dislodge the image from his mind, but it fastened on his imagination more persistently, more luridly, as each day passed.

If nothing happened soon, he promised himself, he would find a way to smoke them out. A strike of some sort, perhaps an ambush. It would be messy, he thought dismally, it could be dangerous, and, more than anything else, it offended his sensibilities.

'Rupert, darling, you're looking quite morose,' said Merise, coming to join him at the ship's railing and laying a hand on his sleeve. 'Still no news, my love?' She now knew the details of Rupert's scheme and if her interest in the treasure was perfunctory, her concern for Julia, much as it surprised her, was not.

'None,' he admitted. 'She's still in Istanbul and hasn't made a move.'

'Istanbul,' said Merise thoughtfully. 'You know, I've never been there.'

'Hmmm,' murmured Rupert, equally thoughtful.

For Julia, time passed in a golden blur. There were two Tariks, she discovered: the rough, earthy, primitive Tarik who took her swiftly, almost brutally, on the silk sheets in his bedroom, and the bizarrely inventive lover in the room of gold. There, no carnal act was too fantastic, too extravagant for his imagination. One night he filled her with gold, forcing a string of gold beads into her anus, another into her vagina and, when she would have screamed with the delicious agony, he stopped her mouth with a gentle kiss. Another night he spent hours stroking her breasts with the horns of a drinking cup in the shape of a ram

144

until she came in a shuddering burst of suspended pleasure; afterwards they drank champagne from the cup. She became as inventive as he, wrapping the links of gold chains around his massive prick, impaling herself on his gilded flesh.

In the bedroom, they were silent, coupled with wordless violence.

The room of gold echoed with moans and laughter, screams of pleasure, the subdued murmurs of passion fulfilled.

It was there, fittingly enough, that Tarik finally agreed to take her to the treasure.

Chapter Eight

*T*he raid took place in the early hours of the morning, in the dark, still hours before dawn when the moon reigns, when even Istanbul, a city that never sleeps, is quiet.

Six figures, dressed all in black, swarmed up the outer walls of the palace like huge insects, their movements graceful and controlled. It was a ballet of black against white, of supple motion against still, unyielding concrete. Anyone watching would have admired the deft economy and synchronisation of movement as they scaled the wall, seemingly unsupported, but only the moon observed their swift ascent.

Dmitri was fast asleep, snoring gently beneath his newspaper to the strains of Billy Joel and The Doors.

Noiselessly they dropped, cat-like, to the inner courtyard. They crouched silently in the shadows, becoming the shadows, absorbed, waiting. Nothing stirred but the warm night air.

In wordless accord, they stood.

Blue-grey steel gleamed menacingly in the moon-light as weapons were raised.

Like wraiths they fanned through the endless corridors, silent and deadly, and left no trace of their passing.

They worked slowly and methodically in the dim light.

The austere, minimal furnishings of the palace aided their search.

Gloved hands parted draperies, fingered polished surfaces, opened drawers and cupboards.

Not a single sound betrayed their presence as they passed from room to room.

Only the room of gold, recessed in the heart of the palace, remained undiscovered and inviolate.

The private chambers were approached with caution, semi-automatic weapons trained on beds and divans.

Beds and divans that were found to be empty.

Frustration mounted as it became apparent, room after room, that the palace was deserted.

They departed as silently as they had arrived, observed not only by the moon, but also by Dmitri.

'Shit, shit, shit!' Rupert exclaimed furiously, scanning the flimsy telex and running a hand through his long, dark hair. He had been awakened by a soft tap on his door at the cruelly unreasonable hour of six o'clock, and an obnoxiously alert cabin boy had passed him the message. If the young man had been surprised to see their most scandalous passenger, Merise Isabella Van Asche, sharing the purser's bed, he had had no time to register his amazement; Rupert had slammed the door in his face with an explosive oath as soon as he had snatched the paper from his hands.

'What is it darling?' asked Merise sleepily, squirming against the rumpled sheets.

'It's from Dmitri,' he said abstractedly. 'They've entered the palace, searched it.'

'What a good idea,' yawned Merise. 'So your friends, or your people, or whatever you call them, have captured the master villain and Julia's safe and sound. How nice.' She rolled over on to her side and plumped a pillow beneath her head. 'Can we go back to sleep now?'

'No. That's just it,' said Rupert bleakly. 'They weren't my friends, or my people. And Julia and Tarik have vanished.'

'I feel like I've been kidnapped,' protested Julia, as Tarik's Jaguar cut through the night.

'Perhaps you have,' said Tarik.

'But why are you in such a hurry? And why, for God's sake, in the middle of the night?' she asked. 'And where, exactly, are we going?'

He had acted like a whirlwind, sweeping her from the room of gold and then from the palace, barely allowing her time to pack her few belongings and then almost thrusting her into the waiting car.

At first it was exciting, a sort of strange continuation of their lovemaking, where he led and she followed, and, following, discovered her own realm.

But this was different.

And, in some subtle way, he was different.

She had no choice, no opportunity to contact Rupert. As she hastily made herself ready, she could think of no plausible excuse to use the phone, let alone ask for a telex or fax machine; he would be suspicious, and rightly so.

Now she could only trust to luck, surrender to events, follow her instincts, and hope that the strange, tenuous bond she felt with Tarik would protect her.

'To my treasure, Julia, and yours,' he said.

'But at this time of night? So your departure won't be noticed? or so I won't be able to see where we're going?' she probed shrewdly.

'I said I would show you the treasure,' said Tarik equably. 'I never promised to show you its exact location.'

'But – ' she interjected.

'Until our business is concluded,' he finished. 'And then, my dear, you will have your discovery.'

When he had received the hundreds of millions of American dollars she had offered him, she thought with a sudden chill; the hundreds of millions of American dollars she had no access to; the hundreds of millions of American dollars which, in fact, did not exist. She pushed the thought aside.

'What do you mean, you'll show me the treasure, but not where it is?' Julia asked, uncomfortably aware that her voice was a little shrill with nerves.

She felt like a sleepwalker awaking from a dream. This was not the Tarik of the room of gold, nor even the Tarik of the bedroom. Suddenly he was remote, a stranger.

'Just that, my dear,' replied Tarik imperturbably. 'Someone as delightfully ready to double-cross her employer as you are shouldn't be surprised if I take a few precautions.'

'Precautions?' Her voice rose unsteadily. 'You're not going to drug me, are you?'

'Don't get hysterical, Julia,' said Tarik, laying a heavy hand on her thigh. A hand that had, only, what, an hour before rested tenderly on her breast? Now it squeezed harshly. In his bedroom, under the chased lamp, amidst silken sheets, that touch would have been foreplay; in the confines of the speeding Jaguar it was a warning. 'And it's quite obvious where we're going. You can see the lights of the airport ahead.'

She could, barely, straining her eyes, and as she did she also became aware of the lights behind them, a set of lights that had followed them since they had left the palace.

'Tarik, Tarik, I think we're being followed,' she said hastily. 'Look, those lights behind us. They've been with us ever since we left.'

'I should hope so,' Tarik said, glancing lazily in the rear-view mirror. 'My men,' he explained. 'They shadow every move I make. And now yours too, of course.'

'Of course,' she echoed, wondering if her voice sounded as hollow to his ears as it did to her own.

At the airport, in the section reserved for private planes, there were few formalities and even fewer questions. The pilot emerged from a cargo shed to greet Tarik deferentially; a weary customs official, either bribed or simply tired, merely waved them on.

The plane was larger than the little Cessna that had brought her to Istanbul, Julia realised, large enough to accommodate a bedroom at the back and a spacious lounge decorated in shades of crimson and pewter where normally there would have been rows of seats. Still, it was small enough that she felt the reverberations of the engines through the skin of the plane as the pilot readied for take-off. They reminded her of the pulsing thrum of the zodiac as Rupert had steered her away from *Calypso* a lifetime ago. Then she had felt the thrum as a palpable sexual excitement; now she felt the same tension mixed with apprehension.

Tarik was at the front of the plane, conversing in a low voice with the two men who had accompanied them on board. Both were tall and dark and wore black suits that failed to disguise suspicious bulges beneath the armpit. She thought suddenly of the little pistol Rupert had given her and rummaged through her hastily packed tote bag. She was not much surprised to find it missing.

'A drink, Julia?' asked Tarik, coming to stand beside her. 'We'll be taking off shortly.'

'Please,' she replied. 'Scotch, if you have it.'

It was an old single malt that warmed with a smooth fire. She drained it in one swallow and immediately felt better. Holding out her glass for a refill, she smiled at Tarik and said lightly, 'So much mystery. Now that we're on our way, will you tell me about the treasure?'

Tarik cocked his head, apparently listening to the sound of the engines. 'Almost on our way,' he said. 'Come with me.' With his hand on the small of her back, he led her to the bedroom and closed the door. He removed his tie and jacket and sprawled on the pewter-coloured counterpane, gesturing to her to do the same.

'The treasure,' she repeated, settling herself beside him. There was something reassuring in the familiar weight of his body next to hers.

'Mmm. Do you remember what Schliemann said when he uncovered the shaft graves at Mycenae and found the three warriors, their skulls preserved beneath masks of gold?'

'I have gazed upon the face of Agamemnon,' quoted Julia.

'Yes. And I, I have gazed upon the face of Helen, the most beautiful woman in the world,' gloated Tarik.

'Helen?' echoed Julia, confused. 'It's in Greece, then?'

'No, not in Greece,' said Tarik absently.

'But Helen returned to Sparta with Menelaos after the war,' Julia began to object, then stopped herself.

'At the sack of Troy, Menelaos wanted to kill her, and I'm sure he did,' continued Tarik. 'It's the only possible explanation. She is so beautiful, so incredibly beautiful.'

'But – ' Julia bit off her words. Obviously Tarik, like Schliemann himself, was a romantic who believed only what he wanted to believe. It was ludicrous to imagine that a figure culled from literature and mythology could be identified with physical remains. Still, she felt a rising wave of excitement.

'So beautiful,' Tarik said again. He turned to her and with the utmost gentleness began to caress the contours of her face, the curve of her jaw, the arch of her cheekbones, the swell of her lips. His gaze was at once fiercely concentrated yet strangely distant and it occurred to her that he was seeing someone else – his mythical Helen.

His touch was subtle and delicate as he traced her features with his fingertips, lingering on the curve of her mouth. She felt herself responding as though to a kiss.

'Covered in gold,' he murmured, his hands shifting to her throat and then to her breasts, then down her belly to her thighs with a tenderness she had never

152

felt from him before; a tenderness, she knew, that was not meant for her.

'It's a burial, then,' Julia prompted softly.

His hands fell away and his face regained its customary expression of reserve. 'Her tomb,' he said shortly, drawing away from her and reaching for his scotch.

'And it is at Troy, isn't it?' she persisted, regretting, a little, the loss of his touch.

'Yes,' said Tarik abruptly. 'Enough, Julia. I have promised to take you there, and I shall. It's a short flight, try and get some sleep.' He rose from the bed and left the room.

Disconcerted by his sudden change of mood, Julia drained her scotch, poured another, and tried to think. A female burial – a tomb – in Troy, that Tarik was convinced was the grave of Helen. There would be a mass of grave goods, she speculated, not just gold but other everyday objects that would help to date the trove. He had said that it was at Troy; it must be misleadingly obvious or exceptionally well hidden to have avoided discovery for so long.

She felt the shudder of the plane's engines as it began to taxi down the runway. She parted one of the pewter silk curtains on the wall but could see nothing from the tiny window. On impulse she went to the door and tried the handle. It was locked.

She finished her drink and, without bothering to undress, covered herself with the pewter silk spread and tried to sleep.

In a tilled field not far from Ciplak, two jeeps were parked. The drivers, Tarik's employees alerted earlier from Istanbul, waited, lounging against the jeeps, smoking and chatting intermittently. Although each was armed, it was more from habit than anything else. In the dead of night, in a deserted field, there was no danger and little need for caution.

One of the drivers produced some rather good brandy. His last conscious thought, as stars danced before his eyes and he blacked out, was that perhaps he had drunk more than he'd thought.

The unconscious bodies were neatly tied, gagged, and dumped into a ditch.

Two men took their places beside the jeep; another four fanned out along the perimeter of the field.

Julia was dreaming, a dim, diffuse, erotic dream tinged with gold, a mélange of images of tangled limbs and golden bodies. Rupert appeared, and then Merise, and then Tarik, all entwined in a carnal conspiracy, a golden web whose tendrils ensnared her, licking and caressing, enfolding her.

There was a sweet, tingling warmth, surrounding her, suffusing her, like a blush of pure pleasure. She was growing rounder, fuller, warmer, ripening to gold. A thousand flickering lights glowed beneath her skin, pooled, then splintered.

She woke at the moment of climax to find Tarik's dark black eyes inches from her own.

He had meant merely to awaken her and then rejoin his men before they disembarked, but her obvious arousal had triggered his own. He had watched her sleeping body gently rock in unconscious pleasure and felt the sly titillation of the voyeur; he was already hard when orgasm roused her from her dreams.

He stripped himself quickly then fumbled with the buttons of her pants. No foreplay; he was too hard, too eager, too ready. He entered her in one swift, numbing thrust.

For Julia, it was a seamless spiral from dream to reality. She was wet and heated, still pulsing with the dying contractions of her climax; he filled her, convulsing her again with the power of his thrusts.

When he moved, she could feel him everywhere, as if he overpowered the rhythms of her body with his own, dispelling the sweet dreamy bliss with a plunging, driving force that obliterated everything except the heat of his next thrust.

She lunged against him, meeting him stroke for stroke in a struggle for climax.

It was over quickly; they came together almost at once.

Outside, the four men crept closer, surrounding the plane.

The pilot, wanting to stretch his legs, released the doors and let down the steps.

Tarik's men, with a knowing grin at the closed door of the bedroom, decided to go outside for a cigarette.

It was over quickly; faced with six men armed with submachine guns, they surrendered almost at once.

'Bitch!' spat Tarik, as venomously as possible while struggling against his bonds in the back of the jeep that had just careened into a deep pot hole. 'Double-triple-crossing bitch. You'll regret this, I promise you.' he glared at Julia.

'Idiot,' she spat back, losing her fear in fury.

They had been taken in the bedroom, two guns trained on their half-naked bodies, two pairs of lascivious, mocking eyes enjoying their embarrassed, inarticulate rage as their bodies parted, prodded by a gun barrel.

'No more talking,' advised one of the gunmen lazily from the front of the jeep, casually waving his gun for emphasis.

Julia closed her eyes, wincing as the jeep shuddered its way over the deeply rutted roads. Beside her Tarik subsided into silent, impotent fury. Their bodies clashed together as the jeep gained speed.

'This has nothing to do with me,' she whispered to him as they rounded a curve, forcing them together at the side of the jeep. 'Nothing, I swear it. If it did, would they have tossed me back here with you, bound my arms and legs at gunpoint? For God's sake, think.'

'It's a trick,' he hissed back, unconvinced. 'Who are these men? Yours? Your employer's? You bitch.'

'You fool,' she snapped back. Another curve of the road jolted Tarik's body hard against hers, his weight pinning her to the ribbed metal floor of the jeep. His anger was a tangible thing, like his lust; she could feel it enveloping her. She smelled the hot reek of his sweat, mixed with the dust from the road and the heavy night air, faintly scented with jasmine.

It was, she thought, almost a parody of sex, his body rocking against hers, the ruts of the roads forcing him closer against her, their bodies straining in frustration.

But this was the frustration of forced bondage, not arousal, of mistrust, not compliance.

In the midst of her frustration, in the midst of her fear, Julia clung to a single comforting thought.

She was almost, almost certain that she had recognised the man in the jeep who had so casually brandished his gun.

Mabik.

Another reckless curve; another clash as she and Tarik were thrown against the side of the jeep; and then nothing but deep, dark, instant oblivion as her head snapped against the metal floor.

'Bitch. Double-crossing bitch.'

She heard the familiar, hateful words from far away and twisted to escape them, wanting to stay in the thick, dark cocoon of unconsciousness that enfolded her. It was safe there, unfeeling, unthreatening.

But rough hands were shaking her awake, dragging her across a rough dirt floor, fumbling at her clothing, slapping slight, stinging blows across her cheeks.

Reflexively she tried to fight back, kick or claw, but her hands and ankles were still bound.

'You betrayed us. Betrayed me,' accused the unseen man's voice.

She bucked against him, shaking her head to clear it.

'Maybe I'll have you for it, just as you had me,' threatened the voice. He was straddling her, one hand toying with the fastening of her pants, the other implacable, holding a gun to her head.

Memory returned in a flash and for a moment she was at the banks of the muddy, slow-flowing river, sunlight dappling the shadows, the fertile, loamy smell of the earth in her nostrils, a knife in her hand, and the young, eager body of Mabik beneath her.

She had teased him then, held a knife to his throat, joked about being merciless; now he held a gun to her head, was straddling her as she had straddled him and this time it was no laughing matter.

'Mabik, no,' Julia protested, squirming beneath him.

She could feel the rod of his erection, heavy against her thigh. 'I didn't betray you, how could I?'

'You brought him here,' he hissed, his fingers digging into her through her clothing. 'When we found you you were rutting like animals.'

'Just like you want to do now,' Julia spat back at him, bucking against him, knowing her movements were increasing his arousal, but unable to lie still. 'What does that mean, what does that prove? Nothing, and you know it.'

'You brought him here,' Mabik repeated in a hard voice. 'I knew you meant to take our gold!'

'*He* brought *me* here. And I don't even know where we are,' cried Julia. 'Mabik, you must believe me.'

'Liar,' he retorted, ripping at the flimsy silk of panties. She arched towardsa him, instinctively.

'No, wait. Please, listen to me,' she pleaded.

For a brief moment he hesitated, caught by the urgency of her voice. He wanted her as much as he despised her, inflamed with lust, inflamed with anger; first she would pay with her body, and then . . .

'He brought me here to show me the treasure.' Julia was speaking rapidly, her words tumbling over in her eagerness to convince him. 'I told you everything before and you believed me. Now he thinks I'm double-crossing my employer. I haven't been able to contact Rupert, you trust Rupert. Please, Mabik. And now it's all for nothing, because we still don't know where the treasure is. Why did you do this? How did you know Tarik was coming here?

Something she said stopped the harsh fingers at her mound; she could sense his confusion.

'It was Celik,' he said slowly. 'He told us that you were leading Tarik to us, to our gold.'

'But it was Celik who arranged for me to go to Istanbul in the first place,' cried Julia. 'This makes no sense at all. And what do you mean, your gold?'

Mabik was silent.

'It's not the same, is it?' asked Julia as realisation dawned. 'There are two troves, aren't there? A cache that the village has hidden away for years, generations, taken from the excavations, and then this new trove, known only to Tarik. I'm right, aren't I? Listen – Tarik described this Trojan gold to me. It's a burial, a female burial. He thinks it's Helen's tomb. The body is still there, draped in gold. A beautiful woman. That's all he told me, that's all I know.'

'A woman? A grave?' repeated Mabik incredulously.

'Then you didn't know?' said Julia. She felt his body relax almost infinitesimally against hers. He was still tense, still hard, but the animal rage had left him and her words were beginning to reach him.

'Celik said only that you had betrayed us, that you must be captured,' Mabik said thoughtfully.

'And Tarik? What have you done with him?' asked Julia.

'Oh, yes, your lover,' sneered Mabik, his fingers tightening convulsively on the barrel of the gun, and the soft flesh between her legs.

It was then that they both became aware of their bodies, fixed together like lovers, his erection hard against her, his fingers pressing against her sex.

'Yes, he was my lover,' she replied simply. 'And so were you. But it's Tarik who is the key to the treasure. What have you done with him?'

'He's safe, nearby,' shrugged Mabik. 'Bound, like you, and gagged. Helpless.'

The thought pleased him, Julia realised. More than pleased him, excited him. The evidence was hard against her.

'Is that what you want?' she asked coldly. 'To take me like this, bound and helpless? Perhaps you should gag me as well.'

'What I want – ' he began thickly. 'What I want – is – damn you, Julia.' Suddenly he rolled away from her, pushing her aside. For long moments the only sound in the tiny hut was his laboured breathing.

Finally he recovered himself. 'If what you say is true,' he began.

'You know it's true,' interrupted Julia. 'We'll have to find a way of making Tarik lead us to the treasure. But first you can untie me.'

With a muttered apology, he bent to her ankles, undid the coarse rope binding them, then freed her wrists. A little stiffly, Julia rose, rubbing her wrists and flexing her fingers to restore the circulation.

'But Celik – he was sure,' said Mabik suspiciously. She noticed that he was still holding the gun, albeit loosely, no longer trained on her but still ready.

'Well, Celik made a mistake,' she retorted. 'Maybe he was trying to set you up, have you thought of that? The most important thing is to find the treasure, and I must get word to Rupert. I don't know what we can do – now Tarik believes I've betrayed him, he won't trust me. God, what a mess.'

'The elders, too, believe Celik,' warned Mabik.

'Well, you'll just have to convince them, won't you?' she retorted with some asperity. There was only one way to do that, she decided. 'They can retain a portion of the treasure when we find it, or they'll have nothing. That should be pretty persuasive.

'And then, for what it's worth, you'll have to confront Tarik. Don't say anything about me. Threaten him, tell him that you know about the treasure, try and make him talk. But I doubt it will work.'

'I don't believe it,' muttered Rupert distractedly, the flimsy telex dangling from his fingers. Another unwelcome awakening too early in the morning by the cabin boy, who craned his neck to peer past him to the bed; more bad news. Julia and Tarik ambushed near Ciplak by Mabik and his party; Tarik taken prisoner; the site of the Trojan gold still unknown.

At least, he comforted himself, they now knew it was there, an undiscovered burial rich in gold somewhere in the ruins of the ancient mound that was Hissarlik. But only Tarik knew precisely where.

And Tarik wasn't talking.

Mabik wasn't a skilled interrogator; he would be crude, possibly violent, and physical pain was unlikely to shake a man like Tarik who used it as a weapon himself. Rupert, who had learnt a little of the art, knew the persuasive effects of sensory deprivation, of continuous light or unending darkness, of discomfort rather than pain. But all that took far, far too long.

It simply wasn't possible to kidnap a wealthy Turkish industrialist without creating waves, attracting the attention of employees, associates and even, God forbid, the police.

Drugs? He shuddered fastidiously at the idea. In a long and often disreputable career he had never resorted to drugs except for purely medicinal purposes.

Torture, he thought, a refined, subtle torture that left no marks, no lasting injuries, yet reduced a man to such a fevered pitch that he was in agony, wept for release, begged and pleaded. He had seen it done once in a brothel in Ceylon when a customer had beaten one of the girls. The madam had been strict, her revenge exact: she had simply turned him over to the girls who had, with lewd enthusiasm and considerable inventiveness, brought him again and again and again to the brink of climax and then prevented his orgasm. Sexual frustration can become a desperate, atavistic need, primal and overpowering, and even more persuasive than drugs or violence.

Not, he thought wryly, the sort of instruction one confided to the telex. He looked over to the bed, where Merise's dark hair was fanned across his pillow. Decadence indeed, he decided, remembering his promise to her.

'Merise, my love, wake up. I have to talk to you,' said Rupert, shaking her gently by the shoulder.

In the event, the telex he sent was simple. 'Remember the first night. Stay with him. Keep cover. Wait for Merise.'

'I don't understand,' complained Mabik, reading over her shoulder. 'What first night? What Merise?'

'Merise is Rupert's friend,' explained Julia, puzzled. 'She's with him on the cruise. He must be sending her here to help, but I don't know how. And the first night – oh, I don't know.'

'I don't like this,' said Mabik. 'Better to shoot him through the knees now. Then he'll talk.'

'No,' said Julia sharply. 'We wait, as Rupert said. You'll have to take me to Tarik. And I suppose you'll have to tie me up again. What has he said?'

'Nothing,' Mabik growled. 'Nothing at all.'

'Did he ask about me?'

'I told you, he said nothing,' repeated Mabik, binding her wrists and ankles.

As he led her outside, she blinked at the sun. It was almost noon and the day was growing hotter. Shuffling awkwardly with her bound ankles, she stumbled behind Mabik to another small hut that lay ahead.

'In here,' he said roughly, opening the door and thrusting her inside. Either from sheer frustration or for the sake of authenticity, he shoved her too hard, and she fell heavily against the prone body of Tarik.

'Tarik, Tarik, are you all right?' she asked anxiously.

'Bitch,' he responded bitterly. 'Did they send you here to plead with me?'

'No,' she protested, 'I told you, I know nothing.' She searched for something to say to lull his suspicions but nothing occurred to her. She thought again of the curious wording of Rupert's telex. The first night. He must mean the night they had spent together on board the *Calypso*, but why?

She remembered how he had prolonged their love-making, curbing her haste, slowing her passion.

Slowly, yes, that was the key.

She would say little; perhaps he would be reassured by her silence. Despite the stifling heat of the tiny hut, she pressed closer to him.

Chapter Nine

*A*s the hours dragged on, it became hotter and hotter inside the tiny hut. They were allowed outside to relieve themselves; their hands were untied to enable them to eat a simple meal of bread, olives, cheese and water under the watchful eye of a masked gunman and swiftly refastened as soon as they had finished; periodically another masked figure Julia was sure was Mabik would enter, alternately demanding and threatening.

'Tell us where it is, what you have come for.'

'I could shoot you now, just through the knees, and you'll never walk again.'

'Tell us where it is, what you have come for.'

'We could shoot the woman, perhaps that will convince you.'

Idle threats, Julia was sure, but there was a note in Mabik's voice that disturbed her. His hatred for Tarik was palpable; understandable since he believed him responsible for his brother's death. But there was a distinct viciousness in his voice when he spoke of her that was both confusing and unsettling.

'Tell us where it is, what you have come for.'

'I could give the woman to my men, make you watch as they took her.'

Not just vicious, thought Julia, but spiteful. This was more than distrust; it was bitterness. Mabik still wanted her, she knew; his fierce, physical reaction to her had been uncontrolled, even though he had disguised it as an act of vengeance. And he had found her with Tarik in the bedroom of the plane, rutting, as he had said, like two animals.

Sexual jealousy was a deep and powerful emotion, primal and atavistic, knowing no logic, no limits. It had been some subtle sexual jealousy of David that had led her to challenge Merise, that had drawn her to Rupert – an erotic exorcism of her own insecurities.

If Mabik's resentment ran so deep, he might well be tempted to carry out his threats against her, Rupert or no Rupert, treasure or no treasure.

And as time passed, she could sense his frustration growing.

'Tell us where it is, what you have come for.'

'We could torture the woman slowly, in front of you. Would you tell us then?'

'Please, for God's sake Tarik, tell them what they want to know,' pleaded Julia after Mabik had left, the tremor in her voice unfeigned. 'Please. I'm frightened.'

'You? Frightened? Of your own people?' he said contemptuously. 'Perhaps you deserve to be.'

'Please, I've told you, I had nothing to with this,' cried Julia.

But Tarik had relapsed into silence.

While Mabik threatened and demanded, Julia pleaded and coaxed; Tarik remained silent, unmoved.

She lost all track of time. Intermittently she lapsed into a light, troubled sleep only to be awakened by Mabik's harsh voice.

'Tell us where it is, what you have come for.'

She had almost decided to end the charade, insist that Mabik release her, when a cool, amused, yet decidedly disdainful voice cut through the stifling air of the hut.

'My dear Julia, how delightful to see you again. And in such a charmingly rustic setting,' drawled Merise.

'Merise,' gasped Julia thankfully, raising herself painfully on one elbow.

'And this is, I presume, your latest mark?' said Merise, ignoring her and turning her eyes to Tarik.

'Your employer, I presume,' said Tarik through gritted teeth.

Julia began to speak, but Merise's voice drowned her own.

'Julia has been with me for some time,' said Merise smoothly. 'An endearing child, with an enchanting tendency to double-cross anyone at the slightest opportunity. Keeping that in mind, I've found her to be the most reliable member of my staff.'

Utterly confused, Julia fell silent.

'Charming and rustic though this is,' continued Merise, 'I'm sure we can find some other accommodation with a little more scope, yes?' she asked, turning to the masked figure at her side. 'Take them there.' She turned and walked out of the hut without a backward glance.

Still bound, they were prodded out of the hut. Julia

166

didn't miss Mabik's vicious, victorious glare as he thrust her into the back of the waiting jeep.

'Well now,' cooed Merise. 'Isn't this cosy?'

It was anything but cosy; a large room with white-washed walls, harshly lit by a naked bulb that descended from the ceiling, furnished with only a large wooden table, four chairs, and a single divan, on which Merise reclined. Julia and Tarik sat, bound to the simple wooden chairs.

Julia wondered at the motives that kept her bound beside Tarik. There seemed no obvious reason to continue the charade, but instinct kept her quiet. Merise must have some trick, some ace up her sleeve, that made it necessary.

'I've always thought that there was something delightfully special about bondage, haven't you?' Merise asked airily. 'A sexual victim, pliant and passive, utterly submissive. That's always appealed to me. And to have two victims, a man and a woman, that's even more enticing.'

If she was acting, thought Julia numbly, it was a brilliant performance. The role of dominatrix suited her; she even seemed to have dressed for the part in thin black leather trousers and shirt. Her lush dark hair tumbled over her shoulders and her maenad's eyes gleamed.

'It's a common fantasy between lovers, a game. But it's still a fantasy. The chains are by consent, the pain to enhance pleasure. But you haven't consented, have you? And that makes it all the more interesting.'

The husky, sensual, hypnotic voice continued. Julia had fallen under the spell of that voice once before, succumbed to the sexual heat that flowed from

Merise, the provocative promise of utter carnality. But this was different. There was something darker, more dangerous than she had felt before. Cat and mouse yet again, but on a different plane, in a different realm. And it was not a game Julia was sure she was prepared to play. Yet she was still conscious of an unwilling fascination.

'Pain, the exquisite pain of unfulfilled need, the ache of frustration – it's a truly rarefied torture. Women, of course, are so much more of a challenge. With men it's easy, so remarkably easy. Too easy. But with a little careful humiliation, a little degradation, it's so much more satisfying.'

'You expect me to fear you,' said Tarik flatly.

Merise smiled and widened her eyes. 'I know you'll fear me,' she replied softly.

'You expect me to take you to the treasure.'

'I know you'll take me to the treasure,' corrected Merise, still smiling.

'You'll pay. In American dollars, as agreed?' asked Tarik, feeling his way, playing for time.

'Oh, no,' said Merise mildly. 'I'll pay for nothing. I think, eventually, you'll be quite pleased simply to give it to me.'

Tarik narrowed his eyes. The woman unnerved him by her calm, her absolute self-possession, and by the faint air of depravity that clung to her like a musky perfume. It was the lascivious way she spoke of pain, the hot glow in her eyes. He recognised the killer instinct that went beyond simple lust, simple greed.

And, like Julia, he was unwillingly fascinated.

'I'll make you rouse to me,' Merise said softly. 'You won't be able to stop yourself any more than you can stop the beating of your heart. I'll make you hard,

168

harder than you've ever been, with my mouth, with my tongue, with my teeth. It will be soft and warm, and tight and wet, everything you want. You'll feel the blood surge to your prick, the need begin to pulse faster and faster, the tightening in your balls, the ache deep at the base of your spine. You'll be mindless, nothing more than your cock, desperate. And I'll keep you there as long as I please. Julia knows that I can, don't you Julia?' asked Merise, her eyes never leaving Tarik's face.

'No, I mean, yes. Merise, I don't – '

'Because it's what you wanted, isn't it? The power. The sensual power.'

'No, Merise, not like – '

'Oh, yes, like this.'

Languidly she rose from the divan and came to stand by Tarik's chair. Calmly, almost impersonally she unzipped his trousers, slid down his shorts, and released his prick. There was nothing seductive in her movements; it was a demonstration of pure power.

In a sudden flashback, Julia saw David and Merise, highlighted against the white screen of the lecture hall, his phallus thick and engorged from her mouth.

Then, as now, her hands and lips moved ceaselessly, the rhythms ever changing, soft and fluttering, hard and pulsing. She sucked him deep into her mouth, pressing him hard against her palate, releasing him to blow gently on the swelling tip of his penis, swirling her tongue against the sensitive slit before drawing him back into the cavern of her mouth.

And Tarik found, as she had promised, he could no more stop rousing to her touch than he could stop the beating of his heart. He strained against his bonds, but it was only to thrust harder against the flickering heat of her mouth, the delicate scrape of her teeth.

When she left the engorged length of his prick to trail her tongue along the inside of his thighs to his testicles, he could barely prevent himself from groaning.

Julia closed her eyes, trying to curb her own, unwilling arousal. It had been different with David and Merise, when she had watched, alone and invisible. This was too close, far, far too close.

Merise was relentless, the flickering expertise of her tongue like a trail of fire along his shaft, the rapid pulse of her fingers clasping and unclasping him. Tarik strained to find his rhythm, but as soon as his body began to succumb to the straining suction of her mouth it was replaced by the sharpness of her teeth.

Climax was coiling deep in the base of his spine, an urgent roiling need as desperate as she had promised. He felt the first faint quivers as his body readied, and then arched in a sudden jolt as she pressed one long nail into the mouth of his anus, freezing his orgasm in shock.

Merise laughed softly. 'So easy, you see?' she purred. 'And so obvious. There are other ways. Julia and I can show you together.'

Julia's eyes flew open. 'No, Merise,' she said sharply. 'I won't. This is enough. Untie me now, let me go.'

'But darling Julia, why should I?' asked Merise mockingly. 'I've only just begun to enjoy myself.'

Tarik muttered something unintelligible under his breath. Casting a swift glance at him, Julia saw his forehead beaded in sweat, his massive prick held tight and twitching between Merise's hands.

'Because I ask you to,' replied Julia firmly. 'Because this is not your game alone. I'll leave you with Tarik, as long as you promise not to hurt him.' The words came out in an unexpected rush. 'But, now – let me go.'

'Is the dull little prude surfacing, frightened of its own shadow?' mocked Merise.

'Not at all,' Julia said flatly. 'I make my choices now, and I don't choose the shadows. Not even yours. Now, for the last time, let me go.'

'Ah,' commented Merise with a faint glimmer of respect in her eyes. She loosened her grip on Tarik, and, rising, went to stand behind Julia. Gently Merise stroked her hair, then let her hands fall to her shoulders, drifting lightly across the tops of her breasts. 'It's the bonds that disturb you. You might grow to like it, you know.'

'Yes,' agreed Julia. She could not deny it; her nipples were already hardening at Merise's touch. 'But the real fantasy is the bond, the covenant that we both agree to. And I didn't agree to this.'

'I know. That's why it appeals,' said Merise regretfully. Still, she bent down and unfastened the thick rope binding Julia's wrists and then her ankles to the chair.

Julia rose unsteadily, rubbing her wrists. Merise had already returned to Tarik, and knelt by his side.

'You don't want to stay?' coaxed Merise. 'Just to watch? You might find it interesting.'

'No,' said Julia carefully. 'Thank you, but no.'

There was a door at the end of the room. She opened it clumsily and stumbled through, to find Mabik and a confusing number of Turks, drinking tea and smoking, their guns loose at their sides. In a voice of calm authority, Julia said bluntly, 'I want some water to wash. Some food. And then a bed. Now.'

Exhausted as she was, she had thought, once she reached the room under the eaves and its large feather bed, that she would sleep at once. Instead she lay restlessly, returning in her imagination again and again to the room below.

A small, salacious part of her regretted that she had left Merise and Tarik alone, had not stayed even to watch the sensual torment Merise would create. Still another part was shocked by her response.

She tossed and turned. The pillow was too hard, the mattress too soft. The coarse cotton sheet chafed against her skin. She made a silent litany of complaint knowing that the real reason she could not sleep was the itch of curiosity, of arousal.

Lurid, lewd images teased her. She saw Tarik, his big, powerful body straining against his bonds as Merise knelt to him. She had spoken of pain, of humiliation. Julia's mind shied from the words. She couldn't bear to think of Tarik hurt, Tarik degraded. They needed to know the site of the treasure trove. If only Mabik and his men hadn't ambushed their plane they would even now have been exploring Helen's tomb. Why the ambush?

It was Celik, the mysterious Celik who had prompted the ambush, frightened the villagers into kidnapping Tarik. Yet it was Celik who had arranged for her to go to Istanbul and meet Tarik. Could he be playing both sides against each other? Or was Rupert somewhere in the background, pulling strings, making them dance like puppets to his own obscure choreography? Perhaps that explained the sudden appearance of Merise, Merise who had seemed to have no interest in the treasure or Rupert's plots and schemes. Or was that too just a ploy?

She found herself straining her ears for some sound from the room below, a groan, a moan, a cry. Was she imagining that faint, guttural echo? She felt the hairs on the back of her neck stand up. Her body recognised that sound.

Irritably she pushed aside the covers. It was warm in the little room, but not hot, not hot enough to account for the sweat beading her brow, the heat of her skin. She remembered Tarik's harsh, hoarse groan as he thrust into her, the intense surge of his body straining against hers.

She slipped a hand between her thighs; she was wet, her body answering the guttural call, real or imagined, of her lover.

On a sudden impulse, without turning on the light, she reached down to the side of the bed and felt for her tote bag. She rummaged through it, her fingers recognising silk and canvas, the outlines of her cosmetic case. The rosette had slipped to the bottom. She drew it out, rubbing the embossed surface between her thumb and forefinger.

A golden disc that had adorned the shroud of a princess, that Tarik had placed against her breasts, her thighs. Almost unconsciously her hand moved to her breast to trace the hardening point of her nipple with the rosette. Not the warm moist wash of mouth and tongue, but the hard, cool friction of gold against sensitive flesh. She felt the tingling flush rippling beneath her skin, arcing to her groin.

Her lower lips were already slick and swollen. With the embossed gold rosette, she explored herself slowly, parting her inner and outer lips, finding the taut bud of her clitoris and releasing it from its protective flesh.

Sensation contracted to the lightly abrasive brush of the golden rosette against her core. Faster and faster, harder and harder, until the flickering heat pooled and swelled, enveloping her. As she came, she was sure she heard Tarik's voice raised in a hoarse cry.

'No!' grunted Tarik harshly, straining against his bonds. Merise had caught him just at the crest of his climax, pressing her thumb and forefinger hard at the base of his penis, a sudden, intense pressure that interrupted the rhythms of his body and prevented his seed from spilling.

'Ah, but yes,' laughed Merise throatily. She eyed him with satisfaction. With the help of two armed Turks, she had released him from the chair and forced him to remove his clothes at gunpoint. Now he lay nude, spreadeagled across the divan, wrists and ankles secured to its carved wooden legs.

She admired his body, the coarse pelt of dark hair that covered his chest and exploded in a dense tangle at his groin, the hairy, muscular thighs, the large, purplish organ that quivered under her hand.

She admired, too, the strength of will that made him continue to resist her despite the pain and frustration.

Not a weak man, nor one easily coerced, she thought idly, running a long, pointed fingernail down his throat to his nipple. If circumstances had been different, she might have enjoyed his strength, allowed herself to succumb to it for just a little while.

And still she might, she thought to herself, rising to stand before him.

Leisurely she began to undo the buttons of her shirt.

'We can negotiate,' offered Tarik roughly, his eyes fixed on her. Without the pressure of her hand, he felt his cock begin to slowly subside. 'Return to our original terms. You can't believe I'll let you take it all for nothing.'

Her shirt fell to the floor. She heard the sharp intake of his breath at the diamond at her navel and smiled. 'Think of it as my fee,' she advised him lightly. 'Can you imagine how much you would pay for this night in Singapore or Hong Kong?' Black trousers joined the shirt on the floor. She opened herself to him, displaying the flash of tiny diamonds embedded in her labia.

'Not a queen's treasure,' countered Tarik. But he felt his pulse quicken and his cock twitch at the sight of her naked body and the flash of diamonds at her core.

'We shall see,' said Merise, thinking that soon, yes, very soon, she would have to compromise, but not just yet, not before she had tasted his submission.

He waited for the hot rape of her mouth on his prick, readied himself for the agonising ache of frustration as she brought him swiftly to the brink of orgasm and then denied it. But instead, with strict discipline, she avoided his groin, avoided even his nipples, and confined herself to the more subtle erogenous zones, tonguing the soles of his feet, lightly sucking his toes, his fingers, delicately swarming over his body until he would have given anything, almost anything, to have felt the hard, pulling pressure of her mouth.

And despite his bonds, despite his frustration, when

he felt the soft swell of her breast against his mouth he opened his lips blindly, reflexively to her nipple.

Merise felt a surge of triumph. She had him now, though he didn't know it yet. It had been a calculated risk, exposing her flesh to his mouth, his teeth; he hadn't even thought to bite, to exact pain for pain.

Tarik had lost.

Savouring his surrender, all the more sweet because he was unaware of it, she lowered herself to his mouth, knowing that soon he would beg to come inside her.

Julia roused to a soft scratch at her door. She had been drowsing, lulled by the languor of afterglow, but she came swiftly awake at the noise.

'Yes?' she called out. 'Who is it?'

'It is I, Mabik,' replied a soft voice. 'May I enter?'

Hastily Julia drew the bedclothes up around her and, rather hesitantly, agreed; she hadn't forgotten the vicious look he had given her as he had prodded her into the jeep. 'Well, yes, I suppose. Has something happened?'

'I have brought you some tea,' said Mabik indirectly, coming into the room and handing her a glass. 'It's almost dawn.' He parted the curtains of the tiny window, letting in the early morning light.

'Where is Merise? And Tarik?' asked Julia, sipping the smoky tea.

'Still below,' answered Mabik with his back to her, not moving from the window. 'The woman, Merise you call her, told us not to enter. But we heard the sounds . . .' his voice trailed away, as if he were embarrassed.

'Yes?' prompted Julia.

176

'She made us untie him from the chair,' he said slowly, turning from the window. 'And then to strip his clothes. The look in his eyes – I was glad I was wearing a mask. And then we bound him again to the divan, and she told us to go. But we kept hearing the sounds. It was pain, but it was not pain. Who is this woman? What does she do to him?'

A question that had been troubling Julia as well.

'You know Merise was sent by Rupert,' said Julia evasively.

'Yes, but, such sounds,' he gestured helplessly. 'This cannot be a good thing.'

'Oh? And what sound does a woman make when she is tortured? Or a man shot through the knees?' she asked sarcastically, reminding him of the threats he had made in the hut.

Mabik shook his head. 'I didn't mean those things,' he protested. 'You must know I didn't.'

'You sounded remarkably sincere to me,' retorted Julia.

'Well, I might have meant it, but I wouldn't have done it,' Mabik answered. He turned back to the window to avoid her eyes. 'I was confused. Angry. I wanted to hurt you. Frighten you.'

Julia felt herself softening. Mabik's blunt simplicity was somehow reassuring; he was so young, and so proud, that the admission must have cost him something.

'I know,' she replied gently.

'How can you know?' he asked bitterly.

'I do know,' Julia said. Far, far too complicated to try and explain the twisted, subterranean compulsions of sexual jealousy; not only years, but culture, divided them. She couldn't even begin to summon the words that might make it right between them.

'And,' he said in the voice of one goaded, 'I am still angry.'

No, words would not suffice. It would be unnecessary and perhaps even unkind to remind him that he had no right, no reason to be angry with her. A furious row might relieve the tension, but would result only in new wounds.

Julia got out of bed and, naked, stood behind him at the window. She slipped her arms around his waist and laid her cheek against his back, fitting herself into the curve of his body.

He turned swiftly, pulling her against him, taking her mouth abruptly in a brutal kiss, his tongue stabbing at her teeth, his lips hard and unforgiving. She made no move to gentle him, merely opening her mouth to his, letting him vent his anger on her lips.

He kissed her again and again, punishing kisses that drove the breath from her body. She felt herself growing dizzy, lightheaded, the blood pounding thickly in her ears. He drove his tongue into her mouth, finding the sensitive spot just below her palate with a bruising pressure that brought tears to her eyes, yet still she made no move to stop him.

She accepted his anger, absorbed it, was even strangely moved by it. The pain he inflicted with his hard mouth and bruising fingers was not calculated, not sophisticated, but the simple, powerful expression of his turbulent feelings, his lust, hurt, passion and jealousy, and so she welcomed it.

If he could purge himself with her body, then let him. She had no urge to fight him; knowing he needed her submission, she gave it freely.

He was young; it was not long before the demands of his temper were overcome by the demands of his body. His hands and mouth were still hard, but with the urgency of desire.

She felt no answering heat, no surge of lust, but a warm, pervasive tenderness that seemed to communicate itself to him, for at last his hands gentled and his mouth softened, and then released hers.

She looked up into his dark eyes and smiled, tentatively running her tongue over her swollen lips.

'Julia,' he said raggedly, 'I'm – I'm sorry.'

'It's all right,' she said softly. 'I understand.' Taking his hand, she led him to the bed and lay naked on the coarse cotton sheets, wordlessly offering herself to him.

Some of his haste and urgency returned; he stripped himself quickly and then seemed almost to erupt against her, tangling his limbs with hers, pressing hot, frantic kisses to her breasts, her belly, her thighs, rocking his pelvis against hers.

She lay passive, still enveloped in that strange, warm tenderness, accepting and absorbing his body as she had his anger, and when she came it was in a soft, suffusing blush.

Afterwards they lay together quietly for a time, until the sounds of the morning became too insistent: the clanging of a cow bell as a herd was driven past the house, a burst of raucous laughter from the men outside. Both Mabik and Julia stiffened as they heard a faint groan from the room below.

'Tarik,' muttered Mabik unnecessarily. 'This can't go on much longer.'

'It won't, I'm sure,' said Julia positively. 'Merise must know what she's doing.'

'And if he tells you where this treasure is? What then?' he asked.

'Well, I'll want to make a preliminary examination of the burial before we contact the authorities,' Julia began.

'The authorities,' interrupted Mabik in dismay, raising himself on one elbow to look at her. 'We can't have them here. It's too dangerous.'

'But we must,' argued Julia. 'The trove belongs to the Turkish government. It must be surrendered to them intact and undisturbed. There's no need for them to know of anything else,' she added reassuringly.

To herself she acknowledged that he was right to be concerned; the site would come under careful scrutiny from the archaeological service, from foreign schools, academics and journalists. The village's secret cache of artefacts might well come to light. Perversely, the thought troubled her and for the first time she became aware that her loyalties were uncomfortably divided. Mabik's next question only confirmed that disturbing notion.

'And Tarik?' he asked.

'Well, I suppose, the authorities, the police,' she foundered. She didn't want to imagine Tarik in custody, perhaps in prison. It would be like caging a force of nature; wrong, unthinkable. And she, Julia, would be directly responsible. She couldn't let it happen – yet she had no choice.

Perhaps some solution could be found, some compromise reached, she found herself thinking.

Merise was mercilessly inventive, alternately harsh and gentle, demanding and persuading, bringing

Tarik again and again to the brink of climax. He must be close to breaking, she judged; his body was slick with sweat, and great cords stood out on either side of his neck. He was strong; he was stubborn; but no man could endure for long the agony of frustration that she inflicted so expertly.

'A split,' he ground out, arching to her mouth.

'What sort of a split?' she asked, refusing him her lips, blowing gently on the swollen tip of his penis.

'I'll give you a share, a small share, for nothing,' he shuddered.

'Ah, we progress,' she murmured, letting her tongue snake out to rest against him for one whirring moment.

The men on guard were becoming restless. The sounds they heard were explicitly sexual, the groans of need, of frustration. At first they joked lewdly amongst themselves, but the laughter quickly became forced, then died away altogether. None of them was immune to the echoes of a heated struggle they could only imagine.

Tarik's harsh cries made them uncomfortable, uneasy. On some subliminal level too deep to be understood, they felt his gnawing, aching need, and it disturbed them.

As the sun rose, they drank endless cups of tea, smoked cigarette after cigarette, and chatted desultorily, trying to ignore the frisson of sexual tension in the air.

Julia and Mabik joined them, but Julia's presence made them more uncomfortable still. She caught the sly, speculative glances that were cast her way and was uneasily aware of being the only woman among so many men; men who were listening avidly to the sounds of sex.

She remembered Mabik's threat, to give her to his men, and wondered whether they were thinking of it too. Of course, she reminded herself, that had never been a real possibility; Mabik hadn't meant it, wouldn't have done it, but the thought was enough to drive her away, outside, to the tiny garden at the back of the house, where chickens were scratching at the dusty earth.

So she was alone, under the shade of a gnarled old tree, when at last she heard the harsh, primal cry of Tarik's surrender, a scream of rage and release, exultant yet defeated.

Chapter Ten

Merise emerged, faintly flushed and eyes sparkling, startling the guards who seemed, for a brief moment, to have frozen, transfixed by the awful, powerful cry of Tarik's release. 'You can untie him now,' she said. 'Take him away, let him dress and wash. And then we'll want food; I'm starving.'

Mabik jostled the others aside, quickly translating her words. 'He's told you then?' he asked impatiently.

'Told me?' echoed Merise, sounding faintly puzzled.

'The gold, the treasure,' he said.

'Oh, yes, of course, the treasure,' she agreed. She stretched, sinuous as a cat. 'He'll take Julia to it. Where is she?'

'In the garden, I think,' replied Mabik, as Julia appeared at the wooden doors that led outside.

'Ah, Julia,' said Merise, catching sight of her. 'I'll join you there, it's rather cramped with all of us here.' She let her eyes rove over the guards, who were staring at her in fascination, and then dismissed them. 'And I'll want food and something to drink.'

'Quaint and rustic indeed,' commented Merise, eyeing the chickens with some disfavour as she walked into the garden.

'Merise,' Julia began hesitantly.

'And some chairs,' added Merise, unheeding, making it clear that she would say little more until her wishes were met. Rickety wooden chairs were duly fetched and set in the shade, and Mabik hastily produced bread and cheese, cold lamb and olives, and a bottle of white wine.

'Ah, that's better,' said Merise, after she had taken a swallow of her wine.

'Merise, how is Tarik?' asked Julia.

'A definite six, darling, possibly even a seven,' replied Merise.

'A six? A seven? What do you mean?'

'Of course, I was forgetting,' said Merise obscurely. No reason for Julia, whom she had once dismissed as a miserable one, to know of her rating scheme. 'Tarik is actually rather good. Though I'd rather thought that you would have found that out for yourself.'

'No, I mean, is he all right?' Julia asked.

'I'm sure he's fine,' Merise said nonchantly, taking an olive.

'You didn't hurt him?' Julia pursued.

'Such concern for our villain,' mocked Merise. 'I'm surprised at you, Julia. Surely you should be more interested in the site of the treasure, and how to locate it, but no, you're all tender solicitude for the master criminal.'

'Merise.' Julia's voice was flat, undaunted by her mockery.

'Ah, well, since you ask, yes. I hurt him.' Merise raised her eyes to look directly into Julia's. 'And I think, eventually, he enjoyed it very much.'

'Oh. Oh, I see,' Julia replied, subdued.

'I wonder, he's a strong man. In the end I had to bargain for your gold,' said Merise. 'This cheese is actually rather good.'

'What do you mean, bargain?' asked Julia.

'He's agreed to show us the site, provided that you and he alone uncover the treasure. Oh, and I promised him half of it. Is it goat's cheese, do you think?'

'Half of it?' cried Julia, shocked. 'Merise, you can't do that. It belongs to the people of Turkey. It must be handed over to the proper authorities as soon as it's been verified. Surely that's what Rupert planned all along?'

Merise smiled sceptically and remained pointedly silent.

'I knew – I mean, at first, I wondered, oh – damn!' said Julia, exasperated. Rising from her chair, she began to pace around the tiny garden, scattering chickens in her wake.

'We can't plunder the site and then expose it. Think of the information that would be lost, a country's heritage. It would be unethical, wrong,' persisted Julia.

Merise yawned. 'Has it only just struck you that there's something a little unethical about this whole scheme? My dear Julia. Shall we contact Rupert now and see what he has to say?'

'No,' said Julia sharply, and then repeated in a softer tone, 'No. Not yet. I think we should wait until I've seen it. After all, we really don't know anything yet,' she added in explanation. Suddenly she was most reluctant to involve Rupert in this dilemma. It wasn't, she thought distractedly, that she didn't trust him. It was just that look in Merise's eyes. That look said as clearly as if the words had been spoken that Rupert had never intended to hand the entire treasure over to the authorities.

Angrily she jammed her fingers into her pockets, scraping her knuckle against a hard, jagged edge. It was the gold rosette Tarik had given her, part of his private, highly illegal collection. The rosette that she had every intention of keeping for herself.

So, she was no better than Rupert, no better even than Tarik. It was simply a matter of degree. The thought appalled her. Somewhere along the line she had jettisoned her academic ethics without even noticing, she realised, as her fingers closed protectively around the rosette.

There was a slight commotion at the end of the garden, and Julia looked up to see Tarik enter, encircled by the masked guards.

'Perhaps we could dispense with the armoury,' he enquired sardonically, 'Now that our negotiations are concluded.'

He looked a little pale, thought Julia sickly, and his Armani suit was rumpled and stained. Still, he moved with his usual powerful assurance as he walked over to Merise and claimed the chair Julia had abandoned.

'But can we trust you?' asked Merise sweetly.

'I never renege on a business deal,' Tarik said briefly.

Julia felt sicker.

'My men remain as they are,' said Mabik, coming into the garden. Julia saw that he had resumed wearing his mask.

Tarik glanced at Merise, expecting her to countermand the order, but she merely shrugged.

'Yes, please, at least make them put the guns away,' said Julia.

Tarik's unreadable gaze rested for a moment on her face. She was astonished to see his brief smile.

'It seems your employees are as – shall we say, unconventional as your business dealings?' observed Tarik to Merise.

'I have never been conventional,' replied Merise vaguely, offering him a glass of wine.

Obviously Merise was intent on preserving the guise of wealthy collector, thought Julia; was she perhaps just as intent on recovering a portion of the treasure for Rupert? She would be more convincing in her chosen role if she were to demonstrate some interest in the artefacts she was supposed to be so avidly collecting, but Tarik seemed to find nothing amiss in her attitude. Indeed, he seemed almost unnaturally composed, chatting inconsequentially with Merise, drinking wine and eating olives under the watchful eyes of six armed Turks whose guns remained trained on him.

'Tarik,' ventured Julia, 'you're – you're not angry?'

'I learned long ago when to cut my losses,' Tarik replied evenly – too evenly, she thought. Or was she merely becoming suspicious of everyone?

'So,' Julia said hesitantly, 'The treasure – the site – you'll tell us now? You mentioned a female burial – I mean, the grave of Helen.' She hastily corrected herself at his expression. 'But there must be more.'

'Yes, there is more,' he said. 'Walls and rooms, the remains of a Bronze Age palace, but the only treasure is Helen's gold.'

Yes, it was only the gold that interested him; he had just summarily dismissed one of the greatest finds of the century in a few words. Walls, rooms, a palace. She felt a rising tide of excitement. 'But where?' she asked.

'You know the plan of the site?' said Tarik.

'Quite well,' replied Julia. She dropped to her knees and in the dust at their feet began to sketch a rough diagram of Homeric Troy: the circular course of the walls; the three main gates and towers; the paved street from the south gate which ascended the terraces of the city to the king's palace.

'Not quite,' said Tarik, bending down to erase the line that formed part of the wall. 'The northern circuit was demolished by Schliemann in the early excavations and the true extent of the city walls was never determined. It lies further to the north, here,' he said, pointing.

'The remains of another palace, you mean?' asked Julia, frowning at her sketch. 'Because the burial must lie beyond the city walls. And the cemetery for Troy V was discovered here, to the south. And the houses that were found were all clustered around the southern circuit of the wall.'

'Because the area to the north was never excavated and used as a rubbish dump,' replied Tarik. 'The tomb lies beyond the north wall, concealed by the rubble, undisturbed for centuries.'

'But how do you know all this?' asked Julia, puzzled. 'You can't have dug the area yourself.'

'Modern technology,' explained Tarik. 'A rather sophisticated combination of sonar scanning and computer imaging. Just here, at the outskirts of the site.'

'You can't be serious,' said Julia, incredulously.

'The equipment was installed some time ago,' said Tarik. 'A similar sort of probe was used on the pyramids in Egypt.'

'Yes, yes, I think I remember reading something about that,' said Julia slowly. 'But this is incredible. I mean, how did you do it?'

'People see what they expect to see,' said Tarik. 'A simple shepherd's hut – we sank a shaft beneath it to bedrock to create a control room for the equipment. The scanning probe generates 3D images of the area and we found that, quite by chance, the shaft connected with a series of tunnels leading to the palace and beyond.'

'So you've already mapped out the site,' said Julia in some wonder. 'You know the plan already, without even having seen it.'

'Yes,' said Tarik.

'And you'll take me there? You'll show me the probe, the plans?' she asked eagerly.

'We shall open the tomb together,' said Tarik. A strange, hot look flared in his eyes. 'Tonight, when the tourists have left and the custodians are sleeping. I shall take you there tonight.'

Alone, in the tiny bedroom under the eaves, trying to rest, Julia was wracked with indecision. Now that they knew the approximate location of the tomb, she should contact the authorities, reveal the existence of Tarik's probe. There couldn't be many shepherd's huts on the northern boundaries of the site; they could find it easily enough. That was the right course of action, the proper thing to do. Skulking around in the dark, illegally examining the remains, opening a tomb like

189

some modern-day grave robber was wrong, undeniably wrong.

And undeniably exciting.

To be the first to see that gleam of gold, to breathe the air of the Ancients, to touch and feel for herself.

She drifted off to a light, uneasy sleep, knowing that she had already made her decision.

In the dark, illuminated only by the wavering light from the headlamps of the jeep as it shuddered over the uneven ground, the landscape looked almost surreal.

'How much further?' asked Julia, clutching at the dashboard for support as the vehicle careened around a corner.

'Not far now,' Tarik replied shortly, struggling to bring the jeep under control.

They were alone together for the first time since the ambush. Although Mabik had been determined to accompany them, along with his armed guards, Tarik had been equally determined that he and Julia should open the tomb alone, and Tarik had prevailed.

She was conscious now of a tension between them, an underlying constraint that manifested itself in an intense physical awareness of each other. She could sense his growing excitement and knew that it was at least partly sexual. With all she knew of him, she could not doubt that he intended to take her in the tomb, slake his fantasy of the most beautiful woman in the world with her body, have his revenge for the sexual torment Merise had inflicted on him, for the role that Julia had played.

Another sharp curve and she was thrown against his body. The hardness of the impact startled her, reminding her of his strong, well-muscled arms and thighs. She felt an answering surge of response, as unexpected as it was powerful.

'Can't you go more slowly?' Julia asked.

Slowly. The word reverberated through her mind. Slowly, Rupert had advised in his cryptic telex, in the prelude to their lovemaking. Slowly. But events had quickly spiralled to this climax, to this rough and hasty journey in the dead of night.

'No,' said Tarik. 'If we're being followed I want to lose them.' So saying, he switched off the head lamps, plunging them into darkness.

'Oh, be careful,' cried Julia. 'We'll never find it like this.'

'You seem to forget I know this area rather well,' said Tarik dryly.

In the dark, Julia lost all sense of direction. They seemed to have left the paved surface of the road and were now juddering over an unploughed field. Again she was tossed against him, but this time he held her to him, removing one hand from the steering wheel and pressing her close to his body. It was a curious gesture, at once protective and menacing. She knew that there would be bruises left by his harsh fingers.

'There,' he said suddenly. 'Just up ahead.'

At first she could see nothing, but as they drew closer, straining her eyes, she could just make out the dim outlines of a small shepherd's hut with a thatched roof. The jeep ground to a halt.

For a moment he was still, obviously listening for sounds of pursuit. Held hard against his body, Julia had a sudden clarity of perception, as if her consciousness had fragmented into a number of separate sensations: the fine weave of his linen suit against her cheek; the salty, dusty smell of his body; the dull thud of his heartbeat; the rise and fall of his breathing. The sensations swirled and coalesced; she felt herself melting into him in a warm, pulsing darkness.

She was abruptly jolted from her strange reverie as Tarik opened the door of the jeep and pulled her to her feet.

'Here, this way,' said Tarik, unnecessarily, as he kept her firmly at his side. She stumbled beside him over rocks and stones, the discarded rubble of centuries.

Inside the hut it was dark, warm and close. She listened to him as he moved around, then gasped as the hut was flooded with light. Of course, she thought dimly, there must be a generator, something to provide the power for his scanning probe.

'So now we begin,' said Tarik, looking straight into her eyes. His black eyes were hot, shining with excitement and a kind of vindictive triumph.

'Yes,' said Julia, feeling her anticipation rise to match his own.

'You know there is a price you'll pay for this?' said Tarik bluntly.

'I know,' answered Julia calmly. 'And I will pay.'

He nodded once, then turned away to the back of the hut. With one foot he scuffed aside some of the earth of the dirt flooring to reveal a wooden trap door. He grasped the large metal ring at its centre and pulled it to one side, revealing the gaping mouth of a shaft.

'You go first,' he ordered Julia.

There were metal bars affixed to the side of the shaft forming a crude stepladder. Julia descended gingerly, feeling her way, half expecting the bars to

192

give way at any moment. The only light was from above and the scope of its illumination was limited. It failed her about halfway down, and she made the rest of her journey in darkness. At last she reached the bottom and stood with her back against the wall, waiting for Tarik.

It occurred to her then that it would be a simple matter for him to replace the trap door and drive away, leaving her stranded and his precious treasure intact. With a sudden chill she wondered if that was what he had meant by a price to pay.

No, he was coming; she could hear his heavy steps on the metal bars. She pressed closer to the wall as he dropped lightly to his feet beside her.

She heard the sound of his fingers fumbling against the wall and then the room lit up before her eyes. Julia caught her breath in amazement. They were in a large room floored with concrete. Three walls were covered with an impressive array of sophisticated-looking computer equipment, screens and consoles and interconnecting terminals bristling with buttons, switches and wires; there was a gaping hole in the fourth wall that obviously led to some passageway.

With the ease of one who knew exactly what he was doing, Tarik flipped switches and pressed buttons and the complicated machinery whirred into life, the screens glowing a luminescent green, red lights flashing. He tapped in a series of commands on a console, and the pulsing green light of the huge screens contracted to a series of images. One had a continuous clockwise scan centred on two flashing blips of light, like a radar scan; another showed a complex series of wavy lines; a third displayed a 3D image of two figures, obviously herself and Tarik; on the fourth appeared a complicated plan of the site in all its phases.

It was like being caught in the middle of a computer game, thought Julia, fascinated. The room belonged to the control centre of a space ship, to the pages of science fiction; the contrast with the rude shepherd's hut above them was ludicrous.

'Yes, you are here,' said Tarik ironically, gesturing to the screen where their images were shown.

She listened with half an ear to his brief explanation of the workings of the scanning probe and resonance imaging, her attention focused on the plan of the site. Distinguishing the superimposed phases was too confusing; she tried to orientate herself by the gates and the great tower but it was no use.

'Can you reduce that to the Homeric period, around 1250?' she asked, interrupting Tarik.

'Of course,' said Tarik. 'Watch.'

Lines wavered and reformed and the familiar site appeared, but this time extended to the north, showing the outlines of a great Megaron hall, a mighty palace of the Late Bronze Age.

'Look here,' said Tarik, gesturing to the 3D screen. Their figures had disappeared, replaced by the image of the palace. There was the great hall, a warren of smaller rooms, storage rooms filled with huge clay *pithoi*.

'I don't understand,' said Julia. 'So the programme reconstructs as it goes along?'

'No, it simply reproduces the images,' said Tarik. 'Look.'

She saw the line of the street leading beyond the palace, the great course of the wall, a long, dromos-style passageway cut beneath it that led to a great vaulted tomb. The interior was revealed to show the figure of a woman lying on a stone bier.

The imaging narrowed to focus on her face and Julia gasped in astonishment.

It was a funeral mask of beaten gold. Unlike the other death masks she had seen, with blunt, coarsely modelled features, this was delicately moulded to portray a heart-shaped face with a smooth, curving brow, high cheekbones, an arched nose and beautifully shaped lips. In life she would have been stunning; in death she was magnificent. Julia could almost see why Tarik believed he had gazed on the face of Helen.

And from the tip of the diadem that rested above the mask to the soles of her feet, she was draped in gold.

'My God,' Julia breathed.

'Yes,' said Tarik triumphantly. 'Now, come with me.' Taking her by the hand, he led her towards the gaping black hole of the passageway.

It was dark and cool in the passageway, the only source of light a powerful torch that Tarik produced. It cast an eerie glow on the closely fitted limestone blocks that faced the passage and on the rough paving stones beneath their feet. Gradually it dawned on Julia that they were following the course of an ancient street. There were intersecting tunnels leading in all directions but Tarik made his way confidently. It occurred to her that this was a journey he must have made in his mind many times before.

At last they reached a section of the wall with a deeply undercut tunnel that she realised must be the passage to the tomb. She bent down, bumping her head on a piece of jutting masonry.

Tarik urged her along impatiently. She was conscious of a gradual incline in the ground level and noticed that the flooring was now beaten earth.

He stopped at last before a massive boulder that guarded the entrance to the tomb. It had shifted slightly from the wall; there was, Julia judged, just barely room for them to slip past. She knew that her breathing had quickened with excitement and that despite the cool air her shirt was sticking to her back. Pressed against the boulder, she hesitated, overcome by some obscure scruple, but he pushed her forward and so, slithering awkwardly against the rock, she entered the vaulted chamber.

There was no light but the erratic play of Tarik's torch as he struggled with the boulder, and then he too was inside.

He let the torchlight play on the bier and for a moment they were both silent, awed by the beauty of the golden figure lying there.

And then, before she could divine his intent, he strode up to the bier and put his hand to the mask.

'No, no,' cried Julia, her voice echoing strangely in the vaulted cavern. 'You mustn't disturb her.'

It was as though the sound of her voice broke some spell, unleashed some potent, powerful emotion. He turned and dragged her against him, all bruising mouth and stabbing fingers, swiftly firing her own response.

Madness flared between them.

They struggled with their clothing, Tarik ripping at the buttons of her shirt, Julia's fingers desperate and urgent at his flies. Grappling, they fell to the ground.

It was a heated struggle for power, for dominance, for orgasm. She bucked and writhed beneath him, trying to capture his rod between her thighs. She was already slippery with want, tumid and engorged, eager for the filling thrust into the warm, wet, waiting void, but he eluded her, turning her on to her stomach, slipping his cock between the cleft of her buttocks.

She felt the head of his penis slide between the slick folds of her labia, then return to her other entrance, exploring the sensitive flesh between the channels of her body, imprinting himself on her body.

There was a dark, delicious pain as he nudged at the mouth of her anus and she felt her inner muscles begin to spasm in response. He moved then to her core and thrust inside as she convulsed around him, her body wracked with the blinding flash of climax.

She held on to him tightly as the heated waves diminished, almost sobbing with relief and pleasure.

But for Tarik, it was only the beginning. Again and again he claimed her, sometimes with his mouth, sometimes with his fingers, sometimes with his prick, dragging her from climax to climax until she was exhausted and lay trembling and sated.

She thought vaguely, when her senses returned, that he must have learned something from Merise but not quite mastered the trick of it; this was no devious sensual torture but a magnificent onslaught.

However, there was no need for him to know that.

'Did I hurt you?' he asked at last.

She gave him the answer she thought he wanted. 'Yes,' she replied.

He fumbled for the torch and trained it on her face. She blinked, but said nothing. At last, with something that sounded like a sigh, he set the torch on the ground and began to dress.

'And so the treasure,' he said, when they had both managed to struggle back into their clothing.

Taking the torch from him, Julia trained it on the bier, carefully taking note of the heavy necklaces and bracelets, the shower of gold discs covering the body, the cache of grave goods at the foot of the bier, gold drinking cups and knives and pottery vessels.

'Oh, yes, she's real, it's authentic, I'm sure of it. And it's the right period for Homer's Troy. Look at the curving swirls of painted decoration on the jar,' she said, moving the torch light to the pottery jugs. 'It's certainly late Helladic.'

'And now we divide the gold,' said Tarik, coming to stand beside her.

'No, impossible,' Julia retaliated. 'Nothing must be touched, nothing can be moved. It has to be properly photographed, properly recorded.'

'At last, some faint respect for archaeological procedure,' drawled a voice from behind them. It was a man's voice, deceptively casual, lightly accented, and completely unfamiliar.

At least to Julia.

Tarik turned with a roar, grabbing the torch from Julia and waving it crazily. 'Celik, you bastard! What are you doing here? How did you get here?'

The light from the torch caught the blue steel of the snub-nosed pistol aimed directly at them. 'What a welcome,' he returned mildly. 'Although I didn't expect that you would be pleased to see me. Especially when you learned that I represent the International Antiquities – '

He got no further. Tarik swung the torch; there was

a blinding flash of light and the smell of cordite; a rush of bodies; Julia was flung back against the bier, hitting her head on the sharp corner and lapsing immediately into unconsciousness.

She roused to the soft, rhythmic slap of a hand against her cheeks and a stream of foul obscenities that ceased when she opened her eyes.

'At last,' said the voice. 'You were out cold.'

'Celik?' she asked hazily.

'Actually, Robert Marchant,' he corrected her. 'But Celik will do. Can you stand?'

'What happened? Where is Tarik?' asked Julia.

'Gone,' he said flatly. 'I lost him in this damned labyrinth. I was afraid he'd double back for the gold, so I returned here. And to make sure you were all right.'

She started to laugh at the palpable afterthought, but winced at the pain.

'Can you get up?' he said again.

'I don't think so,' she answered candidly. 'My head is swimming.'

'Well, try,' he said callously. 'Otherwise we'll be here all night. And while some people seem to find tombs attractive for all sorts of reasons – ' the innuendo in his voice was clear ' – I do not.'

'How long were you there?' asked Julia, disconcerted.

'Long enough,' he replied, confirming her fears. 'I couldn't see much – fortunately voyeurism has never been my thing. But what I could see – and hear – gave me a terrible hard-on,' he added reminiscently.

'How unprofessional,' commented Julia coldly, rising unsteadily to her feet.

'As for unprofessional – well, why don't we leave the discussion of ethics for later while you do your professional best to get us out of here,' retorted Celik.

'Where's the torch?' she asked dubiously.

'Smashed,' said Celik succinctly.

It was by the frail illumination of a disposable plastic lighter that they made their way back down the sloping passage to the wall.

'For a spy, you're not very well organised,' Julia said acidly as the light flickered and died.

'Spy?' he disclaimed unconvincingly, flicking at the lighter until it caught. 'A simple desk man, that's me. International Antiquities and Forgeries Squad. You wouldn't believe the paperwork.'

His breezy insouciance was both irritating and reassuring. It reminded her of someone. Rupert. She ducked under the wall and was pleased to hear him swear as he hit his head.

'But you're supposed to be one of the villagers,' Julia said. 'And then I thought that you were working for Tarik.'

'So did Tarik, for a time,' replied Celik. 'I imagine I'm no longer on the payroll.'

Relying on her memory and Celik's fickle lighter, Julia led them down the ancient street. She made a few wrong turnings, fascinated to find the remains of rooms and walls, a much more extensive network of structures than she had imagined. Celik greeted her cries of delight rather sourly, she thought.

'And it was you who arranged that stupid ambush,' accused Julia as they extricated themselves from a storeroom and returned to the path.

'Not one of my more shining moments,' agreed Celik equably. 'But by then I was more or less convinced that Tarik had turned you. Rupert said no, but I couldn't take the chance.'

'Rupert,' echoed Julia.

'He does like to dabble,' agreed Celik. 'One can only trust he hasn't overplayed his hand and summoned the world press to Ciplak. There's a lot to do.'

With relief Julia saw a dim glow of light ahead and realised that they had reached the computer room.

'Like what?' she asked.

'Dismantling this junk, for a start,' Celik replied with a dismissive glance at the equipment.

'Why?' she asked, taking a good look at him for the first time. He was tall and slender, with a shock of brown hair, liquid brown eyes, and a thin, clever face. His features were pleasing but indeterminate; he could pass for almost any Mediterranean type.

'It doesn't really add an air of authenticity to a chance find, now, does it?' he replied sarcastically.

'A chance find? Then you're not going to expose Tarik and his installation?' Julia said, surprised, stopping with one foot poised on the metal bracket of the bottom step.

'All things in good time,' he assured her, patting her bottom with a rather abstracted air, as if he was simultaneously urging her up the steps and assessing the rounded curve of her buttocks. 'By now he's probably halfway to Istanbul.'

An early dawn was edging the sky as they emerged from the shepherd's hut.

'I must have been out much longer than I thought,' said Julia, glancing up at the sky.

'You were,' Celik agreed briefly. 'Damn his black soul, Tarik's taken the jeep.'

'But how did you get out here?' asked Julia, puzzled.

'Clinging on to the back of the damn jeep, how else?' Celik replied.

This time Julia couldn't restrain her laughter, despite the pain in her head. 'A rough ride,' she smiled.

'Believe it,' he replied.

She wasn't smiling when, hours later, they finally reached Ciplak. Numb with fatigue, stumbling with exhaustion, sweaty, dirty and with a pounding headache, she reeled into the house Celik led her to and collapsed on the divan.

Chapter Eleven

*I*n one of the tiny rooms under the eaves, Merise stirred, half awakened by the noise from downstairs, a door slamming, the sound of footsteps, a soft babble of voices. Julia and Tarik had returned, she thought drowsily. She really should get up, go down and greet them, find out about the treasure. But for the moment she was content just to lie here, on the narrow bed with rough white cotton sheets, next to the warm, sleeping body of Mabik.

She breathed deeply, inhaling the sweet, musky, unique scent of sex, the perfume of passion spent, and smiled lazily. He had been wary at first, even apprehensive, remembering the hoarse, tortured cries that Tarik had uttered, but his unwilling fascination had prevailed. Merise herself had been carried away on a wave of wanton energy catalysed by her domination of Tarik, a wave so pure and powerful that she could almost feel it zipping through her bloodstream, a lust so exhilarating, so intoxicating, so fluorescent that it could be assuaged only by climax after climax.

Mabik, hesitant and unsure, had succumbed awkwardly but inevitably, thrusting into her immediately with all the vigour of his youth. She allowed him that first thrust, that swift, filling surge, then put her hands on his hips, pushing him backwards until his cock was just at the mouth of her vagina. She held him there for several taut, tense seconds before she released her hold, letting him re-enter her in a thrust more powerful than the first.

Again and again she repeated the move, making him plunge deep and then withdraw almost completely, feeling him grow harder and harder, until her inner walls began to pulse. Then she pushed him hard, so that his prick was free. Taking it in her hands, she guided it up the sensitive flesh to her clitoris, then further up. to her navel, then drew it back to her clitoris, then to the mouth of her vagina, where he plunged deep.

After each thrust she made him withdraw completely; sometimes keeping him between her legs, rubbing his prick between the slick leaves of her labia; sometimes drawing him up to her belly, relishing the hot, hard length against her flesh, feeding the excruciating, pulsing need to have him back inside her.

When she sensed that his climax was close, she squirmed beneath him, drawing his penis to her breasts and then her mouth, delicately nipping the head of his prick with her teeth, not hard enough to cause him pain, but enough to delay his orgasm, to prolong the fierce anticipation.

He had stiffened in shock, in sudden fear, but she

had reassured him, taking the head of his cock in her mouth, easing the scrape of her teeth with the warm, rhythmic wash of her tongue before releasing him, drawing him back down to her breasts, circling her hardened nipples with the glistening, engorged tip of his penis, then cradling him between her breasts.

It was then that Mabik roused himself to touch her in turn, grasping her breasts with his hands, clasping and unclasping them, massaging himself firmly with the soft mounds. Merise felt herself swelling with pleasure.

Young and untutored he might be, but Mabik caught on quickly, using his penis as a second mouth, another hand, rubbing it over her breasts and belly, pausing at the downy thatch of her mound until she arched her hips just slightly, just enough to allow him to slide down to her clitoris.

She kept the head of his penis there, a meeting of two tumescences, for she was as engorged as he, and raised her hips so that the whole length of the underside of his prick lay against the furrow of her mound, and began to rock against him.

For Mabik, it was a unique frustration, enclosed yet not enclosed, held by her thighs and the soft, slick petals of her sex curling around his shaft. He could feel her pulsing against him, not the tight, hard friction of penetration, but a soft, rhythmic pressure that seemed to radiate along his cock.

Beneath him, Merise began to move faster. Always in control of the rhythms of her body, she let the tingling splinters of impending orgasm cluster, rubbing the hot head of his prick against her clitoris, the hard length of him heavy against the sensitive folds of her flesh, the pulsing emptiness of her inner walls.

She felt the burning heat pool and then glow, engulfing her just as she arched, taking him into her.

Now, remembering, she smiled a little complacently, then frowned, recalling Mabik's hoarse cry as he found his own release. 'Julia' he had shouted, 'Julia'.

Thinking of the old quip about the various types of orgasm, she smiled again, a little wryly. There was the negative orgasm, signalled by the cry of, 'Oh no! Oh no!': the religious orgasm, 'Oh, God! Oh God!' – and the fake orgasm, cynically defined by the name of whatever partner you happened to be with. And while she had never considered Mabik as anything other than a body to be used, it was still disconcerting to hear Julia's name at such a moment. Especially Julia's.

And then she remembered the night on *Calypso* before Julia left the cruise, remembered the long, lascivious lessons she had given her, and decided that, in its own way, Mabik's cry had been something of a compliment. Indirect, to be sure, but a compliment nevertheless.

Merise stretched a little, luxuriating in the dim, pleasurable aches of a body well-used, and got out of the narrow bed. Mabik didn't stir and there was no need to disturb him. Distastefully she eyed the heap of black clothing draped over the wooden chair in the corner. Not for as long as she could remember had Merise Van Asche ever worn the same clothes twice in a row.

Idly she fingered the coarse cotton shirt Mabik had dropped on the floor. It hung almost to mid-thigh and smelled quite fresh. She slipped it on, ran her fingers through her hair, and decided to go downstairs. Coffee and croissants, she thought, no, perhaps not croissants. Did they have croissants in the wilds of Turkey?

Opening the door on this thought, she stepped out into the narrow hall and almost collided with a man she had never seen before with Julia slung over his shoulders like a sack of potatoes.

'Jesus, watch out. Shit.'

'What the hell?'

For a few moments they staggered drunkenly together until they crashed against the wall, Merise pinned against it by the combined weight of Julia and the man. Julia lolled between them, barely conscious.

'Is she all right?' asked Merise in surprised concern. 'Who are you? What are you doing with her?'

'She's okay, she just weights a ton,' the man reassured her briefly. 'Who are you?'

As haughtily as possible while wearing nothing but a man's shirt, and pressed against a wall by an inert female and a dusty stranger, Merise replied, 'I am Merise Isabella Van Asche.'

'Oh yeah? I heard about you.' The stranger gave her a shrewd, speculative stare. 'Let me put her to bed and I'll see you downstairs.'

'Chicken soup?' snorted Merise. 'No one drinks chicken soup for breakfast.'

'They do here,' he said, gulping soup with a hideously enthusiastic slurping sound.

'It's repulsive,' complained Merise.

'So don't drink it,' he shrugged.

They were sitting in the tiny backyard garden on rickety wooden chairs under the shade of the gnarled old tree where only yesterday Julia had traced the lines of ancient Troy in the dusty earth. Merise looked at the chickens scratching for food in the dust, re-examined the contents of her cup, and set it aside.

'Coffee,' she said positively. 'Even Turkish coffee will do. Some croissants or pastries or something. And some fresh fruit. And some answers.'

'Kitchen's there,' he replied laconically, nodding towards the house.

'Indeed,' said Merise frostily. The thought of fumbling around the primitive kitchen, trying to light the fire, no doubt chipping her nails and ruining her manicure in the process – no. Especially not under the sarcastic, mocking brown eyes of the man sitting next to her.

She was at a loss to explain his antagonism, his careless rudeness, his curt inattention to her thinly veiled orders. Few men were immune to the lure of her sensuality, the promise of her body. In her world, they vied for the privilege of gratifying her needs, fulfilling her merest whim; more to the point, she couldn't remember the last time she had been inside a kitchen. 'Just who are you anyway?' she asked curiously. 'And what's happened to Julia? And Tarik?' she added.

The bare essentials emerged under her pointed, persistent questioning; the descent to the tomb; the treasure; Tarik's flight.

'International Antiquities and Forgeries?' asked Merise sceptically when he had finished. 'You? I don't believe it.'

A slow grin spread across his face. 'Yeah, well, Rupert may be a little surprised too.'

'Rupert,' Merise started. 'My God, Rupert. I'll have to telex the ship immediately. And what do you mean, he'll be surprised?'

'Let's just say he knows Celik, not Robert Marchant,' he replied. 'And I'll take care of contacting him. I'm keeping you, Merise Isabella Van Asche, under my eye from now on.'

'Really?' she replied disdainfully, raising her eyebrows. 'Whatever for?'

'Two reasons. First, I don't trust you. You're a Van Asche, you've got money, you're a friend of Rupert's – who knows? Maybe this rich collector scam wasn't just a smokescreen. Second, you might be useful bait.'

'Bait?' repeated Merise icily.

'Bait. Like you leave a hunk of raw meat or a tethered goat to lure a tiger,' he explained. 'For Tarik.'

'It's not often that I find myself compared to a hunk of raw meat or a tethered goat,' she said with a false smile. 'Anyway, you said Tarik had escaped.'

'We don't know how far he's gone. My gut tells me he's not finished yet. And if he makes another stab at it, it's quite possible he might make a grab for you.'

'What on earth for?'

'Listen, babe, I was here the whole time, outside the door with the rest of them. We heard what you did to him. If I was him, I'd be back. Either for more of the same or to wring your neck. Maybe both.'

An intriguing possibility, Merise conceded. This Celik, or Robert, or whoever he was, was no sexual innocent, hinting at that most dangerous of sexual tricks, semi-asphyxiation to enhance orgasm. It was not a practice she indulged in or approved of; there were other ways, other means; that one too often resulted in disfiguring bruises, or, in less expert hands, an unexpected and sometimes ignominious end. It was a blunt and unsophisticated effort to achieve the effects she could create much more inventively, best left to cross-dressing cabinet ministers or rural English vicars.

Still, it was interesting that he had mentioned it, she decided, looking up at him.

Their eyes caught and clashed. She read in his a cynical admiration coupled with a strangely impersonal lust. This was a man who thought he had conquered his cock, she realised, and smiled inwardly. That creature didn't exist, unless he was very, very old, very, very ill, or dead.

He saw the smile in her eyes and was taken aback. He had meant to frighten her, just a little, assume the upper hand, let her know that he couldn't be coerced by her sexual intimidation. It might have been a message better left unsent. Because instead of the fear, or disgust, or even distaste he had expected, he read a carnal calculation.

He stood abruptly, knocking over the cup of chicken soup she had placed on the ground. 'I've got things to do,' he said briefly, making his way towards the house.

She was beside him. 'Such as?' asked Merise.

'Take the men out to the site, get to work there. Contact Rupert. Contact my department. Make a few calls.'

'You're going back to the tomb? I'll come with you,' said Merise.

'No,' he replied automatically.

'Why not? I've never been – you and Julia have already seen it. And if it hadn't been for me, you'd never have got the information from Tarik. Besides, you said you wanted to keep an eye on me,' she offered silkily.

Unconsciously his eyes slid to her, taking in the

slim, perfectly toned body evident beneath the voluminous folds of the man's white shirt, the long, spectacularly beautiful legs.

'Or maybe you could just strip me and tie me to a post as bait for Tarik,' she continued, just on the thin edge of sarcasm, knowing that his thoughts would fly to the sight of her body, naked, helpless, bound and waiting.

'Put some clothes on and hurry,' he snapped. 'I want to make this a quick trip; I'm dead on my feet.'

Julia slept undisturbed for almost twenty-four hours.

She had been vaguely aware of Celik carrying her up the stairs, vaguely aware of the clumsy clash of bodies in the hall, dimly conscious while Celik undressed her, stripping off her dusty clothes and rolling her beneath the sheets, faintly aware as he stood by the side of the bed, looking down at her intently as the rich, dark, numbing waves of exhaustion claimed her utterly.

She slept deeply, but she dreamed, strange, dark dreams, exotic and carnal. She was at once both one with the tomb and inside it, a hollow void pierced by alien warmth and strange echoes, a princess whose golden rest was violated by the penetration of another world.

She was the womb, the tomb, the hollow vessel meant to shelter life and death, protecting, nurturing, suddenly invaded, probed by the lancing spear of phallic intent.

She felt the echoes of their cries reverberating through her, arcing from the breast-like dome of her vaulted chamber to the tips of her gold-painted toes, being both tomb and body, knowing only the thrusting, grasping, greedy presence of rapacious bodies seeking to strip her.

It was a rape she was powerless to halt, a rape she conspired in, mute, still and golden. She rose to the pillage, nipples hard as the rock she was made of; her body as hot and fervent as the sun that beat on the earth above them, warming the dirt that enfolded her, warming the blood that had stilled in her veins.

She felt her body rise and lift above itself, insubstantial as morning mist, weightless, dissolving under the hot rays of the sun, felt her moisture flow to dew the cold packed floor of her grave as she came, impaled by the yellow heat, consumed, convulsed.

Still deeply asleep, Julia cried aloud as her body arched in climax, then relaxed as a sweet, voluptuous ease suffused her, enveloped her in a rosy blush of tingling sensation.

Merise, wearing yesterday's black suit, choking on clouds of dust, clutching the side of the jeep for balance as it bounded over the bumpy road, jolted against two Turkish villagers who smelled strongly of goats. She mentally damned Rupert, for getting her involved in this mess, damned Celik, for his appalling driving, and damned the two Turks, who must have slept with their damned goats.

It was past midday and the hot Turkish sun was searing the earth, sending rivulets of sweat down her shoulder blades. The flip side of decadence, she supposed; she definitely felt soiled. She gazed, without much interest, at the stark, uncompromising landscape, the jumbled piles of rocks and boulders, and swore aloud as the jeep crashed into a pot hole.

Hot, sweaty, and now almost certainly bruised,

Merise ground her teeth. Rupert would owe her for this, she promised herself. She had insisted on accompanying Celik, alias Robert Marchant of the International Antiquities and Forgeries Squad, with some vague idea of protecting Rupert's interests, as Celik-Robert seemed to have taken control of the affair, sending faxes and making phone calls, curtly brushing aside her questions.

He was leaving nothing to chance. Following them was another Jeep with six armed Turks who would be left to guard the site while he made his preparations before informing the authorities, before contacting Rupert. On the face of it, there seemed little that she could do.

He didn't trust her, that much was obvious. Was it simply because he didn't trust Rupert, she wondered? And was Celik himself what he claimed to be? Did the International Antiquities and Forgeries Squad actually have their agents masquerading as Turkish peasants? Was there even such an organisation?

Impatiently she dismissed such speculation. At the moment her main concern was to try to stay more or less upright as the jeep bumped and shuddered over the dusty road, and to try to stay as far away as possible from the goat-reeking villagers crammed in next to her.

At last the jeep slowed and finally came to a stop near a small hut with a thatched roof. Thankfully she eased herself out of the jeep, ignoring the hand one of the Turks extended, and looked around. The area seemed flat, almost featureless.

'This is it?' she exclaimed, disappointed.

Celik, who was delivering a rapid-fire stream of instructions in Turkish to the men who surrounded

213

him, ignored her. Gingerly picking her way over the rocks, Merise went to the hut, intending to find some shade.

'Wait,' called Celik abruptly. 'I want to go in first, see if anything's been disturbed.'

The Turks scattered at his orders, fanning out in a large circle surrounding the hut as he made his way over to her, swinging a large torch in one hand. 'This is the access route Tarik cleared to the tomb,' he explained, opening the wooden door and peering inside.

'This?' she exclaimed incredulously, craning her neck over his shoulder and doubtfully examining the bare interior, the wooden floor, the single, naked bulb dangling from the roof. Celik entered the room quickly and was already on his knees, scrabbling in the dirt to find the iron ring of the concealed trap door by the time Merise had walked inside. The trap door opened with a groan, and he swiftly slithered down into the gaping void.

For a moment Merise hesitated, then looked down. She could see nothing except the bobbing light of the torch, intermittently illuminating the metal brackets of a makeshift stepladder fixed to the concrete wall. With a sigh for her manicure, she carefully lowered herself on to the first rung.

The air smelled strange, cool, and somehow old. Celik was cursing, his voice sounding strangely hollow, and the light from the torch weaved erratic circles. Just as she thought her eyes were becoming accustomed to the dark, to the strange play of light and shadow evoked by the torch, there was a sudden burst of illumination and she could see clearly.

Looking down, she saw that she was almost at the

bottom of a narrow shaft that opened out into a room lined with machinery and screens. Celik was frantically jabbing at switches and buttons, cursing fluently in a mixture of Turkish and English.

She reached the last rung, and stepped with some relief on to the floor. To her inexperienced eyes the hulking, grey metal equipment with lifeless screens and protruding wires looked like something that belonged in a boiler room; this was not some ancient tomb, not by a long shot. Anticlimax after anticlimax; what else could you expect from a day that began with chicken soup, she reflected bitterly.

'Something wrong?' she asked Celik, after casting a disparaging glance around the room.

'That bastard,' he spat, unheeding. 'He's been back, deactivated the programme, dismantled something. Shit! I should never have left, damn it. It just won't bloody work.'

'What won't work?' asked Merise.

'Know anything about sonar scanning?' said Celik, ineffectually stabbing out a series of commands on a computer console whose screen remained implacably blank.

'No,' she replied, confused.

'Then shut up, Merise Isabella Van Asche,' he ordered tersely.

Her eyes widened and she was on the verge of flinging out some cutting retort when she realised just how flustered Celik was; his hands were shaking and a thin sheen of sweat had appeared on his forehead.

'It won't gain him much time,' muttered Celik under his breath. 'But if he's been back ... damn it! I should have known he'd never give up so easily.'

'Tarik, you mean?' asked Merise.

'Of course Tarik, who else?' replied Celik, bashing his fist against the console. 'He must have doubled back after he saw us leave – it's been hours, enough time for him to grab the gold and get away again. And without the plan it'll take ages in this damned labyrinth.'

'You mean you can't find it?' said Merise, amused.

'Of course I can find it,' he retorted, stung. 'It's just a question of time. But if he's already disturbed the site – Christ, I'm going to look like a fool.'

'That was my intention,' came a silky voice from the shadows, and Tarik emerged from the dark depths of the passageway into the room. Despite his crumpled and now far-from-white Armani suit, he looked utterly composed and completely in control. And he was pointing a deadly-looking snub-nosed gun directly at Merise.

'Shit,' hissed Celik, whirling to face him.

'Exactly,' nodded Tarik. 'The best-laid plans, and so on. And now, Ms. Van Asche, is it? No, that's far too formal. I shall call you Merise. And now, Merise, if you would just step over here?' he gestured to his side with the gun.

Merise stood absolutely still, too frozen with shock to move.

'I really must insist,' said Tarik pleasantly, firing at the ground at her feet. The report in the small space was deafening; Merise jumped as if the bullet had stung her. 'That's better,' he said smoothly. 'Just a whiff of grapeshot, a small demonstration of power, so much more effective than threats, don't you find? Now come here.'

Shakily Merise made her way over to him. Her numbed brain refused to work.

'You can leave her out of it,' said Celik with a fair attempt at authority. 'I'm the one you have to deal with.'

'Ah, yes, Celik, my loyal employee. Or is it Robert Marchant, International Antiquities and Forgeries? In either case, you seem to have outlived your usefulness,' Tarik observed, pointing the pistol at his heart.

In films, thought Merise, dazed, in films, this was the moment that the heroine bravely knocks the gun out of his hand and wrestles him to the floor, while her ally dives for the gun, and the good guys win. But this was not a film: this was horribly, dangerously real, and the man with a gun was a man she had subjected to the most refined, sophisticated sexual tortures she could devise.

'You won't kill me, Tarik,' said Celik with more assurance than he felt.

'No?' asked Tarik, in a tone of mild interest. 'Why not?'

'Because the penalty for murder is considerably heavier than it is for smuggling antiquities,' Celik pointed out. 'And as it is, we haven't even got a case for that yet, and you know it. If you leave the treasure undisturbed, we can't prove a thing.'

Something flickered in Tarik's eyes. 'Indeed. And how long have you been in my employ? Some eighteen months? And tracking me for much longer, I assume?'

'Yes,' confirmed Celik.

'And you can prove nothing? You must be singularly incompetent.' Tarik smiled. He moved the gun slightly so that it was now pointed at Celik's head. 'I wonder if I would spill any brains at all with a head shot?'

217

'I can offer you immunity,' Celik promised hastily. 'In this case, at least. No one will have to know. Kill me now, in front of a witness, and you'll only be making trouble for yourself. You'd have to – ' he stopped himself short, cursing his own stupidity.

'Kill her too?' prompted Tarik with one of his small, infrequent smiles. 'The thought had occurred to me, and, believe me, it's not one I find completely distasteful.'

Merise listened with numb disbelief.

'I have men on the ground, surrounding the site,' Celik warned desperately. 'You'd never get away.'

'You never know,' shrugged Tarik. 'But, as it happens, I have several scores to settle.' The gun never wavered as, with his free hand, he delved into his pocket and extracted a length of thin cord. 'Merise, my dear, apt at bondage as you are, I assume you are more than capable of tying up Celik to prevent any sudden moves? If you would be so good?'

She took the cord from him with shaking hands.

'Ankles and wrists, just as you had me tied,' Tarik reminded her. 'No sudden moves, no trick knots, or I really will shoot you both.'

She obeyed him like a sleepwalker.

'Ankles crossed, that's right. Yes, hands behind the back, very good,' Tarik approved. 'Not that there's the remotest possibility that anyone could hear, but, nevertheless.' He stepped forward and stuffed a rather grimy handkerchief into Celik's mouth.

'And now, my dear,' began Tarik, turning to Merise, 'I think we'll begin with an explanation. Who are you and what role are you playing in this charade?'

She licked dry lips and looked him straight in the eye. 'I am Merise Isabella Van Asche,' she said. She felt a little of her confidence return as she pronounced her name.

'So I gathered,' replied Tarik. 'Not a common name,' he observed. 'Vienna? Van Asche Industries? There was a wild child, disowned by the family. You, I presume?'

Merise inclined her head with something of her usual hauteur.

'Yes, you have a certain reputation,' he continued. 'But not, I think, as a collector of antiquities.'

Useless to disagree. 'None at all,' she replied. From the corner of her eye she could see Celik, eyes wild, obviously trying to communicate some warning. She turned her back on him. It was Tarik she had to deal with; Tarik she had to convince. The time for silly subterfuge had passed.

'I had nothing to do with anything of this, really, until the end. It was just another one of Rupert's wild schemes –'

'Rupert?' he interrupted her sharply.

'A friend,' she shrugged.

'Rupert,' he muttered, almost to himself.

Annoyed with herself for revealing his name, Merise continued hastily. 'Julia really is an archaeologist,' she assured him. 'She had nothing to do with Celik. Neither of us did,' she insisted, cheerfully casting Celik to the wolves.

'So,' he said slowly, 'it was all a lie. Even your promise to split the treasure trove. The promise you gave me as you took me in your body, the promise I gave you in pain.'

'No.' She faced him squarely. 'I meant what I said, and I told Julia that those were the terms.'

'But now the roles are reversed,' he observed. 'I have the gun, I have the treasure, and I have you.'

'I've done nothing,' Merise began.

'Nothing? You kept at least one promise – you promised me pain, the ache of frustration, the impotence of bondage – was that nothing? And did you never think that some day you would pay the price for your pleasure? For your arrogance? Remember, you expected me to fear you.' Curiously, Tarik's voice was mild, interested; his words even, not accusatory.

For some reason, he struck a chord. Paying the price for pleasure – she had done so, but in her own coinage. Rebelling against Van Asche propriety, choosing to become a sexual outlaw, following the impulses of her sensual imagination, obeying no one and nothing but the imp that was her libido, had cost her, but no more than she could afford.

She had burned her bridges with a conflagration of lovers; she could never return to the conventional world of monogamy, of marriage, and she was well satisfied with her choice. To exchange infinite variety for stability, even more deadly, for familiarity, would be death to her sexual spirit. Perhaps, once or twice, she had been almost tempted to continue a liaison beyond its natural course, beyond the point when sex became predictable, but she had always resisted. When a lover's touch became familiar, expected, and even worse, enjoyed. Without anticipation, it was time to leave.

Desire dissolved with intimacy. Lovers began to want more than passion, wanted to become more than bodies, offered their dreams and desires, paraded their fears and insecurities, making her complicit in their fate, stifling her with their need.

No.

Never.

Sex and lust she understood and would share; love belonged only to one person. To Rupert. She had never before acknowledged it, not in so many words, not to Rupert, not to herself, but it was true.

The price of pleasure. Expertise in the carnal arts was not casually acquired. It required patience, imagination, a willingness to surrender to sensation, and even a certain courage, to embrace the liquid, lewd, lubricious pleasures of the flesh without shame, guilt or modesty.

And with it came power, the sensual power that Julia craved, the power that Julia had turned away from the night Merise had tortured Tarik. If you craved power, it was because you understood powerlessness, and no tyrant, sexual or otherwise, ever underestimated the reversals of fortune.

If she had known that the tangled sexual skeins of her life would lead to this, would she have done anything differently? Deep in her heart, she knew the answer.

'Well?' said Tarik harshly. 'Answer me!'

She had forgotten the question. 'The price of pleasure?' she said, gathering her thoughts. She tilted her head, considering, and then smiled, honestly amused. 'As I told you, in any brothel in the world you would have had to pay dearly, very dearly, for the pain and pleasure I gave you that night.'

There was no longer the slightest trace of fear in her eyes, Tarik realised, torn between admiration and irritation.

He took careful aim, and fired.

It was as if a hot wire had been laid against the

flesh of her upper arm, a singing, screaming, searing furrow ploughed into her skin. Instinctively, she clasped her hand to her arm, and watched as a tiny line of blood appeared between her fingers.

There was a muffled sound from Celik, choking on his gag.

'That, Merise Isabella Van Asche, is pain,' explained Tarik calmly.

It was a flesh wound, no more, she realised. Strangely, she wasn't scared. This was an accounting of sorts; they could barter. 'How unimaginative,' she returned lightly. 'And do you inflict pleasure so bluntly? I simply must know.'

Again, a strange light flickered behind his eyes. 'Then you will be enlightened. Come here, this way.' In a parody of courtliness, he half bowed, and gestured with his gun to the gaping dark depths of the passageway.

Celik, straining uselessly at the cords that bound him, watched helplessly as Merise and Tarik disappeared into the gloom.

Rupert presided over the elegant luncheon buffet on board *Calypso* with all his usual vivacity and charm, despite his inner conviction that something must have gone seriously wrong at Ciplak. Merise, or Mabik, or even Julia should have contacted him by now; Tarik must have broken. No man – no woman, for that matter – could withstand the techniques of sexual persuasion Merise had mastered; it could only have been a matter of hours.

'The smoked salmon,' he carolled gaily. 'Utterly divine. I personally persuaded the chef to add just the merest hint of dill only for you.'

They had learned those techniques together on an eclectic world tour, Merise's gift for her eighteenth birthday. The brothels of Hong Kong, Singapore, Japan and Paris had proved fertile fields for the erotic imagination. He still remembered, with absolute clarity, how, under the direction of a Zen prostitute, Merise and he had sat far apart on tatami mats, fully clothed, concentrating and summoning all their erotic imagination and energy to bring each other to climax simultaneously without touching. For two essentially selfish pleasure seekers, it had been an emotional and sexual revelation, never to be repeated.

'Mussels fresh this morning,' he chirruped. 'I promise you, I prised them off the hull of the boat myself, along with the oysters.'

Yes, he assured himself, Tarik had broken. But why this continued silence? If only he had been able to go himself – but, he reminded himself, there were very good reasons, very sound reasons, very compelling reasons why he couldn't appear to be too involved, reasons he would never disclose, not even to Merise.

'Indulge yourself,' he trilled at a plump brunette hovering uncertainly near the pastries and gateaux, which were richly decorated with whipping cream, sugared fruits and candied flowers. 'Enjoy, sin a little.'

That had always been his credo, and when it landed him in trouble it was usually of the most enjoyable kind.

Well, not always, but usually.

Once again the vaulted chamber tomb echoed with savage cries. Ever afterwards, Merise would only recall isolated images and sensations. The hardness of the packed-earth floor against her naked body. The urgent brutality of Tarik's body, mauling her, branding her. It was not the disciplined carnality that carefully blends pain with pleasure, but a primitive, violent onslaught of unleashed sexual fury.

Something dark and feral in her rose to meet him, something blind and furious that throbbed as viciously as her wounded arm. Her powerfully honed sensuality counted for nothing; this was primal and raw, a barbaric rite.

She came and came again, endlessly, mindlessly.

'You've been gone for hours,' gabbled Celik furiously as Merise removed the filthy gag from his mouth. 'What happened? Where's Tarik?'

'Nothing happened,' said Merise calmly.

'What?' he cried impatiently, and then paused. Merise was unnaturally pale, her eyes unfocused. She had a strange, distant air, almost as though she were in shock. 'Look, it's okay,' he said more gently. 'Just untie my hands, and then you can tell me everything.'

'Nothing happened,' Merise repeated. 'He's gone; he was never here. And we will never speak of this again.' With clumsy fingers she began working at the cord that bound his wrists.

'He's gone?' Celik rubbed his wrists, wincing as his circulation returned. 'Oh, God, another entrance; I should have thought of that. Maybe the men will catch sight of him. Where is it? Can you lead me to it? Where did he take you? What did he do?'

'No,' said Merise flatly. For the first time she looked at him directly, her eyes steady. 'He told me to give you a message. I'll tell you what he said, but that's all. And we will never discuss this, ever again. No one must know. Do you understand?'

There was something in her eyes that warned him. 'Yes, yes, I understand,' he promised soothingly.

'He's taken the master card for the probe,' Merise said, her voice sounding flat, rehearsed. 'It will never work without it. Have the equipment dismantled and shipped to Istanbul. Release both of his men. Report the site as a chance discovery made by Julia. Forget anything else. Do you understand?'

'That's crazy,' he burst out. 'Impossible. Christ! This means he's looted the tomb, hasn't he? He's taken the gold. But how?'

Merise turned away from him, leaving him to untie his ankles. 'That's all,' she said remotely, almost indifferently.

'That's all!' he said, horrified. 'For God's sake, Merise, what did he do to you?'

'Nothing,' she replied. 'Nothing at all.'

Gathering his wits, Celik rose unsteadily to his feet. 'Poor Merise,' he crooned unconvincingly. 'You've been through a lot, haven't you? And your arm, let me see it. There's a first aid kit in the jeep, we'll get it cleaned and bandaged. Then you'll feel better. And then we can talk.'

Damn the woman, and damn Tarik, thought Celik bitterly as he drove slowly back to Ciplak. He had coaxed, cajoled, persuaded, even turned vaguely threatening; nothing worked. Her silence was impenetrable. Much to his own disgust, he found himself thinking that Tarik had provided him with the perfect solution.

He had been carefully obscure in his preliminary contacts, had revealed nothing that couldn't be explained by a chance discovery; better that than the humiliating possibility of having to explain how he

225

had had Tarik virtually in his grasp, not once, but twice, and let him slip away.

Julia, with her archaeologist's memory, could easily lead him back to the tomb; she had examined the treasure trove, would know what Tarik had taken.

His mind was spinning in circles. In the space of a day he'd been shot at, tied up, and fucked up royally. All he wanted to do now was sleep.

Chapter Twelve

*T*he next morning, Julia woke at dawn to find herself nestled in the warm curve of Celik's body, cuddling spoon-fashion against him, the half tumescent bulge of his early morning erection comfortably wedged between her naked thighs.

She felt blissfully disorientated, confused even as to the date, let alone the place, waking from a dream so rapturously erotic that she still felt buoyed by it, wanted to cling to it as long as possible. Had it been merely a dream? Had Celik made love to her as she slept? It seemed barely possible, she thought hazily, snuggling against him. His arms tightened reflexively, drawing her even closer, and she felt the warm puff of his breath on the nape of her neck.

A faint, warm thrill tingled down her spine at his unconscious caress, and she knew, without knowing how, that Celik had not touched her. But he felt so right, curled against her, as if their bodies had been made for each other. She felt warm, safe, protected.

This sexless intimacy, unthreatening, undemanding, merely enfolding, was exactly what she needed.

No one, she thought drowsily, should have to wake alone, without the reassuring warmth of another body, without the comforting, rhythmic rise and fall of another's breath to bask in.

There was a sweet, innocent yet expectant magic in lying naked next to a sleeping man. A man whose body was unexplored yet now undeniably familiar; a curious, impersonal sensuality in feeling his hair-roughened thighs curled against her, his unconscious arousal nudging at her body. With a small sigh of contentment, she parted her thighs, drawing him to the furrow of her body, and nestled closer.

She smiled, closed her eyes, and reached for the dream.

They awoke together, hours later, to find themselves face to face, sharing the same pillow.

'Morning,' said Julia, through a yawn. 'Or is it afternoon? And what are you doing in my bed?'

Close up, she could see that his brown eyes were shot through with gold flecks and his lashes were long and thick, curling at the ends.

'Early afternoon, I should think,' he replied with an answering yawn. 'And, actually, it's my bed.'

'Oh. Then what am I doing in your bed?' she asked.

'Sleeping,' Celik replied softly. 'So far, only sleeping. What a waste. I like the feel of you in my bed.'

'Mmm. I can tell.'

His prick was hard against her belly. She relaxed against him, enjoying the soft touch of his hand on her hair, the hopeful pressure of his groin against hers. It would take so little, so very little, to arch against him, draw him inside her. But she was reluctant, for

228

some reason she could scarcely define to herself, reluctant to disturb this sleepy, intimate tranquillity with the slick ease of sex.

The adventure was over; indiscriminate sexual gourmandise was suddenly, inexplicably, no longer an option, she realised. It would be easy, too easy to take him now. Like a woman starving, she had feasted on Rupert, on Merise, on Mabik and Tarik; now it was time to fast a little. Perhaps it was merely that Celik was holding her so comfortably, so gently, stroking her hair so easily. It was soothing, like a warm balm on a bruise she hadn't even known was there.

This was special.

Too much and yet not enough lay between them. Only hours ago she had lain with Tarik in the tomb; now she needed an hiatus, a carnal caesura to mark the passage to her relationship with Celik.

Unknowingly, she stiffened a little in his arms, and obligingly Celik loosened his hold, so subtly, so casually that she never noticed, having sensed her mental rejection.

It wasn't physical, Celik thought, no, it couldn't be physical, not when her body melted against his, not when he could feel her nipples peaking against his chest, not when he was hard against her. But he could wait, would wait until the time was right, knowing that time would come.

No, Julia was thinking, perhaps the adventure wasn't over, not yet, not quite. There was still the final period, the final exclamation mark to be affixed on the page that was David. Until she had done that, she couldn't take Celik as a lover. It was irrational, it was illogical, but somehow it made perfect sense to her.

'So, what now, Celik?' Julia asked, stretching luxuriously, and inconspicuously away from him.

A good question, thought Celik. She knew nothing of Tarik's return; he would have to tell her. Subconsciously, as he slept, he had made his decision or it had been made for him; he would report the site as a chance find, have the men dismantle the equipment, present the tomb to the world as a lucky discovery, and never reveal Tarik's involvement. It rankled, unquestionably it rankled, but he couldn't see a way out of it.

As concisely as possible, he told her what had happened and finished by saying, 'So we'll go back to the site, check it out, then finalise arrangements with the authorities, alert the press.'

'I don't believe it,' gasped Julia, her eyes wide. 'He shot Merise! He wouldn't have done a thing like that.'

'It was just a flesh wound,' said Celik dismissively – too dismissively, she thought.

'That's terrible,' she shuddered. 'Is Merise all right?'

'With her, who can tell?' shrugged Celik. 'Anyway, let's get moving, shall we? Unless?' He lifted his eyebrows suggestively and edged a little closer to her.

'Not yet,' replied Julia, shaking her head, hoping that he would understand, seeing from the faint smile in his eyes that he did. 'And I need a coffee. And a shower. And my make-up. And some clean clothes. And I want to see Merise before we do anything.'

The plumbing was primitive, a mere spout located outside in the tiny garden, and the water was cold, but Julia took her time, soaping herself carefully to remove all the dust and grime, and washing her hair twice, watching the suds bubble away into the grated drain. The heat of the sun quickly banished the chill of the water, and when she was finished she felt refreshed and renewed.

Wrapped in a towel, she ascended the rickety stairs at the back of the house to the bedroom, and found coffee and her tote bag awaiting her, along with her freshly laundered jeans and denim shirt. She spared a rueful thought for her favourite white shirt that she had worn the night before, but it was dirty and torn, probably beyond repair.

Torn by Tarik's hands, in the thick, dark blackness of the tomb, as Celik listened and a golden princess, thousands of years dead, lay a mute witness to their mating. So, Tarik had returned to his Helen, she mused. Thinking it over, she was not surprised that he would make a final attempt to retrieve a share of the treasure; much as she hoped he had not plundered the tomb, she was aware of a sneaking relief that he had escaped and might even now be safe in Istanbul, cloistered behind the facade of his Ottoman palace.

But to have shot Merise so cold-bloodedly, so calculatingly – from Celik's description she had a vivid mental picture of the scene: Merise, her chin high, calmly asserting that in any brothel Tarik would have had to pay for pain and pleasure; Tarik, equally calm, raising the gun, a tight, small smile on his lips as he fired, saying, 'That, Merise Isabella Van Asche, is pain.'

Pain and pleasure. Perhaps Tarik and Merise understood each other in a way she never had. Perhaps the sexual techniques that Merise had used were equally cold-blooded, equally calculated. Suddenly she was glad that she had turned away from that scene, had not stayed to observe Tarik in Merise's clutches. Still, she would always wonder. The thought jarred a fragment of memory.

Merise's voice, purring with satisfaction, saying silkily, 'And now you'll always wonder.' Then she had been taunting Julia with her sensual power to seduce David and Julia had succumbed; in a way they had come full circle.

Julia made up her face carefully, remembering Miko's instructions. It seemed years, not days, since she had been on the *Calypso,* and submitted so nervously to the Japanese woman's hands and art. Now her skin was delicately tinged with gold from the hot sun and exhaustion had lent a finer edge to her features; her eyes seemed huge, even without the complimentary shadow, and her cheekbones rose high without the dusting of rose powder.

She paused with the mascara wand at her eyelashes, peering at herself in the murky depths of the old mirror. She had changed, irrevocably, irreversibly. And it had nothing to do with the artful application of coloured powders and gloss.

The woman who looked back at her was strong, sensual, confident; a woman who had discovered unexpected strengths and emerged from the shadows; a woman who had discovered a taste for adventure.

And one who was learning her range. Not sleeping with Celik was just as much an expression of sensual power as sleeping with him would have been, she decided.

She smiled at this new woman, now her creation, not Rupert's, not Merise's, before bending forward to apply a second coat of mascara.

Make-up in place, she dressed hastily, jeans and denim shirt, drank her coffee, now lukewarm, and left the room. On the tiny landing she hesitated, then knocked softly on the wooden door opposite. If Merise was asleep, she didn't want to wake her, but she did want to see for herself that she was all right. She knocked again, and when there was no response, carefully opened the door.

Merise was lying in bed, her eyes half-closed, her hands at her breasts, wearing a secret, dreamy expression that Julia had never seen before.

'Merise,' she called softly. 'It's me, Julia. How are you?'

Merise blinked and shook her head, as if emerging from some private reverie. 'Julia,' she answered. 'I'm fine. And you?'

'Celik told me what happened,' said Julia, coming over to stand by the side of the bed. 'Your arm, is it very painful?'

'Just enough,' said Merise sarcastically. The throbbing heat had ebbed, leaving it tender and sore. In a perverse way, she would be sorry when it healed; it was a tangible reminder of Tarik, a symbol of pain and pleasure.

'I'm so sorry,' said Julia helplessly. 'What happened? Celik said you wouldn't say anything. Did Tarik take you to the tomb? Did you see the gold? Do you think he managed to take any of it with him?'

'So many questions,' said Merise dismissively, propping herself up on the pillows. The sheet slid down, exposing her breasts, and Julia almost gasped as she saw the faint teeth marks circling her nipples. 'It was dark,' Merise added. 'And I told Celik that nothing had happened.'

'That's nothing?' echoed Julia in disbelief.

'We paid each other in our coin,' said Merise

233

indifferently, catching the direction of Julia's gaze and glancing down. A soft, secretive smile curved her lips as she drew the sheet up. 'You don't really want to know more, do you Julia?'

'No – no, I guess not,' Julia replied slowly.

She could feel the weight of Tarik's gold rosette in her breast pocket as if it was burning into her skin.

Out at the site, Celik's men laboured, patiently trying to disassemble the unfamiliar equipment, reducing the sophisticated scanner into the component parts that would fit through the shaft. It was a clumsy, awkward process, with men stationed at intervals along the ladder bracketed to the wall of the shaft, trying to hoist the equipment to the surface. With all the bangs and scrapes Julia privately doubted it would ever function again.

Celik called a brief halt to the work so that they could make their way down the shaft.

'It'll never work, you know,' she said stopping halfway down and running her fingers over the concrete facing of the shaft. 'This is obviously modern; there's no way this can be passed off as a chance discovery.'

'I know,' said Celik, nearly stepping on her fingers as he continued down the ladder. 'That's why you're going to find the other entrance after you lead me to the tomb.'

'Other entrance?' asked Julia, hastily snatching her hand back.

'The one Tarik must have used to escape,' he explained. 'After the equipment has been dismantled, we'll block up the shaft and seal the passageway.'

'This other entrance could be anywhere,' Julia protested as she reached the bottom. 'And I'm not exactly certain how to get to the tomb.'

'You'll find it,' Celik assured her. 'And if you can't, once we've got the location set, we'll dig a hole at the top of the vault, and you can say you fell in.'

'Not on your life,' retorted Julia as she reached the bottom of the shaft. 'Chance discovery is one thing, touristic idiocy is another. I'm a professional, remember? I'll say I noticed something suspicious in the contours of the landscape – there's no way I'd just fall into something. And you can't disturb the capstone.'

'Then let's hope this other entrance isn't hard to find,' was all Celik would say, joining her on the ground and passing her a torch. 'Lead the way.'

It was not as difficult as she had feared to retrace the steps she and Tarik had taken. Fortunately she was able to recall the plan of the site from the computer graphics Tarik had shown her reasonably well. Her memory failed her once or twice, leading her into empty caverns or storage rooms, but at last she found the break in the wall that led out of the city to the tomb.

She slipped easily underneath, then stopped, struck by a sudden thought.

'What if he's still here?' she whispered to Celik. 'What if there is no other entrance? What if he's waiting for us?' She had a bizarre vision of Tarik standing guard over the funeral bier, gun in hand, guarding his Helen, idly caressing her golden brow.

'Don't worry,' Celik assured her in normal tones as they walked up the dromos-style passage that led to the tomb. 'This time I'm ready. And I'll go first.'

At the huge boulder guarding the entrance he paused to extract a gun from his pocket and then,

235

holding the torch between his teeth, squirmed through the narrow gap. His exultant cry echoed through the chamber.

'All right. It's okay, Julia, it's all here, we've got it.'

Hastily she scrambled through to join him. She shone her torch directly onto the bier, ignoring Celik's excited stream of self-congratulation.

It was as she remembered: the body draped in golden discs; the gold diadem; the necklaces; the jumble of cups and other offerings at one end.

But the gold death mask was missing, revealing the ivory skull beneath.

Oblivious to her sudden stillness, Celik chattered on. 'Must have been too much, too heavy, he wasn't prepared. Excellent, excellent.'

So Celik hadn't noticed the mask was missing, she realised. This was his first real look at the trove; he obviously hadn't had time to take much in before Tarik had ambushed him. Looking more closely, Julia thought that the golden discs covering the body seemed disarranged, and surely she remembered another necklace?

Should she tell him? If she did, would he renew his efforts to pursue and arrest Tarik? Wouldn't it be wiser, safer even, for all of them, if she simply pretended that the treasure was intact?

Celik caught her in his arms in an exuberant hug, kissing her enthusiastically. She returned his embrace automatically, struggling with her conscience. With a tiny, detached portion of her mind, she noticed that his lips were warm and firm.

'It's great, isn't it?' he said, kissing her again.

'Great,' she repeated hollowly.

'Now we scout around for the other entrance; I'll

have a guard posted, get back to the house, make the arrangements – '

'Yes, yes,' Julia interrupted. 'Why don't you take a look first? There may be another path leading outside the wall, maybe at the foot of the dromos. I'll just stay here for a moment.'

'You okay?' he asked with quick concern.

'Of course,' she replied with a laugh. Did it sound as brittle to his ears as it did to hers, she wondered. 'I just want to examine the treasure more closely.'

'Right,' he agreed with alacrity. 'I'll just check the passageway and come back for you.'

Finally alone in the vaulted chamber tomb, Julia sank to the floor and sat cross-legged in front of the bier, keeping her torch trained on the luminous ivory skull of Tarik's Helen, the most beautiful woman in the world, a face the world would never see if she kept silent.

She imagined Tarik in Istanbul, in his room of gold, caressing that exquisite golden face, his large, rough hands gently, reverently tracing its contours, warming the cool gold with his touch, placing the death mask on some anonymous woman who would become his Helen, paying tribute with his body to her image.

She remembered how she had felt, wearing a gold death mask, the dizzy, light-headed blur as her senses pooled to his touch, remembered the bizarre inventiveness of his lovemaking in that room, how he had decked her body in gold, roused her to gilded climax after gilded climax.

Her body warmed with the memory. She had once thought that there were two Tariks; the rough, earthy lover who took her on silk sheets, and the carnally fantastic man of the room of gold. She had once thought she might even be falling a little in love with him.

Now she realised there was a third Tarik, a Tarik she had never known, one capable of shooting Merise in cold blood. Had he always been there, or had Merise created him?

She shook her head, impatient with the turn of her thoughts.

Tarik was gone, leaving the trove almost intact, allowing her its 'discovery'. She owed him for that, and for her memories from the room of gold.

It had been a unique experience, one she would treasure – she smiled at the inadvertent pun – forever.

Thoughtfully she regarded the skeleton on the bier. It had once been a woman, flesh and blood, alive to all the pleasures of passion. What would she prefer? The strange, sensual homage of a man like Tarik, or the impersonal admiration of crowds of tourists? To remain inviolate, untouched and untouchable behind a wired-glass case, an object, or a living memory still inspiring lust and desire?

'Julia, Julia!'

Celik's voice was coming closer. She had only moments to decide.

'Julia?' Celik craned his neck to peer around the boulder. 'What are you doing, just sitting there? The treasure, it is okay, isn't it?'

'Fine,' she said after a slight pause, crossing her fingers in an instinctive, childish gesture. Professional pride made her add, 'Some slight sign of disturbance, but that could be the result of subsidence, a mild earthquake, even an early attempt to loot the tomb.'

'Well then, let's get moving,' he urged. 'I think I've

found a path leading to the surface, veering to the north – the air seems fresher, anyway, come on.'

'Yes, all right, I'm coming,' she replied. She rose to her feet and looked at the bier one last time.

Helen would approve, she thought.

'Rupert is *aux anges*,' announced Celik, reading from the fax he had just received. 'He is *delirious* with delight, simply *ecstatic*, almost *nympholeptic*.' He broke off from his reading and squinted at the page. 'That can't be right.'

It was dusk, and they were all sitting in the tiny garden drinking wine, Julia and Merise seated on the rickety wooden chairs, Mabik hunkered down in the dust between them. The other Turks were out at the site, so the atmosphere was more relaxed, and the smell of lamb roasting on an open grill at the end of the garden perfumed the air.

'Caught by the nymphs,' explained Julia. 'I think he's just trying to say he's pleased.'

'Always over the top – why couldn't he just say so?' grumbled Celik. 'The news that the Antiquities and Forgeries Squad was involved left him completely *bouleversé* but after profound reflection – *bouleversé*?'

'Upset,' supplied Merise.

'Mphm,' snorted Celik. 'So it should. Anyway. Profound reflection. This is a heritage that belongs to humanity, a priceless gift we bestow to the world. I don't believe that for a minute, he must be seething,' he said in aside. 'He showers us all with kisses, congratulations and huglets – huglets?'

'Little hugs, I imagine,' smiled Merise. 'He does tend to get awfully camp when he's excited.'

Celik arched a mocking brow and continued to

read. '*Calypso* will be docking at Piraeus the day after tomorrow; he will be waiting there for you with open arms and simply oodles of champagne. The *dénouement –* '

'Ending, outcome,' interrupted Julia.

'I know what a *dénouement* is, thank you,' said Celik a little acerbically. 'It will be especially sweet as David, he assures you, Julia, is as pompous and profligate as ever – who is David?'

There was a small pause and then Julia answered briefly. 'A colleague. The ship's lecturer. It smells as though the lamb is almost done,' she continued brightly. 'When do we eat?'

Celik eyed her suspiciously before returning to the fax. 'Local papers, local press, stringers from the big leagues will pick up the story,' he muttered, obviously abbreviating. 'Pitch it small and let it grow. Not a bad idea.'

'I don't want anything to come out until I'm back on *Calypso*,' said Julia suddenly.

Her silly fantasies, as flamboyant and overblown as Rupert's prose style, returned to her: Julia in the spotlight, David for once relegated to the fringes, Julia triumphant, David burning with envy. Still, there was no reason she shouldn't taste her revenge, return to David as the recovering invalid, resume the pose of comfortable shadow, see for herself his disbelief turn to fury, to outrage and finally to bitterness when he discovered that she had been pivotal in the archaeological coup of the century.

She wanted one last night as David's Julia, a Julia meek, mild and submissive who would defer to him in public. And then seduce him, astound and astonish him with her newfound erotic skills and imagination, leaving him with the memory of the new Julia, self-confident and sensual, a memory that would taunt him and haunt him for the rest of his life.

That was symmetry; that was justice.

It occurred to her suddenly that perhaps it was as cold-blooded and calculating as anything Merise would devise. She wasn't sure if the thought pleased or disturbed her.

'Why not?' asked Celik.

'That's what I'm thinking,' replied Julia, her eyes speculative. 'I mean, why not?'

'I don't understand,' said Celik. 'Why wait until you're back in Athens?'

'Purely for effect,' shrugged Julia.

They remained in the garden for dinner, eating off cracked plates with supple tin cutlery that seemed to be pierced by the food, rather than the other way round, but the grilled lamb was delicious, fragrant with mint and tender with smoke, with unleavened bread and a salad of aubergines, onions, tomatoes and olives. The wine flowed freely, and not even Merise commented on the crockery.

Conversation centred largely on the plans for the next day, but Julia let it wash over her, preoccupied with her thoughts. She was aware that Celik's eyes darted to her every so often, appraising, and tried to rouse herself to take part, but she felt curiously distant and detached.

As soon as she had finished her lamb, she rose, pleading tiredness, and went upstairs to the bedroom. It was there Celik found her, sitting on the edge of the bed, staring into space, mindlessly fingering the gold rosette.

'You're not that tired,' he said, coming to sit beside her. It was a statement, not a question.

'No, not really, just preoccupied, I guess,' she replied, surreptitiously pocketing the rosette.

'Worried about tomorrow?' he asked. 'Don't, it'll be a breeze. We'll have a prepared statement, you'll answer a few questions, they'll take a few photos. And the Turkish authorities will be there.'

'No, it's not that, especially,' Julia said.

'You're thinking about David,' Celik probed. He shrugged at her start of surprise. 'I asked Merise,' he explained. 'She said he was your almost-but-not-quite-fiancé. That's a new one. He's the reason you got mixed up in all this?'

'Sort of,' she replied vaguely, then hesitated. 'Well, yes,' she admitted in a stronger voice. 'But "was" is the operative word here. It's almost finished.'

'Is that why you wouldn't make love with me this morning? Because of David?' he asked acutely.

Julia bit her lip and refused to answer.

'But you went with Tarik,' he pointed out bluntly.

'That was different. Don't ask me to explain, because I can't. But it was different. And why are you asking me all these questions? It's none of your business.' She had meant her voice to sound cutting; instead the words came out softly questioning.

'Of course it's my business,' he corrected, laying his hand against her cheek, turning her head so that she was forced to look directly into his eyes. 'We're going to be lovers; I want to know everything about you.'

Faintly stunned, Julia was still as he lowered his mouth to hers. He made no move to kiss her, but delicately traced the contours of her lips with the tip of his tongue, a soft, subtle exploration, gently teasing, flirting with her, licking her into arousal, making her want to taste his mouth. There was something sweetly tantalising in the muted wash of his tongue against her lips.

He made no move to touch her, to deepen the kiss, seemingly content with this fragile exploration. Even when she opened her mouth, inviting more, his tongue was tentative, merely touching the inner rims of her lips, sliding gently back and forth, little by little establishing an intimacy of taste and touch.

She could feel the pulses of her body quickening, roused by his delicate sensitivity, his gentleness. He was questioning, not demanding, seeking her response, not forcing it, despite the bluntness of his words, and she felt herself warming to him.

She let her tongue meet his and only then did he lower his lips to hers, his mouth firm, his tongue stroking, caressing, plunging and retreating in the unmistakable rhythm of sex. And she was rising to it, joining her mouth with his, kissing him back as her body responded to the promise of his lips.

When at last he lifted his mouth from hers, she tilted her head back, and began to say, 'Celik –'

'Robert,' he corrected, his breath warm against her ear. 'Robert. I want you to call me by my real name.'

'Robert, then,' she agreed, trying to restrain a shiver as his teeth grazed her ear lobe before drawing it into his mouth and sucking on it as if it were a nipple.

'Relax,' he said softly, his hand at the nape of her neck, gently massaging the muscles there. 'You're tense – relax. It's a kiss, Julia, just a kiss.'

He smiled at her, an amused smile that mocked her misgivings, and she couldn't help smiling back.

Just a kiss. It had been so long since she was kissed,

she thought hazily, as his mouth descended to trace the line of her jaw, outline the curve of her other ear, wander to her eyes, gently covering her lids and brows and lashes with the warm, languorous brush of his tongue. He was learning her contours, painting her with his mouth, weaving a tapestry of kisses; kisses light as a feather that barely touched her skin; kisses hot and slow and deep that consumed her senses.

Under his clever, skilful tongue she felt herself relaxing, melting, growing warm. Succumbing to the pressure of his mouth she lay back on the bed and he eased himself to her side, never interrupting the sweet flow of kisses that became gradually bolder, slipping down to the pulse at the base of her throat, down to the valley between her breasts until his mouth met the barrier of her shirt, then retreating to the column of her throat.

He made no attempt to undress her but lavished kisses on the bare skin exposed to him, her neck, the sensitive flesh just behind her ears, a slow, meticulous, tantalising exploration. When she reached up to touch his cheek, he caught her thumb between his teeth, nipping it lightly before drawing it deep into the cavern of his mouth, sucking hard with a piercing insistency, a fierce pulling pressure, swirling his tongue back and forth, back and forth in a movement so sensually suggestive, so rhythmically compelling that her nipples peaked and hardened in response.

He toyed with her thumb as if it were her nipples, her clitoris, flicking his tongue rapidly against the tip, nibbling gently with his teeth, explicitly, wordlessly promising to lavish the same caress on her breasts, between her thighs.

Still he made no move to touch her with his hands,

or his body, using only his mouth, his tongue, his teeth, keeping a small but maddening distance between them, easing away from her when she tried to press closer to him, until Julia finally realised that Celik – no he was Robert now, Robert – was keeping his promise. A kiss, just a kiss.

If she wanted more, she would have to ask for it, she realised. And she did want more, but it would be wrong, incomprehensibly wrong, for some reason that she couldn't quite remember.

'Just a kiss,' she said softly, looking at him and seeing the golden flecks of his dark-brown eyes.

'Yes,' he nodded, smiling.

With her free hand she slowly unfastened the buttons of her shirt, baring her breasts to him, nipples already hardening against the white silk and lace of her bra.

He released her thumb and bent his head to her, tracing the outlines of her bra with his tongue, delicately exploring the swell and slope of her breasts just as he had first kissed her mouth, outlining it with the merest tip of his tongue. She felt her flesh blossoming, nipples puckering into hard points, engorged with blood, her lower lips swelling in response.

His mouth brushed lightly against one breast and then the other, a caress so faint she might almost have imagined it had not the tingling heat streaked through her body, arcing to her groin. Sensitised to his kisses, her body responded eagerly, hungrily. He was restrained, merely circling one aureola with his tongue, and then the other, making a circle of painful sweetness, holding back, making her crave the hot, sucking, pulling pressure he had given her thumb.

For long, aching minutes he explored her silk-covered breasts with his tongue, gently, discreetly, tonguing the soft underswell, pressing nibbling kisses against the white silk.

Eyes closed, quiescent, Julia waited for his mouth to claim her, for the urgent suction, but he kept her hovering, denying her the suckling she craved. Her breasts felt ripe and swollen, engorged and newly sensitive, and when at last she felt his lips close cautiously over her nipple she moaned in relief.

Still he was gentle, too gentle, until she brought her hand to the nape of his neck, pressing him against her, urging him. Then he unleashed the power of his mouth, sucking deep, fixing the sensitive tip of her silk-covered nipple against the hardness of his palate, scraping her with his teeth, bathing her in the swirling rhythm of his tongue, focusing all her body's pleasure to the searing heat of his mouth.

Just when she thought she might climax from the scalding pleasure, he shifted to her other breast, subjecting it to the same initial tender caution, tormenting her nipple with light, delicate kisses before drawing it deep into his mouth.

He would not use his hands; he shifted away from her touch; when, impatiently, she tried to drag the sodden white silk from her breasts, offering him her flesh, he refused it, drawing her bra back over her nipples with his teeth, silencing her protests with a bruising kiss.

'Just a kiss,' he reminded her, drawing back and raising himself on one elbow. His breathing was ragged and his eyes were very bright.

Ripe with arousal, swollen with anticipation, Julia opened her eyes in disbelief. Was he taunting her, mocking her with her response, her obvious arousal?

No, there was something else lurking in those gold-flecked eyes, something warmer, but still provocative, still challenging.

'Yes, that's right,' she agreed, a little unsteadily.

She could meet provocation with provocation. She rose from the bed and leisurely discarded her shirt, dropping it on the floor, reaching behind her to unclasp her bra, unsnapping her jeans, her movements languid, unhurried, until she stood before him clad in nothing but the white silk scrap of her panties.

He was lying fully clothed on top of the bedcovers; she slipped in between the sheets beside him, leaned over to give him a brief, impersonal kiss on the cheek, and said, 'Good night, then, Robert,' before turning her back to him and snuggling down into the pillows.

A soft chuckle disturbed the hair at the nape of her neck. 'Good night Julia,' he replied.

Eyes resolutely shut, she heard him rise from the bed, the faint, popping sound as buttons were freed, the whisper of his zipper, the faint rustle as his clothes fell to the floor, and then he was beside her under the sheets, his back and buttocks warm against hers.

She waited for the tides of her body to lessen, for the heat to diffuse, wondering at him. She could feel the taut tension of his body next to hers and knew that he was as aroused as she; he must have known, must have sensed that she was on the verge of capitulation. How very strange, she thought, puzzled. And how very nice.

She rolled over, gently kissed him between his shoulder blades, and settled herself for sleep.

She slept fitfully, dozing only to waken minutes later, tossing and turning. Robert's body seemed attuned to hers, turning as she turned, unconsciously following her restless movements, clasping her close to him. If she disturbed him, he gave no sign of it, no grunts of irritation, no peevish protests. He was a most accommodating bedmate, she thought gratefully. And unlike David, he didn't snore.

From the bedroom across the hall she could hear other sounds, unmistakably sexual, soft cries and moans punctuated by the creaking rasp of ancient bedsprings. Merise and Mabik, she decided, bemused.

She tried to divert herself by mentally composing a statement for the press, how wandering beyond the perimeter of the excavated site she had just happened to notice a contour too regular to be natural, had gone closer to investigate, and happened, just accidentally, to dislodge a boulder ... In the middle of a sentence that had become strangely convoluted she fell fast asleep.

They woke together the next morning as they had the day before, face to face, sharing the same pillow, his prick hard against her belly, a comfortable, promising pressure.

'Good morning,' he yawned.

'Good morning,' she replied. 'You're up early,' she added, and immediately regretted the *double entendre* as she saw the smile in his eyes and felt him nudging against her.

'Lots to do,' he said, stretching. Bending to her, he brushed a light kiss on her mouth, a mere phantom of the tantalising kisses he had given her last night, and got out of bed.

Julia, obscurely and perversely annoyed and relieved, watched him as he walked unselfconsciously naked around the room, engorged penis swinging jauntily before him, picking up discarded clothes and rummaging in an old chest of drawers for fresh ones.

'Lots to do?' she asked, admiring the strong, taut lines of his spine as he bent to retrieve an errant shirt.

'Statements, meetings, forms – prepare to meet officialdom at its most officious,' he explained. 'We'll cobble together a statement this morning, before they descend on us. If you want a shower and breakfast first, you'd better scoot.'

She scooted.

The day passed in a bureaucratic blur. Robert hadn't exaggerated the officiousness of officialdom; without his status as a representative of the International Antiquities and Forgeries Squad, Julia doubted whether she would have survived the exhaustive interviews, although his mere presence created suspicion.

'Was he on the trail of some smuggling ring? What had brought him here?'

'My fiancée and I,' he explained, directing a meaningful glare at Julia, 'were merely playing tourist.'

Julia, in a fog of confusion, kept quiet. That hadn't featured in the covering statement they had hastily prepared, but there was no point in objecting. She had lost track of the various departments and inspectorates involved almost immediately; disputes and controversies about procedures and areas of jurisdiction had broken out even before the site was examined. One uniformed official seemed inclined to arrest her for surveying without a permit even as another showered her with questions and congratulations.

It was fortunate that Merise had decided to lie low. Julia's passport was seized, her credentials examined, her identity queried in a mix of Turkish and English that left her head aching. But that was nothing compared to the deluge that broke out at the site when she and Robert led them to the chamber tomb.

There was one moment of unbroken awe as the most senior officials who had squirmed their way past the boulder guarding the entrance gazed at the bier and glow of gold, and then the questions came fast and furious, some practical, some academic, some merely irrelevant. No, she hadn't touched anything; yes, it was exactly as they had found it; she was sure it was Late Helladic; it was far too early to assess the implications of the find; no, she wasn't working for *National Geographic*.

In the midst of this confusion, the press arrived, directed by some well-meaning but incompetent official, and there was a greater flurry, punctuated with the blinding flares of flash photography.

No, she was not working with a government permit; yes, she would be delighted to collaborate with the Turkish authorities and experts; detailed study and excavation would take many years; Homer's Troy? Who could tell?

Yes, if the Turkish officials permitted, she would be happy to pose wearing one of the necklaces, as Sophia Schliemann had done more than a hundred years ago.

And that was how the camera caught them; Julia, her neck bowed, face in profile, as Robert fastened a golden necklace of pendant acorns around her neck, his mouth almost touching her nape as he worked the clasp.

'You didn't have to say your were my fiancé,' complained Julia sleepily many hours later. Her hand ached from signing affidavits and forms in triplicate and her head swam from too much local brandy consumed in the impromptu celebration party that had developed after their return from the site. The reporters and officials had stayed for wine and roast kid and more wine and then brandy and more brandy. She could still hear snatches of laughter and song floating drunkenly on the soft night air.

She was trying, without success, to unbutton her shirt, but her fingers were unaccountably clumsy and the buttons kept going out of focus. She gave up and slumped on the bed.

'Why not?' asked Robert. 'It's better than saying almost-but-not-quite-fiancé. Here let me do that.' Deftly, he undid the buttons on her shirt and eased her out of it, watching as she flopped bonelessly back on the pillows. 'How much of that brandy did you have?'

'Lots and lots,' she replied dreamily. 'But you still shouldn't have said it. It was a lie, and it's a terrible, terrible thing to lie.' She tried to sound severe, but hiccoughed and then giggled instead.

'And it was the local stuff, too,' said Robert, smiling down at her. 'God, you're going to feel terrible in the morning. Stop squirming and let me get these jeans off.'

She was limp and unresisting as he pulled off her jeans. He looked uncertainly at her underwear, and then decided to leave it on. She had worn it in bed last night, obviously wanting to preserve some barrier between their bodies; she might feel better in the morning if she had it on. No, scrap that, nothing was going to make her feel better in the morning, he thought with a grin.

'Terrible, terrible lies,' murmured Julia, thinking dazedly of the golden death mask and Tarik, clumsily snuggling under the sheets and wishing the room would stop spinning.

'If it bothers you that much, we'll get engaged,' Robert offered casually as he took off his shirt. 'What do you think? Julia?'

But peering down at her, he discovered that she was fast asleep. For a moment he let his eyes linger on the golden strands of her hair spread across the pillow, her features, softened by sleep and drink, the rhythmic rise and fall of her lush breasts beneath the sheets. He liked her, he admired her, was physically drawn to her: she had guts, she had brains and a taste for adventure.

In fact, he admitted to himself, he was more than halfway serious about an engagement.

Despite the fact she snored.

Chapter Thirteen

*I*nsulated by a raging hangover, Julia was in no mood to appreciate the sweet poignancy of waking again in her platonic lover's arms, face to face and sharing the same pillow. Her head ached vilely; consciousness was a repulsive, disgusting insult to a system shattered by horrible, fiendish, dreadful Turkish brandy; and it was all his fault.

'How do you feel?' Robert asked in a whisper.

It sounded like a clarion of bells reverberating through her skull, a war cry, a flurry of trumpets.

'Go away,' she croaked, closing her eyes in pain.

'Is that any way to speak to your fiancé?' he reproached, mock aggrieved.

'Fuck off,' she moaned.

Mercifully, after that, he left her alone, and she almost groaned in relief as she heard the door shut. But all too soon he was back, carrying with him a glass of water, a couple of aspirin, and, horror of horrors, a glass of brandy.

'You don't know it, but you'll feel much better after you drink this,' he informed her with what she considered absolute callousness and outrageous optimism.

'Anything, if you'll just go away,' she managed. The aspirin felt like boulders; she nearly gagged at the smell of the brandy, but he was insistent, holding it to her lips, and, too weak to resist, she gulped it down.

The world spun and swirled, refocused.

She drained the glass and, much to her amazement, actually did feel a little better.

'Electrolytes, or something,' Robert nodded. 'A chemical reaction. It really works, the hair of the dog. But only one.'

'Thanks,' Julia essayed tentatively. 'I think.'

'Breakfast?' he suggested.

She shuddered and closed her eyes.

'Go back to sleep,' he said. 'You'll feel better later.'

Julia drowsed through the rest of the day, rousing herself in the late afternoon to go down to the kitchen for water, bread and cheese and then returning to bed. She was vaguely glad that her hangover excused her from dealing with the problems and petty details arising from their discovery of the tomb. Robert could deal with them, she decided sleepily. Merise could amuse herself. Julia was content to be alone and doze the day away.

Robert came to her in the early evening, tired and dusty, carrying a tray with cold meat, fruit, and a bottle of wine, full of news about the site. The gold had been photographed, recorded and removed; conservators were being flown in from Istanbul to deal with the skeleton; a survey team was being assembled;

Julia listened to all of it with half an ear as she nibbled cold roast lamb and gingerly sipped wine.

'What?' she asked, coming to attention at last.

'I said that Rupert's arranged for a private plane to fly you and Merise to Athens tomorrow. But you don't have to go,' he repeated.

'Oh, yes, I do,' Julia replied.

'Why?'

'Symmetry,' she said at last.

'You could stay here with me for a few days,' he insisted. 'Help out at the site, get to know each other better. After all – ' he flashed a grin at her ' – we are officially engaged.'

For a moment she was tempted. 'No, I have to go back,' Julia replied.

'To see David?' he probed.

'Sort of. It's more to see *me*, David's Julia.' She couldn't explain it more clearly, even to herself.

'But you'll come back? Or I could go with you.'

'No – I don't know.'

He made no further attempt to press her with words, but used his mouth to greater effect; persuasive, coaxing kisses nibbled at her lips; demanding, insistent kisses slanted across her face; hot, searing kisses on her nipples; dainty, delicate kisses fluttered between her thighs.

Again he made no attempt to use his hands, confining his caresses to his tongue, teeth and lips; he made no attempt to remove her underwear, content to stroke her through a silken barrier. All during the long, hot night he tongued and licked and explored her with a seamless sea of kisses, suffusing her with the warmth of his mouth, bathing her with his tongue, giving her a climax that unfurled as sweetly as the petals of a flower but left her aching for the hard imprint of his body.

'Just a kiss,' Robert reminded her, drawing away from her clutching hands, smiling a mocking smile.

'Yes,' agreed Julia, swallowing hard. 'Until – '

'Until later. Now kiss me again.'

The next day, dusk was settling as Julia and Merise made their way up *Calypso's* gangplank where Rupert, resplendent in his white uniform, was waiting to greet them.

'Darlings! How wonderful to see you both. Merise, my love, Julia, my dearest, what a coup! What a splash we'll make! You'll be all over tomorrow's papers. Celik sent me a copy of the statement – how clever of you to pose with that necklace! We must have lashings of champagne to celebrate, it's already chilling in my cabin.' He burbled effusively, kissing Merise and then Julia warmly on the lips. 'David doesn't suspect a thing,' he continued, lowering his voice conspiratorially. 'I only told him you were well enough to travel and would be meeting us here in Athens. I can't wait to see the look on his face. What are you going to tell him? Julia, you are a sly puss – when did you and Celik get engaged? Congratulations, congratulations. I want all the yummy details.'

'Oh, that,' said Julia, a little overwhelmed. 'We're not really – '

'Darling Merise,' interrupted Rupert, unheeding, 'Perhaps it would be best if you ever so discreetly disappeared before David arrives to greet our invalid? And it's the captain's farewell dinner, you'll want to, um, change?' he suggested, eyeing Merise's black pants and shirt with disfavour. 'You do look just the teeniest bit travel worn, my love.'

'Champagne first,' said Merise firmly. 'I'll see you in your cabin.'

'Rupert,' Julia began.

'Aha,' he muttered under his breath. 'Our esteemed professor approaches. What shall we – '

'Just stick to the story,' said Julia hastily as David arrived, raising her voice as he came near. 'Thank you, I'm feeling so much better now.'

'Julia, my dear,' said David awkwardly. 'How are you? You're looking extraordinarily well,' he added uneasily.

He hadn't particularly missed her; her presence was so unobtrusive that her absence was barely noticeable, especially with the throng of wealthy widows and divorcées willing to hang on his every word. But now the cruise was at an end, he was really quite pleased to have her back. Yes, undeniably pleased. She was a sweet little thing, Julia, comfortable and, well, useful. Her bent for dry, academic detail was occasionally helpful in fleshing out his broad, synthetic interpretations, and her uncritical admiration was satisfying in a way he had never troubled to define.

But she looked different, somehow. Instead of the pallid invalid he had expected, Julia looked tanned and healthy, almost glowing. There was a new aura of vitality, of *presence*, that he found faintly disturbing.

'Thank you, David,' said Julia shyly, dropping her eyes.

'All better now?' he said heartily, trying to remember what had been wrong with her.

'Quite recovered,' Julia replied with a small, demure smile.

'Good, good,' David enthused. 'Such a shame you had to miss the cruise. It went very well, very well indeed. I think I really managed to capture the spirit of the ancient world, bring it alive for our passengers,' he continued getting into his stride. 'I'm sorry you weren't here, I know you would have enjoyed listening.'

Julia stopped listening. Instead she looked at David calmly and critically, masking her scrutiny with a wide-eyed adoring gaze. He was attractive, she admitted, with that shock of prematurely grey hair contrasting with his unlined face, his deep brown eyes, his air of vigorous enthusiasm.

Mentally she found herself comparing him, feature by feature, to Robert, barely aware of Rupert fluttering away, murmuring something about 'leaving you two love birds alone.'

Robert's eyes were brown, but they had deep gold flecks, and they changed, became warm or cold, fired or iced by his thoughts, his emotions. David's eyes were shallow.

'And when we were at Mycenae, I – '

David's lips were full, pursed lovingly around the word 'I'. Robert's mouth was firm, fastened teasingly on her nipples.

Symmetry, she reminded herself, symmetry.

'You must have been wonderful,' Julia breathed adoringly. 'Why don't we go to our cabin and you can tell me all about it?'

In the cabin she pottered about, apparently aimlessly, unpacking her tote bag, half undressing to prepare for a shower and then stopping, as if distracted and enthralled by David's stories. It was a calculated striptease, a subtle display of her body designed to arouse him only subliminally, make him aware of her without him consciously realising that he was. And so, her eyes fixed on his, she unbuttoned her shirt slowly, letting her fingers dwell artlessly on the slopes of her breasts as if she was transfixed by his words.

She saw the faint flicker in his eyes when at last she discarded her shirt, revealing the skimpy, lacy bra she wore.

'Tell me more about what you said when you were at Mycenae,' she encouraged.

Ego warred with libido; she could almost smell his nascent arousal even as he babbled on eagerly, describing his lectures, his insights, his triumphs.

How could I have been so blind, thought Julia in wonder, as she slowly slipped off her jeans. What she had seen as charm, as charisma, as vitality, was the self-confident enthusiasm of self-love; what she had admired as poise and verve was the buoyancy of sheer ego.

Not once had he betrayed the smallest interest in her fictitious illness; not once did he interrupt his catalogue of self-congratulation to express any concern for her. David really was, as Merise had once described all men, a prick; and that part of him was not immune to her scantily clad body, she realised with an inward smile. His eyes were darting from her breasts to the silken vee between her thighs and the path of his gaze reminded her of the hot trail of Robert's kisses.

The thought was strangely exciting.

'Tell me all about where you went on the mainland,'

Julia invited, walking over to the mirror to brush her hair, offering him a view of her back. She watched his eyes in the mirror as they swept down her spine and fastened furtively on her buttocks. Robert's mouth had traced the same path, lingering at the nape of her neck, carefully tonguing each vertebra, dipping into the cleft between the globes of her buttocks, probing for the taut mouth of her anus, using the scanty silken barrier of her panties for greater stimulation. She could feel herself dampening at the memory.

'I really must shower,' said Julia abruptly, forgetting, for a moment, her role as rapt listener and cutting David off in mid-sentence. She saw the surprised look that crossed his face and hastened to add, 'It all sounds so thrilling, I'm dying to hear the rest of it, but we can't be late for dinner, can we? And I'm sure all the passengers will be wanting to see you one last time.'

It was the right note to take.

'Yes, you're quite right,' David agreed, preening himself a little at the thought. 'I'll just get changed and then meet you in the lounge, shall I?'

'Perfect,' approved Julia, retreating to the bathroom and locking the door. She didn't want to see David's naked body as he exchanged his khakis for formal dinner wear; it would shatter the spell.

She took a long, blissfully hot shower, glorying in the delights of civilized plumbing, washing herself thoroughly with scented soap, shaving her legs and armpits, conditioning her hair. Only when she was reasonably certain that David had gone did she turn off the water and step out of the shower. She towelled herself off briskly, fixing a turban over her damp hair and wrapping herself in a terry bathrobe before unlocking the door and peeking into the cabin.

It was empty.

Relieved, Julia went to the mini-bar and extracted a split of champagne. The golden wine foamed over the glass; she held it aloft in a silent toast to Rupert and Merise, to Tarik and Mabik, to Robert and, finally, to Helen of Troy, before draining it.

Pouring another glass, she wandered over to the wardrobe and inspected the clothes hanging there. Dull, dull, dull and dowdy; she was dowdy, she realised. She had become so accustomed to the superbly cut, subtly provocative clothes Merise had chosen for her that her old wardrobe came as something of a surprise.

She must have been a willing accomplice in her own annihilation, she decided, eyeing the dreary colours, fawns and taupes and greys.

With a grin she selected a shapeless linen shift in a particularly drab brown and held it up against her, seeing how it sallowed her skin and swallowed her curves.

Perfect.

She rummaged in the drawers, eventually finding a pair of white cotton briefs and a bra, serviceable and sensible, and put them on before dropping the shift over her head. She unwrapped the turban from her head and combed out her hair, deliberately omitting to scrunch and fluff it for more body. No make-up, she decided, not even so much as a touch of mascara. This was David's Julia, Julia the Invisible; but not even the drabness of her dress could dim the triumphant glitter of her green eyes. Well, she'd just have to keep her lashes lowered.

Strangely, she felt no tug of familiarity with the image in the mirror; it was as if she were wearing a disguise.

'Julia, darling, what have you done to yourself?' hissed Rupert as she hovered at the entrance to the lounge, looking for David. 'You look terrible! Where does it hurt?'

'Ssh!' she hissed back. 'I'm invisible.'

'Julia, darling, I can see you perfectly well,' Rupert reassured her. 'What have you been drinking? Tequila? It takes some people that way, don't worry, we'll have you right as rain in no time, a little black coffee, and – '

'Don't be silly, I'm fine,' Julia muttered. 'Stop making a fuss, somebody will notice.'

'Not if you're invisible,' Rupert retorted with some asperity.

'Just watch, you'll see,' she assured him, drifting away to join David at the bar.

There was, as usual, a throng of passengers surrounding him. David acknowledged her with a brief wink and a smile, leaving her on the fringes. Once she would have felt uncomfortable and awkward, nervous of the social chitchat that seemed to paralyse her tongue; now it struck her as simply banal and boring. Once she would have retreated to her fantasy world, played the game of mental seduction; now she had memories instead of fantasies.

She maintained her demure, unobtrusive, shyly retiring persona throughout dinner, murmuring almost inaudibly in response to any remark addressed to her, letting David bask in the attention he garnered so effortlessly. Rupert, at another table, cast her the odd, puzzled look. Merise sent her a fleeting, knowing smile that mockingly approved her ploy.

It was her last appearance as David's Julia; she wanted to look the part and play the part perfectly.

The food was elaborate and elegant; a delicate lobster mousse garnished with baby shrimp; a champagne sorbet followed by poached salmon in hollandaise sauce, then a filet of beef stuffed with crab served with new potatoes and fresh baby peas. Perversely Julia found herself longing for the blunt, simple fare of roast lamb and olives. The wines were French; she missed the spicy, aromatic Turkish wine with its hint of resin.

As dinner drew to a close there were speeches and presentations, last-minute instructions on disembarkation procedures, reminders to retrieve all valuables from the ship's safe. Throughout it all Julia sat quietly, a tiny, meaningless smile pasted on her lips, mentally planning the night.

She assumed David would want to linger over coffee and brandy; he did. She assumed he would want to repair to the Starlight Lounge to charm the remaining passengers, reluctant to fully abandon his role on centre stage; he did and he was.

It was long past midnight before she was able to draw him away, back to their cabin, and David was long past sober. That Julia regretted a little; she would have preferred him to retain a crystal-clear memory of her, unclouded by drink. Still, it was rather nice to think of his ensuing hangover in the morning as he scanned the papers that would reveal the new discoveries at Troy and the Trojan gold. Injury to insult, or something like that.

263

Weaving a little, he flopped on to the bed fully dressed as Julia turned on the lights.

'Great night,' he proclaimed, scarcely slurring his words. 'What're you doing?' he asked. 'I can do that.'

'Of course you can, David,' soothed Julia, unfastening his tie and easing open the buttons of his dress shirt. 'I just thought I could help.'

Her hands were sly and clever as she undressed him, brushing softly against his nipples as she removed his shirt, tracing the limp outline of his shaft through his trousers, making him twitch and stiffen. by the time he was completely naked he was hard, and he pulled her to him clumsily, groping for her breast.

For some reason that annoyed her; David's hands shouldn't rest where Robert's mouth had last been, where Robert's hands had never been. She pulled away with a soft laugh to disguise her irritation, and slowly drew the drab linen shift over her head, discarding the sensible cotton underwear she would never wear again.

She turned off the light and joined David in bed. It was not difficult to divert his questing hands; he had never cared as much for her pleasure as he had for his own, and he willingly submitted to her lips, her tongue, her fingers.

Alternately gentle and then rough she explored him, claiming his prick with her mouth, sucking him hard and then releasing him to blow softly on the sensitive skin of his testicles. Scratching at the mouth of his anus as she swirled her tongue on the tip of his penis. She knew to vary her rhythms to delay his climax, never allowing his body to relax and succumb to a repeated, expected caress.

Everything she had learned from Rupert and Merise, from Mabik and Tarik, she put to use on David's body; the long, slow, strokes; the heated flutter of fingers; the seductive ripple of flesh against flesh. But she disciplined the movements of her mouth, careful not to bestow anything that might be mistaken for a kiss.

That, too, was symmetry.

She felt no desire for him, no lust, but she revelled in his body's response, drank in his groans with a thrill of sensual triumph, relished her power and his weakness.

Skilfully she brought him to the brink again and again until, in a harsh, hoarse voice she had never heard from him, David begged her to stop, to let him come. Thinking of Merise, she sucked him hard against the roof of her mouth then dragged her mouth away as he began to spurt so that the semen flowed, arcing through the air to her lips.

Symmetry.

Julia awoke the next morning conscious of a tingling, fizzing excitement as if the blood in her veins had turned to champagne. Careful not to disturb David she dressed hastily, not bothering with underwear, merely flinging on the crumpled shift from the night before and then slipping quietly out of the cabin to visit the ship's boutique. The owner, already there checking stock, was persuaded to open early and Julia selected her purchases; fresh lingerie in the style Merise had chosen in emerald green; a tailored white shirt with oversized pockets and gold buttons to replace the one Tarik had torn and a matching skirt that fell to mid-calf and buttoned up the front.

Returning to the cabin she discovered, much to her relief, that David had already left. The drab linen shift was ceremoniously discarded in the waste basket before she showered and dressed in her new clothes. She took pains with her make-up, emphasising her eyes and lips, and carefully styled her hair.

The image in the mirror rewarded her; she looked crisply professional yet subtly provocative, the oversized gold buttons drawing the eye to her breasts and then down. She quickly packed her tote bag, taking only the bare minimum; wallet, passport, make-up. Her fingers closed on the gold rosette and with a smile she dropped it into the pocket over her left breast.

She glanced around the cabin. There was nothing more she needed. The detritus of David's Julia, the dowdy clothes, the sensible underwear – someone else could dispose of them.

Rupert would arrange something, just as he would arrange for her to return to Troy as swiftly as possible. The decision, half-formed in the middle of the night, suddenly crystallised.

With a final, brilliant smile for the creature in the mirror, Julia left the cabin.

She had no clear idea what form her final meeting with David would take, she realised, as she made her way to the breakfast room. Should she casually request a paper, accidentally draw his attention to the relevant article? Should she simply and concisely tell him everything? No, that was impossible – it involved too many other people and too many lies. She couldn't contradict the published version of events. Perhaps she could mix fictions; after she was released from hospital she had decided to visit Troy, noticed the unusual contour in the landscape. But how to account for Robert? She was still puzzling over this as she reached the breakfast room.

In the event, there was no need for words.

David looked up as she approached his table. Spread before him was an early morning edition with Julia's picture emblazoned on the front, the one of her wearing a golden necklace from the treasure trove with a man apparently kissing the nape of her neck.

Speechless, incredulous, he stared at Julia and then at the front page, his eyes darting back and forth disbelievingly.

The look in his eyes was everything she could have wished for: astonished, impotent outrage; shocked fury mingled with confused envy; David was completely baffled.

Julia smiled at him, a warm, sensual, victorious smile, and walked past him without a word, looking for Rupert.

But Rupert was sequestered in his cabin, where, under the indulgent eyes of Merise, he was reverently tracing the smooth, golden brow and beautiful lips of an ancient princess.

'No more chickens,' he gloated.

BLACK LACE NEW BOOKS

Published in October

THE BRACELET
Fredrica Alleyn

Kristina, a successful literary agent may appear to have it all, but her most intimate needs are not being met. She longs for a discreet sexual liaison where – for once – she can relinquish control. Then Kristina is introduced, by her friend Jacqueline, to an elite group devoted to bondage and experimental power games. Soon she is leading a double life – calling the shots at work, but privately wearing the bracelet of bondage.

ISBN 0 352 33110 0

RUNNERS AND RIDERS
Georgina Brown

When a valuable racehorse is stolen from her lover, top showjumper Penny Bennett agrees to infiltrate a syndicate suspected of the theft. As Penny jets between locations as varied and exotic as France, Sri Lanka and Kentucky in an attempt to solve the mystery, she discovers that the members of the syndicate have sophisticated sexual tastes, and are eager for her to participate in their imaginatively kinky fantasies.

ISBN 0 352 33117 8

Published in November

PASSION FLOWERS
Celia Parker

A revolutionary sex therapy clinic, on an idyllic Caribbean island is the mystery destination to which Katherine – a brilliant lawyer – is sent, by her boss, for a well-earned holiday. For the first time in her life, Katherine feels free to indulge in all manner of sybaritic pleasures. But will she be able to retain this sense of liberation when it's time to leave?

ISBN 0 352 33118 6

ODYSSEY
Katrina Vincenzi-Thyne

Historian Julia Symonds agrees to join the sexually sophisticated Merise and Rupert in their quest for the lost treasures of Ancient Troy. Having used her powers of seduction to extract the necessary information from the leader of a ruthless criminal fraternity, Julia soon finds herself relishing the ensuing game of erotic deception – as well as the hedonistic pleasures to which her new associates introduce her.

ISBN 0 352 33111 9

To be published in December

CONTINUUM
Portia Da Costa

When Joanna takes a well-earned break from work, she also takes her first step into a new continuum of strange experiences. She discovers a clandestine, decadent parallel world of bizarre coincidences, unusual pleasures and erotic suffering. Can her working life ever be the same again?

ISBN 0 352 33120 8

THE ACTRESS
Vivienne LaFay

1920. When Milly Belfort renounces the life of a bluestocking in favour of more fleshly pleasures, her adventures in the Jazz Age take her from the risqué fringes of the film industry to the erotic excesses of the yachting set. When, however, she falls for a young man who knows nothing of her past, she finds herself faced with a crisis and a very difficult choice.

ISBN 0 352 33119 4

ÎLE DE PARADIS
Mercedes Kelly

Shipwrecked on a remote tropical island at the turn of the century, the innocent and lovely Angeline comes to enjoy the eroticism of local ways. Life is sweetly hedonistic until some of her friends and lovers are captured by a depraved band of pirates and taken to the harem of Jezebel – slave mistress of nearby Dragon Island. Angeline and her handmaidens, however, are swift to join the rescue party.

ISBN 0 352 33121 6

If you would like a complete list of plot summaries of Black Lace titles, please fill out the questionnaire overleaf or send a stamped addressed envelope to:-

Black Lace, 332 Ladbroke Grove, London W10 5AH

BLACK LACE BACKLIST

All books are prices £4.99 unless another price is given.

---------- ✂ ----------------------

Please send me the books I have ticked above.

Name   ....

Address   ....

            ....

            ....

            .... Post Code   ....

Send to: **Cash Sales, Black Lace Books, 332 Ladbroke Grove, London W10 5AH.**

Please enclose a cheque or postal order, made payable to **Virgin Publishing Ltd**, to the value of the books you have ordered plus postage and packing costs as follows:

UK and BFPO – £1.00 for the first book, 50p for each subsequent book.

Overseas (including Republic of Ireland) – £2.00 for the first book, £1.00 each subsequent book.

If you would prefer to pay by VISA or ACCESS/ MASTERCARD, please write your card number and expiry date here:

....

Please allow up to 28 days for delivery.

Signature   ....

---------- ✂ ----------------------

WE NEED YOUR HELP . . .
to plan the future of women's erotic fiction –

– and no stamp required!

Yours are the only opinions that matter.

Black Lace is the first series of books devoted to erotic fiction by women for women.

We intend to keep providing the best-written, sexiest books you can buy. And we'd appreciate your help and valued opinion of the books so far. Tell us what you want to read.

THE BLACK LACE QUESTIONNAIRE

SECTION ONE: ABOUT YOU

1.1 Sex *(we presume you are female, but so as not to discriminate)*
Are you?

Male	☐
Female	☐

1.2 Age

under 21	☐	21–30	☐
31–40	☐	41–50	☐
51–60	☐	over 60	☐

1.3 At what age did you leave full-time education?

still in education	☐	16 or younger	☐
17–19	☐	20 or older	☐

1.4 Occupation _____

1.5 Annual household income
     under £10,000   ☐   £10–£20,000   ☐
     £20–£30,000   ☐   £30–£40,000   ☐
     over £40,000   ☐

1.6 We are perfectly happy for you to remain anonymous;
but if you would like to receive information on other
publications available, please insert your name and
address

_____

_____

_____

_____

SECTION TWO: ABOUT BUYING BLACK LACE BOOKS

2.1 How did you acquire this copy of *Odyssey*?
    I bought it myself   ☐   My partner bought it   ☐
    I borrowed/found it   ☐

2.2 How did you find out about Black Lace books?
    I saw them in a shop   ☐
    I saw them advertised in a magazine   ☐
    I saw the London Underground posters   ☐
    I read about them in _____
    Other _____

2.3 Please tick the following statements you agree with:
    I would be less embarrassed about buying Black
    Lace books if the cover pictures were less explicit   ☐
    I think that in general the pictures on Black
    Lace books are about right   ☐
    I think Black Lace cover pictures should be as
    explicit as possible   ☐

2.4 Would you read a Black Lace book in a public place – on
a train for instance?
    Yes   ☐   No   ☐

SECTION THREE: ABOUT THIS BLACK LACE BOOK

3.1 Do you think the sex content in this book is:
    Too much ☐   About right ☐
    Not enough ☐

3.2 Do you think the writing style in this book is:
    Too unreal/escapist ☐   About right ☐
    Too down to earth ☐

3.3 Do you think the story in this book is:
    Too complicated ☐   About right ☐
    Too boring/simple ☐

3.4 Do you think the cover of this book is:
    Too explicit ☐   About right ☐
    Not explicit enough ☐

Here's a space for any other comments:

SECTION FOUR: ABOUT OTHER BLACK LACE BOOKS

4.1 How many Black Lace books have you read? ☐

4.2 If more than one, which one did you prefer?

4.3 Why?

SECTION FIVE: ABOUT YOUR IDEAL EROTIC NOVEL

We want to publish the books you want to read – so this is your chance to tell us exactly what your ideal erotic novel would be like.

5.1 Using a scale of 1 to 5 (1 = no interest at all, 5 = your ideal), please rate the following possible settings for an erotic novel:

Medieval/barbarian/sword 'n' sorcery □
Renaissance/Elizabethan/Restoration □
Victorian/Edwardian □
1920s & 1930s – the Jazz Age □
Present day □
Future/Science Fiction □

5.2 Using the same scale of 1 to 5, please rate the following themes you may find in an erotic novel:

Submissive male/dominant female □
Submissive female/dominant male □
Lesbianism □
Bondage/fetishism □
Romantic love □
Experimental sex e.g. anal/watersports/sex toys □
Gay male sex □
Group sex □

Using the same scale of 1 to 5, please rate the following styles in which an erotic novel could be written:

Realistic, down to earth, set in real life □
Escapist fantasy, but just about believable □
Completely unreal, impressionistic, dreamlike □

5.3 Would you prefer your ideal erotic novel to be written from the viewpoint of the main male characters or the main female characters?

Male □   Female □
Both □

5.4 What would your ideal Black Lace heroine be like? Tick as many as you like:

Dominant	☐	Glamorous	☐
Extroverted	☐	Contemporary	☐
Independent	☐	Bisexual	☐
Adventurous	☐	Naive	☐
Intellectual	☐	Introverted	☐
Professional	☐	Kinky	☐
Submissive	☐	Anything else?	☐
Ordinary	☐	_____	

5.5 What would your ideal male lead character be like? Again, tick as many as you like:

Rugged	☐		
Athletic	☐	Caring	☐
Sophisticated	☐	Cruel	☐
Retiring	☐	Debonair	☐
Outdoor-type	☐	Naive	☐
Executive-type	☐	Intellectual	☐
Ordinary	☐	Professional	☐
Kinky	☐	Romantic	☐
Hunky	☐		
Sexually dominant	☐	Anything else?	☐
Sexually submissive	☐	_____	

5.6 Is there one particular setting or subject matter that your ideal erotic novel would contain?

_____

SECTION SIX: LAST WORDS

6.1 What do you like best about Black Lace books?

_____

6.2 What do you most dislike about Black Lace books?

_____

6.3 In what way, if any, would you like to change Black Lace covers?

_____

6.4 Here's a space for any other comments:

_____

_____

_____

_____

Thank you for completing this questionnaire. Now tear it out of the book – carefully! – put it in an envelope and send it to:

Black Lace
FREEPOST
London
W10 5BR

No stamp is required if you are resident in the U.K.